Mardi Gras Madness

by

Lynn Shurr

The Mardi Gras Series

Mardi Gras Madness

Cover Art by *Diana Carlile*

The Wild Rose Press, Inc.
PO Box 708
Adams Basin, NY 14410-0708
Visit us at www.thewildrosepress.com

Publishing History
First Champagne Rose Edition, 2014
Print ISBN 978-1-62830-650-7
Digital ISBN 978-1-62830-651-4

The Mardi Gras Series

"You're crying."

With a touch of his hand, Robert LeBlanc turned her face back toward a sliver of moonlight coming through the branches. "Don't do this. Be the woman who took a tough job in a strange place despite Tante Lil. Be the one who Vivien can't grind into the dirt. I want that woman. I'd give her back all she lost and more."

He placed his lips against her partly open mouth, licked the salty tears from the rim and deepened the kiss. He pressed her pliant body between the hardness of his and the rough bark of the tree. Tonight with the rush of the festivities, the man who should shave twice a day hadn't, and the abrasive texture of his beard rasped seductively against the skin of her cheek. So male, so close, for a moment she could not recall her dead husband's name or face. When she did, he felt the change—the stiffness of her body pulling away from the trunk of the tree, the turning of her head, the closing of her lips.

"I'll wait until that woman comes back," he said and left her alone beneath the tree in that little sliver of moonlight.

Dedication

For my daughter Cora,
who prefers a little mystery with her romance.

Other books in the Mardi Gras Series
by Lynn Shurr
COURIR DE MARDI GRAS

Anything can happen on Mardi Gras day in the countryside.

Fleeing an obsessive boyfriend, Suzanne Hudson arrives in tiny Port Jefferson, Louisiana, to inventory the antiques of an antebellum home. Full of moonlight and magnolia dreams, she soon finds her job boring and the master of the manor, George St. Julien, dull.

Everything changes during the Mardi Gras ride when Suzanne is playfully abducted by a masked man on a white horse and the famous Magnolia Hill silver disappears shortly thereafter. Determined to discover the rider's identity and solve the mystery of the lost silver, Suzanne unearths small town secrets that might be better left alone and finds her life in jeopardy.

Chapter One

Laura Dickinson sat three feet from her husband's closed coffin and calmly accepted more condolences. Bodies brought up from a helicopter sunken in the Gulf of Mexico did not make pretty corpses. The mourners moved aside, and Laura could see the framed photograph of David sitting on the shining bronze surface of the casket.

Lanky, sandy-haired and sporting a wide grin that said he loved the whole world and most especially Laura, David's image gazed at her. She smiled back just slightly, but even that annoyed David's two sisters who soaked up sympathy and tears with their damp wadded tissues on her right. They were already upset because she'd worn a blue dress, one of David's favorites because its tint made her gray eyes seem almost the same shade as his. Another old friend of the Dickinson family came to stand before her and blocked the view of her husband's face. Laura took the offered hand and murmured a quiet, "Thank you for coming."

Two rows back, friends of her mother-in-law dissected the demeanor of the widow loudly enough for Laura to hear. "Considering they were only married a couple of months, she sure doesn't seem too grieved, does she, Bev?"

"Probably drugged. I'd be bawling my eyes out over losing a fine, handsome young man like that. Now with my Ed, he was way past his time to go, and I still managed to shed a few tears."

Laura stiffened her spine. Their words crawled like black spiders over her back, but she wouldn't weep or get hysterical. That would be bad for the baby. If only she could have told David about it before his death. But then, she hadn't known. Both in their mid-twenties, they had decided to chuck the pills and go for a family right away. She'd been amazed after so many years of using birth control how soon she'd gotten pregnant. Knowing she carried David's child was a comfort not divulged to anyone else yet. Only two weeks late, but in the urgency of planning the funeral, she'd put off getting one of those test kits at the drugstore. She knew. Only that mattered.

The elder Mrs. Dickinson came to take her seat on Laura's left. "The minister is going to deliver the eulogy now," she told her daughter-in-law.

Out of the corner of her eye, Laura saw her own mother take a seat behind her, along with her father and older sister. Her mother lifted a few strands of dark brown hair out of her collar and patted her shoulder. Laura wore her hair loose, the way David loved it, not bunched up in knots like his frumpy over-thirty sisters. Mom shushed the gossiping ladies as the reverend took his place at the podium and began a lengthy series of anecdotes about her husband's short life.

Laura's mind drifted. Two weeks ago, she and David had been eating beignets at Café Du Monde in New Orleans. They'd discussed the housing shortage and whether they should live across the lake or try to get a place in the city where it would be easier for her to find a job as a librarian at one of the universities or in the vast public library system—until they had a baby, of course. Newly hired as a petroleum engineer for one of the large oil companies, David would be offshore a lot. He worried that his wife would be lonely or bored.

"In New Orleans? Dave, this is like visiting a foreign country. How could I be bored?" she'd answered, but mailed off her resume to the State Library the next morning because of her husband's concern.

Sugar had fallen from the hot beignet as she'd lifted the little donut to her lips, and the white powder drifted across her chest. Even now, she could feel her husband's fingers moving across the tops of her full breasts to wipe the sugar away. Those long fingers went into his mouth to be licked one by one. They were back at the hotel making love before their deserted mugs of café au lait cooled on their abandoned table. Certainly, the baby had been conceived that morning.

Laura smiled again. All eyes turned toward her as the minister finished up with—"And let us all support this young woman in her time of sorrow and comfort her with the knowledge that surely her husband, David Lee Dickinson, has gone to a better place, and they shall be reunited in eternity. Amen."

"Did you see?" the old bitch in the third row said to her friend. "She's smiling. How can she smile at a time like this?"

David died the day after that passionate quickie in a fine hotel. The helicopter taking him to an offshore platform crashed, no survivors. So sorry, our condolences, such rotten luck. The oil company paid her airfare home and shipped the body after its recovery. She'd collect a large insurance settlement, naturally. Nausea rose in Laura's throat, but then, pregnancy did that to a woman. She stood up a little dizzy, another sign of the child to come, and followed the coffin on its way to the cemetery.

****

Laura regretted having had any food at all at the post-funeral reception as her parents' small sedan bumped along the crumbling Pennsylvania Turnpike toward home. Being crammed in the backseat with her sister brought back old times when they had gone on family vacations. Just like old times, she felt a little carsick.

Thank God, when her father and mother began their usual debate about which exit to take, her sister had gone to sleep after spending half an hour yammering on her cell. Laura's head throbbed. Dad won the argument. They left the turnpike at Morgantown, skirted the city of Reading on a much better road, and ten miles later, arrived in Lost Spring.

Laura rushed from the car, fumbled her key into the lock of her childhood home and made it to the first floor bathroom before the cramps doubled her up. Blood like bright red tears coursed down her thighs. She was losing David's baby, and all the bottled up grief and hysteria came out with it.

"Laura! Are you okay? Speak to me, honey," her mother begged as she knocked on the door.

No words would come out, only sobs, great gasping sobs. Her father took over, pounding on the door and using his deep authoritative voice. "Answer your mother, young lady. Don't make me get the screwdriver to open the lock."

She felt as if she were twelve again and

embarrassed over having started her first period. Laura looked at the stain in her panties. The headache, the cramps, the slightly ill feeling, she was having her period, late but normal, and she couldn't stop crying.

Through the door, Laura heard her mother on the phone. "So sorry to bother you, doctor. We're just back from the funeral. Not good. She's hysterical. Yes, I can send my husband over to Geiger's Pharmacy to pick up some tranquilizers. I'll bring her in tomorrow. Thank you. Thank you so much."

****

Laura could see that unlike herself, her mother had gotten up bright and early and gone to the hairdresser. Mom's once gray head sprouted in tight, honey-blonde curls sprayed to last.

Her father, wise in the way of marriage after thirty-five years, peered over his Saturday morning paper. "Always wanted to be married to a voluptuous blonde. How about another pancake?"

"Then, why didn't you say so sooner?" her mother carped, shoveling a flapjack onto his plate and flipping another on top of the one sitting uneaten in front of Laura. As her daughter made no move to do so, Mom topped the pancake with a pat of butter and doused maple syrup over the stack. "Eat something, Laura. You are nothing but skin and bones."

Laura looked down at the gray cashmere sweater David had given her for Christmas. He'd liked the way she filled it out, but now, there wasn't much to see but the sharp edge of her collarbone. Finally skinny enough to wear low-rise jeans, she didn't have the energy to shop for them. In fact, she felt like crap—all Dr. Goode's fault because he wouldn't renew the prescription for those dandy capsules that made her all warm and cozy like being wrapped in a soft woolly blanket too comfortable to shed. Although the pills killed her appetite, she slept very well indeed under their influence. Now, she couldn't sleep at all and still didn't feel like eating.

"I'll tell you what, Laura. Since you aren't working right now and your settlement still hasn't come in—three months should be plenty of time—how those insurance companies drag their feet—I'll treat you to a new hairdo. Maybe you could get some streaks to perk up your appearance." Her mother put her hands on her fleshy hips causing her blouse to gap over large breasts. "Eat," she ordered again.

"David liked my hair the way it is."

"He probably liked it washed even better. Honey, it's been three months, one quarter of a year since David's funeral. Consider that you only met your husband a little over a year ago, six months of dating, six months of engagement and bam, a wedding. Time for you to get out, look for another job, socialize a bit. You know, Jay Geiger asks about you every time I go to pick up your prescription. He's the pharmacist now. Didn't you date him in high school?"

"I went out with Jay once." Once too often, Laura thought. An ordinary date for a football game and dance afterwards had turned into a wrestling match under the deserted bleachers with Jay Geiger high on some unknown substance that Laura refused to take. She'd scraped him off and walked home.

"You know, dear, you take things too hard. When Jordan dumped you in college, you didn't date again until you met David. When our old dog Fritzie got hit by a car, you refused to get a new puppy."

"Jordan broke up with me at the end of senior year so he could go off into the world unencumbered, he said. I did my grad work at the School of Library and Information Sciences—not too many men there. And David wasn't a dog." She wanted to snarl herself.

But, she did meet her future husband in a library. Asked to sub in the Science and Engineering area, way out of her comfort zone in the Humanities, when Mr. Bean and Mr. Nelson were both out with flu, she'd spent most of her first afternoon there helping the tall friendly grad student look up information on mud logging and directional drilling. She'd been such a help he offered to take her to dinner. After their engagement, Dave admitted he'd made up the questions about stuff he already knew to get the jump on any other engineering students who might make moves on lovely Laura, the librarian. Lovely Laura. If he could see her now. She needed more of those pills.

"Fine, I'm going for a walk if you don't want me around." Laura scraped her chair back and headed for the kitchen door. Oh, more shades of high school—how could she be so petulant? Because she felt lousy, that's why.

"Laura, don't be that way. Finish your meal."

She slammed the door behind her and headed off to Geiger's Pharmacy. If Jay remembered her so fondly, maybe he would give her a little advance on a new prescription. Fatigued halfway to her destination, she leaned against the window of the Hallmark store on Penn Street to rest. Bad idea. Her reflection in the plate glass told her she should have taken the time to put on some makeup to cover the dark circles under her eyes and at least, brush her lank and greasy hair back into a ponytail. She'd do something about her appearance after she talked to Jay.

Geiger's hadn't changed in twenty years. The pharmacy still maintained a tiny soda fountain where small town kids could get an ice cream cone on a hot summer day. Laura moved past the racks of Whitman's Samplers and over-the-counter remedies Geiger's would deliver anywhere in town to the drug counter at the rear of the store. Jay had moved the boxes of condoms to a shelf outside his domain, she noticed. No more need for teen boys to turn red in the face asking for them. Once his old man retired, Jay would probably make other changes—and raise all the prices.

He lorded over the store from his dais above the customers. Jay's red hair, already receding, stood out in contrast to his white lab coat pulled tight across an expanding midsection. He leaned over the high counter and gave Laura a very white, toothy smile.

"Why, Laura Schumann has come to my humble store in person for a change. What can I do you for?" He acted out the part of her friendly neighborhood pharmacist.

"Ah, Doc Goode is out of town, and I need a refill on my prescription. Could I get a few pills to tide me over?"

"Let's see here." Jay tapped away on a keyboard. "What's the married name? Oh yeah, Dickinson. Hmmm, no more refills. Doc Goode is very unbending about refills."

"Yes, I know. He gave me that old line about Doc Goode knowing what's good for me. He needs to retire. The man gave me my baby shots for heaven's sake."

"Yeah, he knows everything about everybody in town—and so do I. If you really need those pills, we might work something out. Why don't you come over to my place tonight? Oak Hill Apartments, number sixty nine—get it? I picked that unit myself."

"I'll just bet you did. Why your place?"

"I wouldn't want my regular customers to see me slipping you anything under the counter, so to speak."

Fairly sure Jay was trying to look down her sweater from his high seat, she figured he hadn't changed much since high school after all. Well, she hoped he suffered from disappointment because her breasts had dwindled away along with her hips covered in now saggy jeans. God, she felt awful. Laura scrubbed at her face.

"Okay, what time?"

"Oh, sevenish. Don't eat dinner. I'll fix something special for you."

"Seven. I'll be there."

****

"How nice that Jay asked you over to his place," her mom twittered. "You look better already, though that dress is a little baggy on you. We should have gone shopping this afternoon for something new, but you were sleeping again. Take a jacket. The evenings are getting colder. Don't you think you should drive over to Oak Hill? I don't like the idea of your walking home at night."

"I'm fine, Mom. Jay will see I get home safely."

As if anything ever happened in Lost Spring. Besides, she knew she shouldn't drive while taking those pills. Laura tightened the gold belt around her waist another notch and bloused out the top of the black dress to make it look a little better. She'd washed her

9

hair and made an attempt to put some curl into it before drawing the unshaped mop back into a golden clip. Next time, she'd take her mother up on the free haircut. With some concealer under her eyes, a little blush on her now sharp cheekbones and a dash of lip gloss, she looked good enough for Jay Geiger.

Laura set off into the crisp, fall evening. She stopped to sit on a low stone wall half way up Oak Hill to catch her breath, but she did arrive at the apartment right on time. Jay waited for her wearing some sleazy playboy getup, a smoking jacket with satin lapels closed over his bare chest, tight black slacks that cut into his flabby waist, and sockless loafers. He held a glass of champagne in one hand and posed in the doorway for a moment as he looked her over.

"A big improvement over this afternoon, Laura. Seven on the dot. But, my ladies are never late."

Jay stepped aside and closed the door behind her. He handed over the flute of bubbly. Laura took a small sip and winced at the taste of the very cheap, very sour champagne probably left over from a Geiger's New Year's special. He wasn't wasting any money on her.

"I know, I know, an inferior vintage, but I haven't added the twist yet."

He withdrew a capsule from the pocket of his jacket and popped it into her glass. The drug dropped to the bottom of the flute and then rose up seductively on the bubbles. Laura tried to catch it on her tongue but missed. She drained half her glass in pursuit of the pill, but it sank into the narrow neck of the flute.

Jay watched with amusement. "Well, well, well, good little Laura Schumann is a junkie."

"I'm not! I need a little something to get over

David's death, that's all."

"Yeah, all my ladies say that. They need to lose a little weight, feel a little better. You ran out of your last prescription two weeks ahead of schedule, junkie."

"No!"

"Seems to me the last time we were together, you turned down some pretty good stuff and ran out on me. So tonight, you will perform first and get these later." Jay held up a plastic container of capsules.

"Drink up. That first one will get you started on your way to LaLa Land. I'll want you on your knees in a minute." He fumbled with the tight zipper of his fly and released a short chubby penis more normal for a child than a man.

Laura laughed for the first time in months. She tipped her glass, christened his small dick with the remains of the cold champagne and watched it retreat into its hole. With a tap on the bottom of the flute, Laura released the pill. It bounced off the pitiful nubbin. She tossed the cheap drugstore glassware at Jay's fireplace, crackling with fake flames, and enjoyed the satisfying smash.

"I am Laura Dickinson, and I am no junkie."

She turned, slammed the door behind her and headed home. The cold autumn wind slapped at her cheeks, and the first of the fallen leaves crunched under her heels. She passed the stone wall where she had rested while laboring up Oak Hill and kept right on going. If the two cops who patrolled Lost Spring, rousting teens from the lover's lane and giving out tickets for running the one red light in town, had seen her face, they might have stopped to ask if she needed help—and Laura would have answered, "No." She'd gotten over the hump; the rest was all downhill.

****

Two weeks later, Laura coasted into her parents' drive on the three-speed bike of her childhood. With a bottle of water, an autumn-crisp apple and a Lebanon baloney sandwich in the dusty saddlebag, she rode out every morning visiting old haunts she'd never be able to show David. The exercise helped—as did getting away from the house.

Laura wheeled the bike into the garage where her dad worked checking the oil in his car. He looked up as he wiped the dip stick with a paper towel. "That old bicycle cleaned up pretty well. Just needed new tires and a little lubrication. Good to see someone using it again."

He bent under the hood and made Laura too aware of the expanding bald spot in the middle of his thick, gray hair and the slight creak of his joints. He and Mom should be planning their winter trip to the Caribbean, not taking care of their grown daughter. By now, they'd usually booked two weeks in the sun for January, but they wouldn't budge as long as Laura needed them.

As she entered the kitchen from the garage, the air sizzled with the smell of dinner. She hung up her flannel-lined denim jacket and asked, "What's cooking?"

"Fresh pork sausage from Frey's and corn fritters," her mother answered, turning the links over in the pan.

Fried food—Mom's answer to rebuilding Laura. According to Doris Schumann, a size eight should be healthy and normal for a grown woman. Men liked a few curves no matter what the fashion magazines said. Her meals had Laura slowly filling out her jeans and sweaters again.

"There's mail for you from Louisiana. Maybe your settlement check has come."

Mom gestured with her spatula toward an envelope on the kitchen table and sent bright droplets of grease flying through the air. Thinking she needed to leave home before she weighed two-hundred pounds, Laura picked up the letter and opened it with her thumbnail. The letterhead embossed with what she supposed were sugarcane stalks read "Ste. Jeanne d'Arc Parish Library, Chapelle, Louisiana."

Dear Mrs. Dickinson:

The library board of Ste. Jeanne d'Arc Parish is in receipt of your resume forwarded from the State Library of Louisiana. As our librarian of many years, Miss Lilliane LeBlanc, is considering retirement, we would like to interview you at your convenience. We were most impressed by your credentials.

Our town, located in the heart of Cajun country, is small, but has a rich history and friendly people. We offer good benefits. Salary is negotiable. Please contact us at the above number as soon as possible.

Sincerely,

Jules Picard, Board President

Scribbled on the bottom of the typed page was a P.S.—If Miss Lilliane hangs up on you, I can be reached at J.P.'s New and Used Appliances. Myrtle Hill will ring my number for you when you get the exchange.

Laura handed the letter to her mother. "What do you make of this?"

"Some place is very desperate for a librarian, I'd say. I didn't know anywhere in the world still had telephone exchanges. Must be way out in the boonies." Leaving a greasy thumbprint in the corner, she handed back the letter.

"Gee, thanks Mom. I did ace all my library classes. I know one year in an academic library isn't much experience, but if they are willing to give me an interview, I think I should go. I need to stand on my own, and let you and Dad have your lives back."

"What life?" said her father, coming in to scrub up for dinner.

"Laura wants to take a job way off in Louisiana. Do you think that's wise? I hear that state is like a Third World country, and she'd be all alone without—" Doris Schumann caught herself before she uttered David's name, as if the very mention might cause her daughter to relapse.

"It's only an interview. They might not offer me the job."

Ever practical Fred Schumann left the room and returned with the dusty atlas purchased when Laura attended grade school.

"Here we are, a map of Louisiana. What's the name of the town? Chapelle. Let's see. H-6. Well, the place is mighty small and on a river. Not much beyond that but farmland and a great big swamp. A country road ends right there."

"You'd have to be crazy to go, Laura," her mother said.

"I'm going," Laura answered.

Chapter Two

The road snaked insanely across the level landscape, twisting wildly between the walls of cane and slithering suddenly into marshy hollows. Of course, the air conditioner on the rented economy car failed just after departure from the breezy interstate.

"Sure," said the serviceman at the last gas station before oblivion. "This is the Old Chapelle Road. You just go 'til you can't go no more."

Then, the cane fields swallowed the small car and driver again. The air conditioner quit at the exact moment when turning back would have endangered the interview waiting at the end of the journey. Laura stopped at a break in the fields where two parish roads crossed. "Chapelle—10" claimed a sign.

She rolled down every window in the vehicle and continued onward. The road bobbed into a small swamp that had recently defeated the highway department by flooding over the grading. Puddles as large and black as tar pits covered the macadam. The little car bounced in and out of a pool masking a treacherous pothole. Great dollops of inky mud flew into the front seat along with a swarm of small, black and very nasty variety of mosquito. The wind created as the small Ford rounded the next bend and came to open country sucked most of the mosquitoes back to their marshy domain, but the damage had been done. Itchy welts rose on her legs and the dark, muddy spatters spread on her white linen suit.

"Should have worn the navy blue," she chided herself, but the white suit with its lime green piping had seemed so very southern in the motel room near the New Orleans airport. In fact, she had been pleased with her appearance for the first time in months—white straw bag and matching shoes, crisp linen suit, hair curled and double sprayed to withstand the oppressive humidity just beyond the motel door. Despite the lacquer, her newly styled hair had straightened tendril by tendril. With each mile, the armpits of her linen suit grew damper.

At last the fields ended, brought to a halt by an immense gray sugar mill, its hooks and claws hanging over the cane, its shadow blocking the sun from a row of identical gray clapboard shacks. No one stirred in the heat of the day. A clump of black-eyed Susans brightened one yard and a red plastic tricycle sat in another, but basically the houses were all the same in their poverty.

Beyond the quarters began a line of white frame houses—at first shabby with peeling paint, then more neatly kept. The uniform white frame gave way to the glories of aluminum siding in pale blue and bright yellow. Crepe myrtles, exhausted by a summer of bloom, still shaded porches with their yellowed leaves and occasionally offered a garish bouquet of hot cerise or deep purple.

The houses grew larger. Here and there stood a real or fake antebellum mansion and more modern brick homes imitating the old cottages with steep roofs and deep galleries. Abruptly, the road ended. Laura stopped at the first traffic light she'd encountered since leaving the interstate. She faced a village green that might have been in New England if the lawn had been shaded with sugar maples rather than live oaks. A gray and white stucco church sat framed by the trees while the brown water of the bayou flowed sluggishly in the background. On the opposite bank lay a vast cemetery of dead parishioners. The church bells clanged briefly.

Noon. At least one thing had gone right. She had a full hour and a half before the dreaded interview, allowing enough time to repair some of the travel damage, find lunch and a large cold drink. The business district stretched both right and left. She chose left and parked by the village green in the shade of the oaks. A single row of shops ran for a block in both directions. Across from her parking space sat an old service station. "Canal Gasoline" read a rusty sign over ancient pumps. Laura headed for the restroom. No one manned the office, but the facilities were unlocked.

Laura blotted her face with a paper towel dampened at the ladies' room tap, combed back what remained of her coiffure and clipped it with a large barrette. She resisted the urge to scratch the mosquito bites festooning her ankles and instead worked diligently on the mud-stained skirt with cold water. She made an assessment in the speckled mirror—lovely Laura, the efficient, competent and resourceful librarian. Yeah, right. She tossed the towels into a can and emerged into the heat of a Louisiana September afternoon.

An old man wiping his lips with a paper napkin came around from the rear of the station. "Didn't hear no car, me," he accused.

"My car is over there. I'll be sure to fill it here

before I leave, but for now I just needed to use the restroom. Could you tell me if I can get lunch somewhere nearby?" Laura smiled appeasingly.

"Domengeaux's got good boudin, yeah." He waved at a small store on the opposite corner. "You not from here, eh?" Again, it sounded like an accusation.

"No. I came for a job interview. From Pennsylvania," she added, knowing what he would ask next.

"At least you not a damn tourist. Strangers always crawling all over our church, yeah. Say, you know da difference between a Yankee and a damn Yankee?"

She shook her head indicating that she did not.

"A Yankee visits, den goes home. A damn Yankee comes an' stays." He chuckled more at the expression on Laura's face than at his own joke. "You gotta learn to laugh if you want to be a Cajun, *cher*." He thrust out an arthritic hand. "Aldus Thibodeaux, pleased to meet wit' you."

Aware her palms sweated in the heat, Laura took his hand. "Go get you some lunch at Domengeaux's." Aldus waved her across the street.

Laura smiled as she crossed to the café, the tar bubbles in the street popping beneath her shoes. To think two days ago, she had been breathing the cool, clear air of the north and regaining the energy needed to restart her life. Now she swam in this humid atmosphere. She paused beneath the awning shading the store. "Domengeaux's" was spelled out in red lettering shaded with yellow. Aslant in opposite corners of the glass were the words, "HOT BOUDIN" and "NEW ORLEANS STYLE MUFFULETTAS." Painted flames licked the letters of "BOUDIN." Double red lines underscored "NEW ORLEANS." A bell rang as she stepped into the pleasant dimness of the restaurant.

A row of refrigerator cases held offerings of cold cuts, potato and gelatin salads and coleslaw. A bank of soft drink machines vended every beverage from apple juice to RC Cola. Chains of garlic and strings of red peppers hung in available corners while postcard racks, packets of dried shrimp, baskets of pralines and alligator toe key chains accumulated on the counter by the cash register.

Two oil-clothed tables held caddies of salt, pepper, ketchup, and one bottle each of red and green pepper sauce. Most extraordinary among the clutter sat a shrine. In the one free corner stood a pale, blue-robed plaster Virgin Mary. A votive candle in a red glass holder burned at her feet, casting an eerie purple sheen over the statue's blue eyes and tinting the Virgin's blonde hair a light orange. Large bouquets of plastic roses, red and pink, flanked the candle.

Only one other customer occupied the sandwich shop. He leaned against the Formica counter with his back to Laura and did not turn around at her entrance. She formed a tentative line several feet from his worn and nicely filled jeans. David had always teased her about being a connoisseur of men's posteriors, an area in which he could not compete with his long lanky body and flat derriere. She had promised to swear off looking when they married.

The other customer continued to ignore her, giving Laura ample time to notice his stocky build, broad shoulders and the thick, black hair waving just over the collar of his khaki work shirt. With his shirtsleeves rolled up exposing heavy biceps, she noticed more dark hair scattered across deeply tanned forearms. This kind of man probably needed to shave twice a day but did not, Laura thought. She wondered if tiny Chapelle had something in common with New York City where striking up conversations with the natives was somehow wrong. People in the South were supposed to be friendlier, but then she had already met Mr. Thibodeaux across the way.

A large woman clutching a Styrofoam box hustled through a curtained doorway. "Dere you go T-Bob, one catfish po-boy fully dressed wit' my own special potato salad on da side, none of dat packaged stuff in da cooler."

"*Merci*, Miss Lola." The customer pulled a wallet from his hip pocket, stretching the worn denim a little tighter for a moment. He took out a ten and shoved it across the counter. "And a Dr. Pepper, too."

Miss Lola rang up the sale and handed over the change. T-Bob pocketed the bills and dumped the coins into a half-full gallon plastic jar with the photo of a bald, thin, large-eyed child pasted on the outside. A legend written in black marker under the photo read "For Jason Breaux's leukemia treatments."

"That was nice of you," Laura remarked, trying to spark a conversation.

The man turned and glanced briefly at Laura, making her very aware of her limp hair and wrinkled, water-spotted linen. "We take care of our own here in Chapelle. If you stay around, you'll realize that. Ma'am."

He nodded slightly causing a lock of black hair to slip across his forehead. He brushed the hair from eyes of bittersweet brown and strode out of the store to a battered pickup truck parked by the curb. He drove off before the shop door closed.

Well, he had shaved today. Would have been a shame to cover that wonderful cleft chin with a beard, Laura thought.

"Ooh, dat T-Bob is some hunk. Too bad about him." Miss Lola paused, waiting for an invitation to gossip.

Laura could not see a thing wrong with T-Bob—except she didn't care for swarthy men—or men who "ma'amed" her as if she were ninety years old—or men who were not David. With no response coming from Laura, Miss Lola shrugged and asked, "What can I get you, *cher*?"

"I heard you had good boudin, but I couldn't stand anything hot today. How about a New Orleans style muffuletta?" Laura smiled confidently, not at all sure what she had ordered, but she saw no other menu than a small chalk board listing Today's Special as the catfish po-boy with potato salad and drink, $5.95.

"Coming right up. You not from around here?" The waitress vigorously plied a slicing machine. Thin shavings of cheese, ham and salami accumulated quickly into a large mound.

"No, I'm from Pennsylvania. I've come for a job interview."

"You dat new librarian. Lilliane LeBlanc told me to watch out for a young Yankee gal. I'm Lola Domengeaux. Dat's said 'DiMaggio' like dat baseball player, but he don't spell it right." Mrs. Domengeaux split an immense circular bun with her knife and deftly heaped on the cold cuts.

"I haven't gotten the job yet."

"Oh, you will, *cher* heart. Not too many will even come for an interview in a small place like Chapelle, and your qualifications are real good." She sloshed crushed olive salad over the wheel of the sandwich, replaced the top and severed Laura's lunch neatly in half. "Anyt'ing else, *cher*?"

"A large cold drink. My air conditioner broke on the way here."

"Take your pick." Miss Lola pointed to the coolers.

Laura selected a tall Coke in a plastic bottle. Chapelle was certainly not what she'd had in mind when she had sent her resume to the State Library of Louisiana—so much for a nice reference position in a New Orleans university. Laura fought the impulse to tell the motherly Mrs. Domengeaux all.

"Here or to go, hon?"

"To go. I think I'll have a picnic over by the church," the Yankee gal answered, feeling awkward with the robust woman who had probably read her resume. She also believed if she sat at one of the tables, Miss Lola would extract her entire life story and tell her T-Bob's in the next thirty minutes.

"Now, if a skinny little girl like you can eat all dis sandwich, you deserve some *lagniappe*. Dat's a little extra, you understand? Here's a praline for dessert. I make my own. Best in da parish for absolutely free."

As Mrs. Domengeaux handed over the big sack containing the muffuletta wrapped in white waxed paper and one praline in a small plastic bag, Laura selected a tourist guide from the overburdened racks on the counter.

"I might as well learn a little about the town while I'm here."

"You be back, *cher* heart. Now da library is down left of da church along da bayou, dat old Barras place. Miss Barras left dat house to the parish for a library, you see. Come on back now, you hear?"

Laura backed out of the door, hands burdened by sack, drink and book, and into the glaring sunlight. Up and down Main Street, no one stirred except for one aged black woman warding off the sun with a huge red umbrella. This lone companion soon disappeared into Hebert's Penny Saver Grocery.

Alone again, thought Laura, and then reprimanded herself to cancel the pity party and eat her lunch.

She crossed the green to the side of the church where the shade seemed thickest and found a small grotto nestled in the angles of the cruciform building. There stood a statue of St. Francis with his feet entangled in ivy and ferns; his hands offered a bowl of water to a stone dove, but the saint's kindly eyes invited Laura to a seat on a mossy bench by his side.

Knowing she had ordered too much, Laura removed one hunk of the muffuletta from the sack and grasped it in two hands. Olive oil dribbled from the bottom and made a thin track down the front of her jacket. Great, one more mark against her—that and being a Yankee. She mopped her chest with a paper napkin and mostly smeared the oil around. Damn.

Her appetite came on strong, complete with a growling stomach. She wadded the napkin under the base of the sandwich and took a bite—salty and meaty, a taste of New Orleans that made her ravenous for more. She was going in for another mouthful when the ferns at the base of the church rustled furtively. Something black streaked from a fist-sized hole in the foundation. Snake!

Laura jerked her feet up on the stone bench. Her sandwich went flying into the ivy. Everyone knew Louisiana teemed with water moccasins. A nest of vipers probably lived beneath the raised floor of the church. The ivy parted and a coal black kitten went to work claiming its half of the fallen muffuletta. The tiny tongue scraped away the first layer of ham and went after the second.

Laura swung her feet to the ground "Okay, you take that half. I didn't want it anyway." The small cat responded to her invitation by pausing to rub against Laura's calf. The kitten returned to its lunch after two quick passes.

"I'll tell you what, little guy. If I get this job, and you're still camping out here when I return, I'll give you a home. Deal?" She glanced at Saint Francis who wore a look of benign agreement. "I'm not even Catholic, and here I am looking for favors from saints."

She finished her half of the muffuletta and drank the Coke, which had already lost its chill. The kitten sprang up the concrete robes of the statue and lapped water from the saint's bowl. Laura let a bit of the sweet, brown sugar praline dissolve on her tongue while she thumbed the tourist guide of Saint Jeanne d'Arc Parish. The town had more historical landmarks than Laura's free hour could accommodate.

She paged to the section on the church. A short walking tour began by the bronze figure on the green. Laura gathered her purse and the sandwich wrappings and stepped out of the shaded grotto. The kitten bounced by her side, then discouraged by the heat and lulled by a full stomach, retreated into the cool darkness beyond the hole in the church wall. Laura positioned herself at Point One of the walking tour and read the guidebook.

"This spot offers a lovely view of the church of Saint Jeanne d'Arc, oldest structure of its kind in Louisiana. The church rests on the site of an older chapel founded by French priests during their conversion of the local Indian tribes. The first chapel gave the town its name of Chapelle. The current edifice, built in 1810 of native cypress, has resisted the ravages of time. The entire structure was recently restored to its original state with funds from the National Trust for Historic Preservation. The church contains many historical and artistic treasures, among them the birth and death records of the original settlers and their descendants.

"Point Two. A statue of Saint Joan stands directly in front of the church. Created, cast, and donated by Emile Devereaux in 1812, the statue was the artist's thank offering for his escape from the devastations of the French Revolution. Devereaux, a court artist, arrived in Chapelle in 1802 with a large group of French emigres. It is also believed that the statue served as an advertisement of Devereaux's skills. He earned his livelihood sculpting busts of local planters and creating ornate tombs for the wealthy. Many of his works may be seen in the Cemetery of Saint Jeanne d'Arc across from the church."

Laura paused to look closely at Saint Joan. She approved of the classical folds of the drapery and the clean ascetic lines of the face. The eyes of the statue were lifted toward heaven, but her fine nostrils flared and her mouth set grimly as if she could smell the first wisps of smoke from the bronze bonfire at her feet. Clearly, Emile Devereaux had been an excellent artist whom fate had delivered to Chapelle to die in obscurity. Laura glanced at the somnolent town slumbering toward its three-hundredth birthday and laughed to think of both herself and Devereaux "buried alive," as her mother would say, in Chapelle, Louisiana.

Shaking off the grim humor, Laura strolled toward the church, Point Three in the guide. She pushed the wrought iron latch on the heavy wooden door and stepped into the sunny interior so unlike the dark and incense-burdened stone cathedrals of the north. Perhaps, the honey-colored cypress planks and pews gave the church its lightness. The founders, being short on glassmakers, had rimmed only the outer edges of the windows in red and blue stained glass. The sun pierced to the heart of the structure and rebounded off the gold altarpieces and the gilt ornamentation rimming the walls. Above, a turquoise vaulted ceiling held the painted stars of heaven and several brass chandeliers now filled with electric candles. In the right arm of the church, a plain brown niche contained the usual plaster Saint Joseph, but the Mary altar to the left was much more striking.

Laura walked down the aisle to get a better view. The left wing held a gothic altar. Entirely of wood, the carvings of the altarpiece twisted and writhed like souls in hell. Among its contortions sat a statue of the Virgin carved of tawny cypress. With complete serenity, she stood straight against the convoluted background and gazed out at her worshipers. Brown hands clasped in prayer above a slight bulge in her white painted tunic as if she still carried the Christ Child in her womb. Black curls escaped from beneath her veil of sky blue, and her dark eyes looked with understanding and compassion on Laura Dickinson. Strewn about her tiny sandaled feet were plaques of marble and granite reading "*Merci*" or "Thanks" depending on the origin of the giver. One elaborate heart-shaped offering of pink marble bore the inscription "*Merci Beaucoup*-1830."

Laura scanned the guidebook, which went into great detail on all of the fixtures of the church and finally came to Point Thirteen—Mary Altar. "Carved by a free person of color, Celestin Segura, the altar was commissioned by Aurelien LeBlanc to commemorate the birth of his son and heir in 1830. The large, pink marble heart was placed on the altar by his wife, Camille. Segura also carved the statue of the Virgin."

Short shrift to give a work of art as fine as the statue of Saint Joan on the green, thought Laura. More than one good artist had languished in Chapelle. Footsteps sounded hollowly on the cypress planks of the old church. A priest dressed in an old style cassock like a long black dress came toward Laura with a greeting on his lips.

"I'm Father Ardoin. Please let me answer any questions you might have about the church. We are very proud of its restoration."

"I was wondering about the statue of the Virgin. The figure is very moving, but there is so little information in the guide."

"I can tell you a great deal more. I've made a study of the history of this church and did much of the research for the restoration. Please, sit down." They sat side by side on a cypress pew pitted with use.

"Celestin Segura was a free person of color. In the

early days of the colony, wellborn wives were hard to find. A Spanish nobleman, Don Juan Segura, held a large land grant in this area. A childless widower, he came without family to this country. As might be expected, he soon craved a female companion and purchased a mulatto slave named Alma from one of his new neighbors. She kept his house and on the birth of their first son, Antoine, he freed her. Like most men of his status and time, Segura acknowledged his bastards and gave them his name. If you have the time, I can show you the actual records of the baptism of Antoine Segura, f.p.c., in this church."

"F.P.C.?" Laura asked.

"A Free Person of Color. The child took the status of the mother." The priest continued, "Celestin, a second son, was born three years later and also baptized here. Shortly after his birth, one of the planters died, leaving an eligible widow with a large estate. The local priest brought pressure on Don Juan to marry the widow in the church even though she was older than Alma and barren. Alma was given a cottage and land on the edge of the Segura estate. She owned a few slaves to farm for her, and her sons eventually were apprenticed to a cabinetmaker.

"Both boys had amazing talent. Their armoires are still cherished by antique collectors. Celestin, however, was a true artist. He must have been fifteen when his mother gave birth to a daughter, Marie, also fathered by Segura. Despite the scandal, Don Juan acknowledged this child too. I believe his marriage, though blessed by the church, did not make him happy and few blamed him for returning to the comfort Alma offered. Juan Segura died in the same year as his wife. They are buried over in the cemetery on opposite sides of the same Devereaux monument. His grave faces the colored cemetery where Alma lies."

Laura shifted on the hard pew and stole a glance at her watch. The priest showed no sign of running out of information.

"Now, I see Alma as a practical woman. Segura's land passed to a nephew of the same name, and Alma, envied by black and white alike for her prosperous farm and her thriving cabinet shop, was left without protection of the right kind. Too old to attract another lover, Alma still had her daughter, Marie, a beauty of sixteen by then. Alma condoned a liaison between her quadroon daughter and Aurelien LeBlanc."

"The LeBlanc of the altar?" Laura interrupted for the first time.

"Exactly. Celestin Segura, the artist, did not have his mother's worldly outlook. He was enraged at her and LeBlanc for placing Marie into slavery of another sort, though it is said that LeBlanc was kind and generous to the girl. However, Marie died in childbirth at the age of eighteen, her stillborn son buried with her. We have those records here, also."

"At precisely the same time, LeBlanc's wife gave birth to his heir after many unsuccessful pregnancies. LeBlanc wanted a suitable monument for the event and commissioned Celestin to build the altar for the church. Segura was the only local artisan at the time skilled enough to undertake the carving. I am certain that LeBlanc was unaware of the depth of Celestin's feelings against him, or surely he would have sent to New Orleans for another workman."

"The plot thickens." Laura gave the priest a small

smile he took for encouragement.

"When the altar was complete, Celestin placed the statue of the Virgin Mary himself and covered it with a cloth. On the day of the dedication in front of the entire congregation, white and black, because the slaves worshiped in the church loft, he unveiled the statue. Without a doubt, the Virgin portrayed young Marie Segura, pregnant with LeBlanc's child."

"Aha." Laura nodded, checked her watch again.

"Aha, indeed! Keep in mind that we are out of the colonial era now and well into Victorian times. People were no longer as tolerant of the mixing of the races though, of course, this still went on. It is said Camille LeBlanc refused to place the pink granite heart until the statue was removed. A parishioner ran home and brought a poor substitute of a plaster statue to sit on the altar. They placed the beautiful carving outside the door of the church until the ceremony ended. Camille and the white community were appeased. By then, the statue carved by Celestin had been spirited off, no one dared ask where. And that night, Celestin Segura hung himself from the rafters of his shop. Since he could not be interred in the holy ground, no one knows his burial site, though I suspect he lies somewhere on Alma Segura's land." Father Ardoin ended his long narrative not even winded. The romance of by-gone days lighted his pale blue eyes and misted his gold-framed spectacles.

"An interesting story. How was the statue returned?" How idiotic to ask! She would be late for her appointment if she couldn't shake loose soon.

"I see you share my enthusiasm for history." Father Ardoin laughed pleasantly. He was a short, slight and balding priest, but his kind blue eyes did remind her of David. "An ancient colored woman brought the statue to me during the renovations. She is called Tante Lu, the oldest member of the black Seguras and quite an institution around here. She told me the story and said the Virgin belonged here.

"Obviously, the statue was the work of Celestin and matched the altar. Mrs. Domengeaux happily took the other statue for her own shrine. I was able to corroborate the names and dates in the story from the church records and even found an old newspaper account of the dedication of the altar. The incident was glossed over in the article, saying that due to an unfortunate accident, a plaster statue had to be placed on the altar. The editor was sure that Mr. LeBlanc would later provide a finer substitute, but as far as I know, he did not. I still feel I must be careful to whom I tell this story. It would be a tragedy to have the statue displaced again by irate parishioners—but you aren't from around here, of course."

"I've enjoyed our talk, Father. I wish I could spend a week here, but I'm almost late for a job interview." She rose and grabbed her handbag, not wanting to go into her origins again.

"Ah yes, the new librarian."

"Not yet!" replied Laura, slightly annoyed to be caught again.

"Listen, my dear child. When I was transferred to this parish from New Orleans, I thought they had sent me to the ends of the earth to preach to the savages. Not true. Here in this small town are the same currents of history, of passion and love, of life and violence we find in the Old Testament. You can find whatever you want here, too."

Someone had been stationed in Chapelle too long, Laura guessed. She thanked the priest and hurried out by the side door, past the Virgin's altar and under the compassionate dark eyes of Celestin Segura's sister.

Chapter Three

The pendulum clock over the circulation desk ticked away the few remaining minutes until two o'clock. The words "hurry up and wait" came to mind as the hands had long since passed the one-thirty appointment time. Laura thumbed her guidebook at a table directly in front of the timepiece. Her perspiring fingers left small damp marks on the corners of each page. She looked at the clock again and caught the eye of the middle-aged clerk who arranged returned books on a cart for shelving. They exchanged reassuring smiles.

"Miss LeBlanc be back from lunch soon now," the clerk repeated for the third time. The words were softened and slowed by a black cadence still a revelation to Laura. She had assumed when first approaching the clerk that she addressed a person as white as Mrs. Domengeaux. True, Ruby Senegal's lips were a trifle thicker than average and her nose a bit broader, but her black hair curled loosely around the pale ears pierced with ruby studs and the first liver spots of impending old age showed clearly on the backs of her white hands. Those hands went back to sorting.

Laura looked at the only other occupant of the library. The old man snored gently in a comfortable chair in front of a fireplace that once graced the parlor of the rambling frame house before the walls were taken down to make way for book stacks. Now and again, the old gentleman's hands twitched, rustling the pages of the news magazine open on his lap.

Ruby Senegal broke the silence. "I'll soon have to wake old Mr. DeVille. When the kids from Ste. Jeanne's come in, he gets real upset about the noise, so we send him on his way home about two-thirty. His family appreciates that. Well, here come Miss Lilliane."

A huge black Lincoln stopped by the bookmobile garage set back from the rest of the building. Laura watched through the side windows as a man in janitor's overalls came from the garage and opened one of the car doors. Instead of assisting an elderly librarian to exit, he withdrew a folded wheelchair, spread its struts and lifted the partially paralyzed Miss Lilliane into the chair. The janitor wheeled the librarian up a ramp and into the bookmobile area. A moment later, the rear of the library came alive with the whir of the wheelchair and a few muffled curses as the chair collided with office furniture. Ruby Senegal left the front desk and headed toward the commotion.

"Well, send her in!" a crotchety voice bellowed. Ruby returned with another reassuring smile on her lips and softly delivered the message. "Miss Lilliane will see you now."

Laura gathered her belongings and stepped behind the desk to the office area. What had been a dining room was now a glass-walled office with a placard on the door reading Librarian. Beyond the office, the processing area arranged itself comfortably around kitchen counters, a sink, stove, and refrigerator. Two more staff members malingering after their lunch hour cast apprehensive glances at the glass-walled room and rushed to stuff purses into desk drawers and grab the work at hand.

"Berta!" shouted the little lady in the wheelchair. A rotund black woman who had just seized a book for bar coding dropped the volume and waddled to the office. "We'll need some coffee shortly, thank you. Mrs. Dickinson, I'll see you now," she hollered.

Laura hurried into the office and hesitantly took a seat on the edge of a chair matching the scarred wooden desk. Instantly, she realized she had taken what would have been Miss Lilliane's seat if the older librarian had not been confined to a wheelchair. Too late now to shift to a more anonymous piece of furniture. Miss Lilliane eyed her choice of seating, and then returned to scanning a copy of Laura's resume in the center of her desk. She began the interrogation without pleasantries. "Let's see, graduate of Clarion State University, wherever that may be. A year of experience in a university Arts and Humanities Library. Is that all? No administrative experience?"

"That's all, I'm afraid," Laura replied as if she confessed to a hideous crime.

"Can you catalog?"

"I had cataloging courses naturally, but I feel I am stronger in the reference and public service areas. As for administrative experience, I was in charge of the student aides in my department, so I do feel I have some knowledge of personnel management."

"Personnel management! Student aides! Berta, is that coffee ready yet?" Miss Lilliane rapped on the glass of her office.

"Not yet, ma'am. Pretty soon now." Berta's hands assembled a large drip coffeemaker as she stared hard at heating water.

The librarian reached into her desk and seized a pack of cigarettes. Before she could insert a smoke between her wrinkled lips, the old woman broke into a fit of coughing. As soon as the coughing ceased, Miss Lilliane lit the cigarette and inhaled.

"Cigarette?" She shoved the pack toward Laura.

"No, thanks."

"None of you young ones smoke. Well, good for you. My daddy told me it would be my death, and it almost has been and probably will be. Smoking put me here." The librarian tapped on the metallic arm of the wheelchair. "Five years ago, I fell asleep and before I knew it, my bed caught on fire. Like a goddamned ninny, I panicked and jumped out my bedroom window. Broke my back and would have been dead if it hadn't been for the bushes. Never smoke."

She pointed the cigarette held between yellowed fingers at Laura. Laura swallowed the impulse to say "No, ma'am" and let Miss Lilliane resume the interview.

"Well, you can't catalog. Do you know anything about genealogy? That's a big interest here in Chapelle."

"Not too much. I would be willing to take any courses available on the subject. I do have some interest in children's and young adult services. While in graduate school, I assisted in developing the summer reading program for the local library system. I considered going into children's services, but academic libraries offered more opportunities."

"Then why are you here?" Miss Lilliane trapped her deftly.

"There were no openings in my field, and I feel the need for a change. We had planned to settle in Louisiana." Even to Laura, her reasons sounded feeble.

For a moment, the elder librarian suspended her attack. "Yes, I recall the people at State Library told me you were recently widowed. No children, I hope."

"No, no children." She suppressed the urge to tell Miss Lilliane her question was not only illegal, but none of her business.

"Good. You won't have any child care problems then. Chapelle has very little to offer in the way of nursery schools. Coffee time." Miss Lilliane stubbed out her cigarette in an overflowing butt-filled ashtray and led the way, barging her wheelchair through the narrow door.

Both employees worked diligently applying Mylar jackets to a stack of new books. The librarian in charge made brief introductions as she maneuvered through the clutter. "Bobbie Meaux," she nodded at a chubby blonde on her left and "Berta Migues," to the black woman on her right. As they settled at the table set with demitasse cups, tiny teaspoons and a plate of Mrs. Domengeaux's unmistakable pralines, Ruby escorted two men into the room. "Two of our trustees—Jules Picard and Armand Duchamp." Miss Lilliane continued her perfunctory introductions.

The lean and dignified Mr. Duchamp took Laura's hand between both of his and squeezed lightly. He wore a red carnation in the lapel of his black suit and reminded Laura of someone she could not place. "My condolences on your recent bereavement, Mrs. Dickinson."

"Mr. Duchamp owns the finest funeral parlor in

town," prompted Miss Lilliane.

Remembering vividly the funeral director, right down to his red carnation, at David's memorial service, Laura withdrew her hand quickly. As soon as she'd freed her hand, Jules Picard began pumping it with vigor. Short and stout and dressed in a rumpled white suit, Mr. Picard had the style and manner of a Louisiana politician.

"I sell appliances, Laura, J.P.'s New and Used Appliances. If you need a good refrigerator or a microwave oven, see me. I'll give you a real good deal. Anything you need, you call me. I'm related to half the town, and the other half owes me money."

While the trustee still laughed at his own joke, Laura seized her chance. "As a matter of fact, the rental car I drove here has a defective air conditioner. That's why I'm so disheveled. I put the windows down and the mud splashed in—and then there was the muffaletta I had for lunch. It leaked. I know I look awful. Oh well, I was wondering if I could get the AC repaired before returning to New Orleans."

"No matter, no matter at all. I could see you were a charming young woman right off. Miss Lola always goes a little heavy on the olive salad, doesn't drain it properly, but don't say I told you that." Jules Picard waved his pudgy hands in front of Laura as if he could erase all her stains with a flick of his wrist.

"Old Thibodeaux at the Canal station can get it done for you by morning. He and his station don't look like much, but he's a real good mechanic, you see."

"I do have to be on a plane to Pennsylvania by four tomorrow."

"No problem. Stay the night here in Chapelle.

You'll have plenty of time to catch your flight."

"Well, I…"

"She can stay the night with me, Jules," Miss Lilliane intervened.

"Oh, no! I can't, really. Thank you." Laura struggled to extricate herself from the invitation.

"Stay with Miss LeBlanc. She has a wonderful antebellum home," said a third man who approached the table where Lilliane LeBlanc poured the deep black coffee into the flowered demitasse cups.

"This is Dr. Bourgeois. Young Dr. Bourgeois who insists I retire," introduced the parish librarian.

Young Dr. Bourgeois appeared to be at least forty. He smiled tolerantly at his patient. "You've been at this for fifty years, Miss LeBlanc. It's time to relax and enjoy life."

"He thinks I'm dying and doesn't want me to do it in a public place. That would be bad for his practice," Miss LeBlanc snapped.

"Has she been giving you a hard time, Mrs. Dickinson? She always gives me one," said the doctor.

"So how do you like our town, Laura?" Jules Picard plunged into the conversation.

Laura scanned her brain for compliments. "Chapelle's history is fascinating. I've been reading the guidebook and had a very interesting conversation with Father Ardoin at the church."

"Then you're a Catholic?"

"No."

"Baptist?"

"No, Lutheran. Most of the families of German descent where I grew up are."

"Dickinson, that's English like the writer."

"You mean the poet, Emily?"

"No, the writer, Charles Dickinson."

"My maiden name was Schumann," said Laura, unwilling to debate names any further.

"Like the piano player." Or like the cellist, she wanted to add but did not.

"That's right."

"You do *parle vous francais*?"

"No, I'm afraid not. I had two years of French in high school, but I don't really."

"Oh, hush, Jules, neither do I. You know how the teachers frowned on Cajun kids using their French when you and I were young. My own mother spoke perfect Parisian French, but I refused to learn because I wanted to be like everyone else."

This defense from the head librarian surprised Laura, but at least the situation had become clear. While Miss Lilliane's body was ready for retirement, her mind was not. At the moment, the old woman resented her board of trustees more than she resented Laura's application for her job. The old lady fell into another coughing spasm.

Dr. Bourgeois steadied his patient until the spell passed. "Have you been taking your medicine, Miss LeBlanc?"

"It doesn't do me any good. Sit down and drink your coffee." The librarian lit another cigarette.

The group settled around the table, and the interview proceeded more normally with the traditional questions about censorship issues, bookmobile service and previous work experience. Each man downed several servings of the strong black coffee, the tiny cups looking even smaller in their large hands. Laura sipped hers slowly hoping to reach the bottom before someone noticed one demitasse of dark roast coffee was about all that a Yankee could handle. The draining of the coffeepot and the pocketing of the last of the pralines by Jules Picard seemed to signal the end of the interview.

The appliance salesman demanded Laura's car keys and the location of the rental and pushed Laura toward the office. "You just call that rental place and tell them you can't make it in tonight because they gave you a defective unit. I'll get Old Thibodeaux started on this right away. Go on now. Just dial O, and Myrtle Hill over at the exchange will get your number for you."

He shut the door to the office and rushed back to the table where Armand Duchamp was making a point with regal gestures attached. Jules burst into the discussion with a flurry of motion while Dr. Bourgeois nodded sagely whenever he agreed with the others. Miss LeBlanc, lips taut and posture unbent, listened to them as if she were a wooden manikin.

Laura tried reading their lips through the glass walls but was distracted by the chatter of the operator. "So pleased to meet you, Mrs. Dickinson. I'm Myrtle Hill, and you must be the new librarian. I heard you were coming to town today. Come by the exchange and visit with me before you go, you hear? It's just down the road from the library. I'll put your call through to New Orleans, now. We'll bill it to the library. They won't mind."

After many clicks and much more of the voice of Myrtle Hill, the call from Chapelle eventually connected to the greater world ruled by Bell South beyond the cane fields. Laura made her arrangements and noted the board members apparently had made theirs because Miss Lilliane gave a defeated shrug and seemed to shrivel into her wheelchair as if only defiance had held her erect. The old librarian revived, however, as soon as her competition returned to the table.

"Well, they've decided to hire you, qualified or not. Do you want the job?"

"I'll need some time to consider it."

"You see! She's not interested."

"But, I am. I do want the job. I need some time to find a place to live and settle my affairs in Pennsylvania, that's all."

"You're hired," shouted Jules Picard.

"Definitely," said the undertaker.

"Congratulations," contributed Dr. Bourgeois.

"And now that's settled, I suppose I have to take you home with me, too. Berta, tell the rest of the staff I'm leaving early."

Preemptively, Miss Lilliane wheeled toward the bookmobile exit. Leaving the trustees shaking hands among themselves, Laura seized her purse and rushed in her wake. Berta's weary, "Yes, ma'am," followed the librarian out the door.

Chapter Four

Miss LeBlanc waited impatiently in her black behemoth while Laura purchased a toothbrush and a few necessities to get through the night. As soon as Laura reseated herself, the driver jerked the hand controls and swung into the road as if she owned the right of way. A red pickup truck squealed to an agonizing stop a foot from their bumper. The driver cursed the old lady fluently in French. Miss LeBlanc drove grandly on, reaching the edge of town in a matter of minutes. Doubting casual conversation with her fellow librarian was possible Laura tried to absorb herself in the scenery. Suddenly, Lilliane LeBlanc began talking and taking her eyes off the road more than Laura liked to make her points.

"At least you're better than most they've sent me. Kids just out of college! The last one left in tears. Couldn't even get through the interview. And they sent me a colored librarian they thought could run the place. Imagine that! Times change, but they don't change that fast in Chapelle."

Laura remained silent and watched the parade of homes, some grand, some shabby, wedged between the road and the bayou. Shaggy pecan trees preparing for winter dropped their yellow, disease-spotted leaves on the trailers and camps, cabins and mansions. Cane made a wall along the horizon on Miss Lilliane's side of the road.

"You, you at least know what it's like to lose something you care about. It's not easy to adjust to loss, to a handicap, to old age."

"It's not easy to adjust to being alone. Some people never adjust." Laura turned to look at Miss LeBlanc, but now that woman's gaze remained fixed straight ahead. Her aged lips moved.

"You're young. You'll adjust. And in Chapelle, you'll never be alone. Everyone knows everyone else's business and will until Myrtle Hill retires. The police jury here keeps talking about getting a modern phone system, but they won't do it until Myrtle gives up the exchange, and she's not much younger than me. Lives with and supports a mother older than the bayou. Those Hills came down here as carpetbaggers, and there is no getting rid of them. Why, they even got the politicians to chase off the Verizon men when they wanted to put up a few communication towers in the parish. Told people they'd get cancer from the invisible rays." Miss Lilliane snorted.

Laura, relieved the talk had taken a turn away from her, resumed her study of the countryside. The cane land turned to pasture on both sides of the road. Brahman cattle, stalked by flocks of small white egrets, grazed serenely in the fields where neither this type of cow nor that type of bird was native. She'd arrived at a place that took well to immigrants of all species. Maybe she could adjust.

A grove of live oaks standing the midst of the fields marked a home site, but nothing stood among the trees except four stout brick pillars and the central core of a fireplace. "By the size of the trees, that must have been a very old place." Laura pointed to the ruins in the grove.

Miss Lilliane nodded. "Bon Chance, my family's home, built in 1798 by August LeBlanc and destroyed by fire nine years ago. Of course, no one occupied it at the time. When the Chateau was completed in 1835, Bon Chance became the overseer's house. After my nephew insisted on converting the land from cane to cattle, no one lived there. Wasn't a mansion, only your typical French colonial cottage. Still, a pity to see it burn, especially since we were trying to give the old place to the parish for a museum. Arson, they said it was arson."

Beyond the ruins of Bon Chance, wide-girthed live oaks hung over the road at regular intervals forming a leafy corridor to another grove. The black Lincoln followed the line of trees off the main thoroughfare and on to a shell road, the heavy car pulverizing the oyster shucks that pinged up against the vehicle in retaliation.

"My home, Chateau Camille." The old lady's voice rose with pride as she pulled into the circular drive. The house, white-columned and deep verandahed, ablaze in the sunlight, was everything an antebellum mansion should be.

"You have a right to be proud," said Laura.

"Who said I was proud? There are bigger homes, fancier ones right in the area. But this one is mine, that's all." The elderly librarian leaned on the horn. When no one rushed from the huge double doors of the house to her side, Miss Lilliane rolled down her window and bellowed, "Pearl! Pearl! Angelle! T-Bob!" and laid on the horn again. No response came from the house.

"You'll have to go around back and get T-Bob. He's probably in the barn with his damned cows. Who knows where Pearl is hiding!"

"I'm sure I can get you into the house, Miss LeBlanc," Laura offered.

"T-Bob knows how I like things done. Now go around back and find him."

Laura accepted the order as a guest must and took a gravel walk to the rear of the house. She threaded through a formal garden among tree-sized camellias and immense azaleas clipped into tight mounds and came out of the maze at a thick hedge of shiny-leafed ligustrum. A whiff of barnyard and the lowing of cattle hinted at the view the ligustrum blocked. Laura passed through a gate and faced a line of thoroughly modern metal and concrete cattle barns. Holding pens and pasture stretched beyond the buildings. Laura picked her way among the cow patties, though the place was as immaculate as a barnyard could be. She settled on the center of the three buildings to try first because the sounds of animal versus man emitted from there.

"Dammit, hold him tighter!" came followed by a thud of hooves against a wall.

Laura entered the barn and in the instant it took for her eyes to adjust to the interior dimness, her white-shod foot sank into a small mound of fresh manure. Shaking what she could from her sole Laura peered into pen after pen and finally came to the source of the noise near the opposite door.

The black-haired man in the soiled khaki work shirt knelt in the straw. He applied a blue antiseptic with sure strokes of his big, tanned hands to a nasty cut on the foreleg of a half-grown Brahman calf whose head was held by a chocolate-colored man dressed in an identical khaki shirt. The lop-eared, saggy-jowled calf had a look about the eyes of a rebellious adolescent. It lunged backwards and struck out again. As much blue fluid stained the man in the straw as it did the calf. Sweat ran down the fellow's neck and disappeared into the mat of black hair showing at his open shirt collar.

Taking her cue from Miss LeBlanc's tone of voice, Laura addressed the surly, swearing hired man she recognized from the sandwich shop. "T-Bob, Miss LeBlanc needs some help out front." She used her best 'I take no nonsense from students' voice. The chocolate-colored man grinned broadly as if she had just told a tremendously funny joke.

The other man rose, brushing the straw from his knees, and answered without looking at Laura. "Tell Tante Lil I'll be there in a minute. Tony, leave him here a few days. Give that cut a chance to heal. He won't be show material, but someone who wants a good piece of breeding stock will take him. Have the men double check for loose wire."

Tony answered with a "Yes, Boss," emphasizing the word Boss and giving Laura another merry grin. Then, T-Bob turned his eyes directly on her.

Bedroom eyes, the words came swiftly to her mind. That's what one of her earthier college roommates called eyes like those, deep brown eyes with a hint of sorrow, a hint of longing, and an outright promise of passion. The color of the eyes did not matter, really. Laura shifted her own eyes to the calf and refocused her mind on the memory of David. Even so, she resisted the urge to tug down her skirt.

"He gave you a bad time," she said.

"Not really. He was afraid of the pain. We all are scared when we're hurt. That's natural. I'm Robert LeBlanc. Only people over the age of sixty call me T-Bob. It's been Robert or Bob since my father died."

"Laura Dickinson." Wondering where his surliness vanished, she offered her hand, and then noticed it put him at a disadvantage. He wiped his stained hands on a trouser leg and took hers in a warm, hard grip. The horn of the Lincoln sounded again, one long blare reaching all the way to the barns.

"Tante Lil calls." Appearing more amused than insulted, he led the way into the garden.

Chapter Five

T-Bob got the wheelchair out of the car and set it up on the gallery at once. Then, his muscles bunching, he carried the thin old woman up the steps. This casual display of strength left Laura a little breathless. He braced the heavy door with his back while gently tipping the chair over the sill. Laura hurried up the steps too late to be of any real service.

"She refused to let me build a ramp. Said it would mar the exterior," Robert LeBlanc whispered confidentially as they entered the wide hallway together.

Directly after their entrance, the sound of more shells being crushed beneath tires in the drive sounded followed by rapid footsteps on the gallery. With a thud of the door, a young girl with long black curls burst into the house.

"I saw a lady come in. Who is she?" the child questioned with enthusiasm.

Miss LeBlanc spun in her chair. "This is my grandniece, Angelle, T-Bob's girl who sometimes remembers her manners. Angelle, this is Miss Laura who will be taking my place at the library."

"Pleased to meet you, ma'am." Angelle bobbed slightly after being poked from behind by a silent figure in a white servant's uniform.

"Our maid, Pearl. You met her sister, Ruby, at the

library."

Except for the light complexion and single pearl earrings inserted in each lobe, Pearl and Ruby had little in common. The maid stood tall, thin and fine-featured. Her hair was screwed tightly into a bun at the nape of her neck. She showed none of the reassuring motherly qualities of her sister. Without waiting to be questioned, Pearl began a defense.

"You were early today, Miss Lilliane. Mr. Bob gave me his truck to take Angelle into town after school for new under things, hers were getting so bad."

"Well, you certainly had a busy day. There will be one extra for dinner this evening."

"There's plenty." Pearl started for the kitchen.

"And make up the bed in the guestroom."

Pearl disappeared into her region of the house. No one knew if she heard the last of the orders or not. Laura rushed to relieve the awkward moment. "Will your wife be at dinner, Mr. LeBlanc?"

"Not likely. She lives in New Orleans with her parents when she's not at one of her spas. We're divorced."

"Mama isn't coming to dinner, is she?" The child's big, brown eyes went wide with alarm.

"No, *cher* heart." Placing a hand on Angelle's long black curls, he hugged his daughter to him.

"Wait 'til you see my new things. They're in the truck."

"Bring them to my room, Angelle, after you show Miss Laura to the guestroom. I have to clean up. I'll see you at dinner, Mrs. Dickinson."

Laura followed the girl down a long hall on the first floor. She got the impression Angelle would have loved to stay and chat if her father hadn't been waiting to see the wonderful underwear. Frankly, Laura was glad the child dashed away after flinging open the door and saying, "This is your room, right next to mine."

Laura took a seat on an impressive canopied bed so high off the ground her feet didn't touch the floor. She rummaged in her handbag for tissues, all the while reflecting that in one afternoon she had incited hostility in Lilliane LeBlanc, insulted her nephew, caused anxiety in the child, and brought on rudeness from the maid.

"You sure know how to put your foot in it, Laura," she murmured as she attempted to clean cow plop off her white shoes with aloe-infused wipes.

Bearing a pile of fresh linens, Pearl entered without knocking. Laura hastily gathered up the dirty tissues from the bedspread and slid to her stockinged feet. Pearl stripped the spread and shook out a sheet without a word. Going to the other side of the large bed, Laura pulled the sheet across and tucked it as she would have on any Saturday when her mother changed the linens. Women did housework together, at least in Pennsylvania.

Pearl glared at her. "I can do my job. Don't need your help." She slipped a pillow into a case and gathered an end to pull up the spread.

"I could use a bathroom if you'll show me the way," Laura requested, eager to get out of the maid's presence.

"You pass through that door. It's two rooms down."

The sliding door next to a massive armoire led to a small room, obviously once a sleeping place for a servant or a dressing room, but now belonging to Angelle if the abundance of lace, dolls and stuffed toys gave any clue. The next door led to a larger bedroom. Miss Lilliane napped on another four-poster, this one lowered so she could manage it from the wheelchair. Even though the old woman had her head propped on several pillows, her breath came out rough and irregular. The next dressing area had been converted into a bathroom. Beyond its doors, Laura heard Angelle talking to her father.

"Come see, Daddy. Each one has a day of the week on it and a different color and real lace."

She heard Robert LeBlanc rumble an appreciation of the marvelous underwear. "Don't show those to any other boys," he cautioned.

Angelle giggled. "Oh, Daddy! Never ever."

David would have made a good father, too. Laura washed her face with cold water, repaired her makeup and retired to her room as quietly as possible, privately embarrassed over passing through the bedrooms of strangers when she could have been directed to the hall door.

****

The dinner went better than the day. Seated at a heavy mahogany table far too large and ornate for three family members and a guest, Miss Lilliane headed the table while her nephew—cleaned, groomed and freshly shaven—not a hired man at all, sat at the foot. Laura was placed opposite the next generation of LeBlancs, the child Angelle, who sat on a cushion to raise herself to table level.

A crystal chandelier from a more formal era of dining illuminated a simple meal of shrimp stew over rice and a green salad with vinegar dressing. They passed a deep basket of fresh French bread among themselves. Once during the meal, the surly servant Pearl appeared to refill the tall glasses with iced tea. The length of the table made conversation difficult, and Laura found herself speaking mostly to the little girl. That suited her. The afternoon had been full of faux pas from the moment she stepped in the manure. A child would be less likely to notice more blunders.

Lithe Angelle, a vivacious child, obviously preferred talking to eating. She had her father's dark eyes, enormous in her small face. Her curly black hair held back from her face with red barrettes fell to her waist. Despite the early autumn heat, she wore a long-sleeved white blouse and her plaid parochial school kilt. If she had a physical flaw, her complexion was too pallid, saved from being sickly by a sprinkling of freckles across the bridge of the nose. The gaps in her smile where her adult teeth just began to make an appearance added to her seven-year-old charm. She reminded Laura of the wonders of being in third grade and having the ability to read chapter books alone and learning to write script.

"I could write to you in Pennsylvania. I know where that is. Up north," Angelle volunteered.

"I'll be coming here to live, dear, so that won't be necessary."

"Will you live with us? My room is right next to yours. We could visit."

"I believe I'll have to find a place of my own."

"But you are welcome to stay here until you find something," added Robert LeBlanc, now the gracious host and not the catfish po-boy man.

Not freakin' likely, Laura thought. No way could she live here with the man who had bedroom eyes and didn't recall meeting her at Domengeaux's, the man she'd called T-Bob in her best schoolmarm voice. Not to mention Miss Lilliane in her perpetual cloud of smoke, and the hostile Pearl.

Miss Lilliane did not reconfirm the invitation, thank God. She seemed more relaxed among her relatives and lit a cigarette only when dinner ended, but this didn't mean she welcomed Laura as a long-term houseguest.

Pearl started clearing the table and signed to Laura to sit down when she stood and began to stack her plates. "A very tasty meal, Pearl." Laura offered a compliment instead of undesired help.

Pearl did not smile. "Not too spicy for you?"

"Oh, no. David and I used to eat Mexican food all the time. The flavor is a little the same."

"David is your husband?" Robert asked.

"I'm recently widowed." It was the briefest answer she could give. Thankfully, Angelle, who had no interest in marital status, interrupted to ask for dessert.

"Coconut cake or lemon sherbet, Angelle?" Pearl asked the child.

"Oh, coconut cake! Pearl's coconut cake is the best."

"On that advice, I'll try some, too." Laura smiled at both of them.

"Make it three, Pearl." Robert LeBlanc added his order.

"Lemon sherbet for me. It's so cooling after a hot meal," Miss LeBlanc said as if determined to be different. "Afterwards, perhaps Mrs. Dickinson would like to see the house. We have so many tourists asking to see the place that I finally wrote out a tour. Even Pearl and Angelle know it by heart."

"Daddy can do the downstairs, and I'll do the upstairs."

"Your father has paperwork to do. I'll give the downstairs tour myself."

Laura could only regret the paperwork and another hour in Miss Lilliane's company. They began the tour on the front porch.

"Chateau Camille was built from 1830 to 1835 by the slaves of Aurelien LeBlanc. Previously, the family lived at Bon Chance, a French raised cottage recently destroyed by fire. Its remains stand a mile from the Chateau, and the oak alley between the two homes was planted in 1835 also. The slave quarters, now demolished, were down the road from the new house. Only household servants lived on the premises."

In her first departure from the rote tour, Miss LeBlanc eyed Laura wickedly and added, "Yankees always want to know where the slaves were kept. One ass even asked me where we beat them. I told him if I knew, I'd be glad to show him how it was done." She slipped back into the monotone of the tour guide.

"Aurelien LeBlanc made his fortune in sugar and at one time owned three-hundred slaves. Many of the slaves were skilled craftsmen, and the plantation ran almost totally self-sufficiently. Bricks for the house were formed of local clay and baked in kilns on the plantation. Native cypress on the property provided all the lumber. The walls are two feet thick and coated with whitewash. Eight plastered and whitewashed brick columns support an upper gallery. The house possesses fourteen rooms not including servants' quarters and a detached kitchen.

"Although Aurelien and Camille LeBlanc had only one surviving child, they maintained the custom of providing lavishly for houseguests who often stayed for months enjoying their hospitality. LeBlanc, of course, also wished to pass on a house suitable to the status of the family to his son and began building the year of the child's birth. Chateau Camille, unlike other southern mansions, has never passed from the hands of the LeBlancs despite the hardships inflicted by the War Between the States." Miss LeBlanc nailed Laura with a glance as if the war were her Damn Yankee fault.

"Follow me." Swiftly, the old woman reversed and wheeled her chair directly toward the heavy cypress door. Laura dashed ahead to open it, sure Miss Lilliane would crash through the wood in a shower of splinters at her present rate of speed. The image made Laura grin, and Angelle, persuading the chair over the sill, answered the smile with a giggle totally ignored by the wheelchair occupant.

Once in the hallway again, Laura became aware that despite the briskly professional tour, Chateau Camille lacked a museum quality. Its hardwood floors bore scuffs from the child's shoes and the runners of the wheelchair. A Chinese bowl of fresh yellow chrysanthemums hid the chips and scratches in the marble top of a fine pier table set between two tall doors. In the dim corners of the twelve-foot ceilings, small spider webs collected dust as well as insects.

Miss LeBlanc paused before the two portraits hung over the pier table. "The left hand painting done by Emile Devereaux is a portrayal of Aurelien LeBlanc at the age of forty-one. The right hand portrait, also by Devereaux, shows Camille Castille LeBlanc and her son, Adrien. The table below is, of course, a petticoat table with a mirror inset in the base so the ladies of the day could check the condition of their voluminous skirts without being too obvious."

"I've been told the mirror served to project more light into the room," Laura added.

"Who is giving this tour, you or me?" Miss Lilliane stared her down.

The shrewd gray-blue eyes of Aurelien LeBlanc seemed to approve of this put down. His high white collar poked into his meaty, prosperous jowls, but did not appear to be causing him any discomfort. His cleft chin rested on a frothy silk cravat. Despite his age, golden if thinning curls still clustered on his broad white brow. Laura moved her eyes from the master-of-the-manor gaze so aptly captured by the artist and regarded Camille Castille LeBlanc.

She thought Emile Devereaux might have overemphasized the virility and vitality of his rich patron, but if he flattered the master, he had been unkind to the mistress. Camille LeBlanc showed her age in the wings of white in her black hair. While her olive complexion was free of wrinkles, the artist had made no attempt to hide a double chin, the broad bosom, or the wide lap of a middle-aged wife going to fat, not a lovely woman by any standard. The only beauty she possessed rested in the dark eyes shining lovingly down on her only son, a curly-haired imp dressed like a little man and looking more like a doll on her large lap than a small child.

Still, the portrait of the boy was not wooden.

Devereaux had captured the dark-eyed mischief and the merriment in the full lips. The son had the father's cleft chin, though where he had gotten his small, straight nose and handsome high-cheeked face would have been hard to say. Perhaps, Mistress LeBlanc's heavy flesh concealed finer bones.

Miss Lilliane rolled on to the first large room to the right. "This is the parlor. The pocket doors in the rear could be pushed back enlarging the room into a ballroom for parties and dances. At such times, the rosewood and horsehair settees and chairs would be pushed against the walls and the Turkish carpets taken up. A band of slave musicians played their instruments in the space between the two fireplaces."

As Miss Lilliane began enumerating the dates and origins of various antiques, Laura noted the comfortable modern armchair, a small television recessed into an old mahogany cabinet, a doll with a plastic, rather than a porcelain face in the corner of the sofa. She imagined Robert LeBlanc watching the evening news from the one inhabitable chair while Angelle played with her blue-eyed, big-busted doll—or David sitting in that chair while their own blond baby played in front of the fireplace.

A sharp note from Miss Lilliane broke Laura's domestic daydream. "Over the mantel is a self-portrait of Adrien LeBlanc, son of the builders, artist and wastrel. It's no thanks to him that the family still owns the Chateau."

Laura wondered if this outburst was part of the written tour. Probably not. The adult Adrien LeBlanc had Byronic good looks, a floppy white shirt open at the neck and one elegant hand holding a palette, the other a brush. He gazed not at his viewers, but at himself, his full, sensuous lips smiling slightly at his own image in a mirror. Laura dismissed him as one of those "I'm too sexy for my shirt kind of guys," definitely not her type now or a hundred-sixty years ago.

"Come here!" Miss LeBlanc wheeled imperiously to the pocket door and slid it easily aside. Over a matching fireplace in the other half of the ballroom hung yet another ancestral portrait, this one done in the same relaxed, romantic style of the Adrien LeBlanc self-portrait. A beautiful woman with honey-colored hair flowing about her shoulders and clad in a loose white morning gown held a chubby, beruffled baby of her own angelic mold, but of undetermined sex, in her lap. A somber dark-eyed boy stood behind the wicker chair holding his mother and his sibling. He rested one hand possessively on her shoulder. A middle child sat at her mother's feet, dark eyes, black curls, and small face half buried in the full petticoat.

"This is Caroline Montleon LeBlanc, wife of the good-for-nothing Adrien and the savior of Chateau Camille." The words, definitely not part of the tour, spewed from Miss Lilliane with as much bitterness as if Adrien LeBlanc had tried to disinherit her specifically.

"I've read her diaries. She was never at any time fooled by her husband. They met in New Orleans where he had gone to study art after his mother forbade him to go to Paris. He established quite a name for himself painting all the young women and many of the quadroon mistresses of prominent men. Some of the portraits were scandalous nudes painted under more scandalous circumstances, but he never painted

Caroline in any guise except that of his wife and mother of his children.

"It seems they reached an early agreement. She, trained and educated to run a plantation, wanted only a plantation to run. He wanted only to be free of responsibility. They married under those terms. His mother, realizing how badly she had spoiled her only child, approved of his sensible choice. Camille LeBlanc died shortly after her first grandchild came into the world. On her deathbed, she placed the keys to the Chateau in Caroline's hands."

Miss Lilliane paused dramatically. Laura searched for words and came up with "Fascinating story."

"Yes, isn't it?" Miss Lilliane cleared her throat and plunged back into her narrative.

"Old Aurelien LeBlanc still lived and attended to business matters, but he shifted more and more of the burden onto Caroline. The two of them watched Adrien come and go, living on the generous allowance they gave him. He spent enough time at the Chateau to impregnate Caroline seven times in ten years with total disregard for the work required of her. She miscarried three times and lost her second son in infancy. Her surviving children are shown in the painting, Charles, who fortunately took after his mother in business acumen, Catherine who later became a nun and it is said, prayed daily for her father's soul, and the baby, Felice, who married back into the Orleans Parish Montleon line. Why Caroline didn't lock the bedroom door against him, I'll never know!"

"Maybe she enjoyed the sex." The urge to be irreverent of long ancestral lines bubbled up in Laura during the tirade. Immediately sorry, she had completely forgotten the inquisitive seven-year-old tagging along on the tour.

"What you talkin' about? Where babies come from? My friend, Jenny Cavalier says…"

"Angelle, go tell your father I'm too tired to complete the tour."

"Oh good!" The child dashed off to drag her father from his paperwork.

"Let me tell you one more thing about the romantic Adrien. He deserted his wife and children during the War. He passed the time in Paris painting and fornicating. He never returned. He died of well-earned dissipation at the age of forty. And he killed his own father, indirectly, of course—but that does not absolve him. Old Aurelien felt he had to enlist to save the family honor. Nearly seventy, he died of camp fever and left Caroline to face the war and the changed world to come later. I loathe having Adrien LeBlanc in my family history. Loathe it!"

Angelle returned dragging her father along by the sleeve.

"Go to bed, Tante Lil. I'll take over."

Without a parting word, Miss Lilliane wheeled from the room.

"Really, I don't need a tour. I'm keeping you from business." Laura had the urge to escape the amused dark eyes of her host by running to her own bedroom.

"Doesn't take much to upset Tante Lil since the accident. Too many changes for her in too short a time to adjust, most of them my fault, though her opinion of me hasn't fallen to loathsome yet. By the old Napoleonic Code in this state, she is a co-inheritor of this house along with Angelle and myself. She has the right to live here until death, and she will. But, my father was a lawyer. I have complete control of the land. Since my conversion of its use from cane to cattle, we haven't had as much cash to keep up the house in the old manner. This house is all to her."

"Then why did you do it? Stop growing cane, I mean."

"If I go into that, Mrs. Dickinson, your tour won't end until midnight. Let's see, according to Angelle, the tour broke off just when you were going to tell her where babies come from."

Laura rarely blushed, but she did now.

"I think we'll skip that and continue with the heroic Caroline. This was her sitting room. She did her correspondence at that Queen Anne desk in the corner. The wicker furniture is not original to the house. We bought it at Lowe's when the old stuff wore out. We can pass from this area easily into the dining room, convenient when you are having a ball. We haven't had any lately."

Robert LeBlanc had none of the lean, pale romantic elegance of the reprehensible Adrien, though they shared the cleft chin, dark eyes and curly hair of the family. Not very tall, the living owner of Chateau Camille stood around five-eight, broad, muscular and tanned from outdoor work, comfortably masculine, and good casual company as long as the dark eyes remained amused and did not turn their serious, longing look on Laura. No, not a surly hired man at all, but the genial country squire. She packaged him neatly in her mind, put him away and thoroughly enjoyed the rest of the tour.

"Here is the dining room. The table is as small as

we can make it. With leaves in, it seats twenty-four. The chandelier is from Venice, the china we never use from France, the crystal from Germany. At one time, all the food served here was raised on the plantation or harvested nearby from the wild roast duck with rice to ham, yams and fresh seafood from Vermilion Bay. Food bills being what they are, I'd like to see that day come again. At this point, I usually ask for a donation to be placed in the Sevres sugar bowl, but you are exempt.

"On to the guest bedroom, once the bower of Caroline LeBlanc and containing an absolutely authentic Mallard bedroom set given to the bride as a wedding gift from her family in 1851. The acorns on the posts symbolize fertility. Since I am here, it worked."

Laura stood in the doorway of the room where she was to sleep, suddenly in awe of resting in a bed where this man's forebears had made love, given birth, and perhaps died.

"The top bar of the bedstead could be removed and used to fluff the mattress. Or it could have been used to fend off the advances of the lecherous Adrien." T-Bob lifted and waved the heavy bar threateningly.

Angelle, his best audience, giggled some more. "Oh, Daddy! About babies..."

"It didn't work or wasn't used. Caroline LeBlanc gave birth to all of her children in this bed and eventually died here. But don't worry, the mattress is new." He read Laura's thoughts with a teasing gleam in his eyes. "The rest of the downstairs rooms were at one time, the plantation office now too messy to be shown because I sleep there, and a nursery with servants' sleeping closets between each. All are now the private quarters of the LeBlanc family and off-limits to tourists. End of tour. Back to paying the bills."

"Look, I appreciate your time." Laura held out a hand in formal parting. "I did enjoy the tour, especially the last half."

"It's not over yet! May I take her upstairs, please, please?" Angelle begged.

"Sure thing, sugar. I will warn you none of the rooms are furnished, and we have some fire damage. After the accidents, I felt we would all be safer on the ground floor. If this old place should burn, the only way out from the second floor is the kind Tante Lil took, through a window or a dive off the upper gallery."

The yearning look came back into the eyes of Robert LeBlanc. Laura turned away and followed Angelle up a sinuous central staircase, "good for sliding down" the child commented in an almost scholarly way.

A small brass chandelier shone at the head of the stairs, and the last rays of September sun lit the rear of the hall through a large window overlooking the drive and oak alley. Angelle began in the large room with doors opening onto the gallery.

"This was Daddy and Mama's room." Dark patches stood out on the Victorian wallpaper where large pieces of furniture had been removed. The child passed into a smaller adjoining room.

"I slept here when I was a little baby." The small pink rosebuds on the paper were browned and blackened around the doorway on the far side of the room. They passed through the smoke-damaged entry. Glancing back, Laura could see another charred spot on the opposite side of the child's room.

"This is where Tante Lil jumped out the window. I was real little, but I remember. She screamed so loud, and Daddy ran through my room into here to beat out the fire."

In Tante Lil's old room, the burnt wallpaper still gave off the smell of smoke. French doors opened on to a small ornamental balcony overlooking the garden. Below, the huge bushes became black mounds in the gathering dusk. Long, black scars reaching from doorway to doorway traced the line of the fire into the floor. Angelle did not linger. With a toss of dark curls, she went out into the hall.

"This is the bathroom, and these were Grandpa's rooms and all his books before he died, but I was only a baby then."

Laura took a quick glance into the suite, an empty bedroom and a library lined with law books, dusty but in perfect order. A large antique desk with a well-used chair of cracked leather sat in front of the library's balcony window. Angelle quickly lost interest in a set of rooms that held no memories for her. She darted out the gallery door at the far end of the suite. Laura followed her into the soft, humid night.

"You can see all the way to the bayou in the day." The little girl swung on the gallery railing that creaked a warning of its age to small children. Laura pulled Angelle to her, and they passed together into the house and down to the first floor.

"Can I come see you in your room? At night, I'm afraid of ghosts in the guestroom, but Daddy says if there are any ghosts in this house, they are all upstairs. With you right next door, I won't be afraid. And you can tell me where babies come from, maybe?"

Laura passed the rest of the evening meeting Angelle's dolls, including one old Raggedy Ann slightly crisped by the fire of the past. She firmly resisted the child's pleas to learn about the origins of babies and referred her to her father or Tante Lil.

"But they won't tell," pouted Angelle. Once the child settled for the night, Laura used the front hall to reach the bathroom, took two aspirins from the LeBlanc's medicine cabinet and ended the stressful day with restless sleep in a strange huge bed.

In the morning, her rented car was, indeed, repaired. "Only a small leak, *cher.* Jules Picard, he picked up da tab, him," said old Thibodeaux over the phone.

In his battered pickup truck, the master of Chateau Camille drove Laura to the ancient Canal gas station still bearing the sign of a company long out of business. Robert LeBlanc sat behind the wheel and talked pleasantly of cattle and crops, sometimes digressing into a funny anecdote about his daughter. If his guest became a little too aware of the biceps bunched under his rolled shirtsleeves or the occasional dark regard of his eyes that was not his fault. Laura moved closer to the truck door and farther from the warmth of his body. After four months benumbed by grief why had her hormones decided to wake up now on a narrow country road in Louisiana?

T-Bob had asked her a question, and she'd missed it entirely. He repeated the offer to have Laura stay at the Chateau until she found a place of her own. Considering Miss LeBlanc had not appeared at breakfast to bid her good-bye over the grillades and grits, Laura thought not. Awkward, how terribly awkward it would be to share a house with Tante Lil and the nephew who exuded pheromones like one of his bulls. She wished Robert would put on the sunglasses dangling from the windshield visor, but since he didn't, she took her dark glasses from her purse and slid them over her own eyes.

At Thibodeaux's Canal gas station, which now sold Shell, Robert got down and helped her from the truck's cab by placing a strong, callused hand under her elbow. The heat of his touch seemed to flow up her arm and into her cheeks. She thanked him and stepped away.

"Good luck finding a place. My offer stands if you can't find anything."

"I'm sure I will. Thank you again for your hospitality." She waved instead shaking his hand, and he grinned like a black-haired devil as he got into the truck and drove away.

Laura spent the spare hours of the morning apartment hunting and discovered apartment complexes did not exist in Chapelle. Rental houses were available in disreputable neighborhoods. The town had subsidized housing for the poor. Lavish southern homes for sale glutted the real estate market, but she found no practical place to live. After a fruitless search, she took her parting meal at noon in Domengeaux's café, this time sitting at an oil-clothed table and spilling out her problems to Miss Lola's sympathetic ears.

"I tell you what, *cher*. I got me an apartment right above dis store. First Papa and I lived dere, and my daughter before she took off for Baton Rouge. Dat girl, I prayed to da Virgin for her. I said, Blessed Mother, give me a child, and I make you a shrine right here in my store and tell everyone about your miracle. It worked for dat lady, Camille LeBlanc, a hundred years and more ago. I t'ink it work for me too, you know, and it did. So I put up my shrine right here in da store where everyone can see it. Da Holy Mother, she kept her part of da deal. So my daughter grows up, gets married and moves to Baton Rouge. I never see her no more—maybe once a month if I go dere, but I don't like da drive. She never brings my grandkids to see me hardly ever—except on most Sundays. Come, I show you da place."

They took a rickety staircase to the second floor. The apartment had generous space for one person, two large rooms, a small bath and a kitchenette. The hardwood floors and an elaborate ceiling decorated with plaster festoons of fruit and flower garlands came as pleasant surprises. The antiquated plumbing fixtures and ancient gas range did not.

"Dis building, *cher*, is real old. Dem French aristocrats built it when dey found out dey had to stay a while after dat revolution. Papa and me, we put in da bat'room and lights. Dis old armoire, it's always been here."

Lola Domengeaux pointed to a vast cabinet filling one wall of the bedroom. Its inlay of fruits and flowers matched the ceiling design. Laura opened the well-oiled doors. The interior had many wide shelves and small drawers. In one corner of the door, she noticed the carved initials "C.S."

"This must be terribly valuable." Laura ran her fingers over the initials and thought of the Mary altar in the church that could be seen through the French doors in the front room.

"You know it, *cher*. We got lots of offers for it, but how you gonna get it out of here? It must of been brought up t'rue da windows and den in pieces. I figure it belongs here, so here it stays."

"I'm staying, too. You have yourself a tenant."

"I knew you'd get dat job, *cher* heart, and I'm pleased to have you. Now come, let me pack you some pralines to take home for your mama. She ain't gonna like you being so far away, but you tell her Lola Domengeaux will take care of her girl."

Chapter Six

Mrs. Domengeaux knew mothers. Laura's own disapproved of her moving so far from home. "We won't be nearby to help you if…"

"If what?"

"If you should start to feel unwell again. Chapelle has only two doctors—I, uh, checked that for you while you were gone."

"And Lost Spring has only one and the same number of traffic lights. The town is full of mostly nice people who would be glad to help me exactly like here."

"A small town like that—all the men around your age will be married."

"Not all."

Laura saw her sister, tossing a salad for the farewell dinner, raise her eyebrows.

"I mean even Lost Spring has Jay Geiger. There are probably some single men in Chapelle—if I were looking."

"Uh-huh," her sister, Cynthia, said knowingly. "Tell us all about the people you met down there."

Laura kept them laughing with thumbnail sketches of Old Thibodeaux, Miss Lilliane, and Jules Picard. She thought she'd gotten the accents about right and used a thick-sliced French fry with the end dipped in ketchup to simulate a cigarette hanging out the corner of her mouth while she told her niece and nephew never to smoke and made them laugh. She omitted T-Bob from her act. She had no desire to joke about him or share him with her family.

Knowing Cynthia adored old things and could not afford them, Laura got some revenge for putting her on the spot about eligible men with lavish descriptions of the LeBlanc's antiques and the armoire in her apartment. Cruel, true, but she had grown tired of hearing Cissy complain about what a financial drain her son and daughter were when Laura would trade all the armoires and stately homes in the world for one beautiful, healthy child. The old sisterly bickering helped dull her departure pangs.

In the morning, her father hitched the U-Haul trailer to Laura's car. Her mother, who had no gift for parting words said, "Get over David and start a new life then. I wish you'd stayed closer to home."

"Get over David? I will never forget David."

Fuming over her mother's insensitivity Laura pulled hastily away from the curb with only a wave to her bewildered father. Get over David. Forget David when the very trailer she towed contained all the bits and pieces of their brief life together: an extravagant solid brass bedstead purchased with wedding gift money and their well-used old mattress, their wedding album and a box of even more precious candid photos, the delicate miniature oil rig that sat on his desk, the coffee mug he always used, the old shirt she slept in on nights when her grief grew unbearable. She took as much of David as she could to Chapelle.

Dragging her baggage behind her, Laura crossed the Mason-Dixon Line leaving Pennsylvania and entering the Southern States, so designated only because of previous differences on slave holdings, and not because of any great difference in weather, flora or fauna. By evening she had reached the true red dirt south of piney woods and twanging gas station attendants. Her second day on the road brought her to the South of slow drawls and evergreen magnolias, and her third across the Mississippi and deep into Louisiana where David had died and Laura now planned a new life.

The road off the interstate and into Chapelle seemed less hostile this trip, even with the ever-irate Miss LeBlanc waiting at the end of it. A few of the walls of cane had been broken down into wide alleys where machines with claws gathered the severed stalks and loaded them into carts to be hauled in cumbersome loads to the mill. The furnace-like autumn heat had diminished to a pleasant daily warmth, and cooler evenings laid the virulent mosquitoes to rest.

The rambling gray mill had taken on life, its cranes grasping at the cane and gobbling the stems by the cartload. White smoke from its chimneys spread out over the shabby houses in its shadow and left a sticky dew behind. The grinding season had arrived and given its blessings to the quarters. Here new clothes, unfaded, untorn, flapped on a clothesline, and a small child as black as the soil sat on one slanting porch and nurtured a baby doll still robed in a stiff, pink dress and spotless white booties. More people passed on the streets of Chapelle. Most turned to eye Laura's trailer, and one, old Thibodeaux at the former Canal station, raised a friendly hand.

Having volunteered two men in the lunchroom

away from their beer and boudin sausage, Lola Domengeaux supervised the unloading of the trailer. Mrs. Domengeaux pushed her recruits, loaded to the maximum, up and down the narrow stairs, urged along by a steady stream of Cajun French.

Though the brass bed set up by one of the volunteers using Mrs. Domengeaux's screwdriver looked inviting after the day's drive and unpacking, Laura dutifully borrowed the delicatessen phone and called first, her parents, and then the library to announce her arrival.

Miss Lilliane was in fine form. "So, you got here. I suppose you want to start work right away."

"Actually, I could use a few days to get settled. Would Monday be all right?"

"Take all the time you need. I can manage without you. I've been doing it for fifty years." Miss Lilliane hung up.

Trying not to be disturbed by what lay ahead on Monday, Laura made up the bed, smoothing wrinkles from the sheets and absorbing old memories. Lola Domengeaux interrupted these thoughts by showing up at the door with two plastic containers of her "own etouffee from da freezer" and "dat other one is rice."

"Just heat it up, *cher*, pour it over da rice, den get you some rest. I close up at six, but if you need anyt'ing else, you call."

After singeing her fingers in the sudden flare from the old gas range, Laura did enjoy the zesty pink etouffee. She picked out the tender tails of crawfish and left some of the rice. Ice water and fresh fruit from the little travel cooler completed her meal. She chanced lighting the old stove again to brew a cup of relaxing hot tea, but with so much left to unpack, Laura could not rest.

Along one wall, she erected bookshelves of cinder blocks and boards that had served her through college, career and marriage, and sat her television in its center. She filled the empty space with her unlimited supply of books and several small sculptures, David's miniature derrick among them, along with a picture of her lost husband.

The volunteers had placed her tan leather loveseat along the opposite wall. Its simple modern lines and warm color blended nicely with the cypress plank floors, but the ornate ceiling seemed to warrant carved rosewood and brocade. Instead, it got a plain, but solid oak coffee table, lovingly refinished and presented as a parting gift from Cynthia. As Laura arranged a few of the overflow of books on its shining surface, she made a mental note to find something special for Cissy, something the children would not break.

Dishes and pans put away in cupboards that required no wiping thanks to Miss Lola, clothes stored in the closet, the antique armoire stuffed with linens and odds and ends of apparel, Laura rested at last on the big brass bed, her body wrapped in David's old shirt, her mind full of his image. Halfway through the night, she jerked herself out of a dream where a man with dark eyes and black hair laid beside her and caressed her breasts with callused hands. She rebuttoned the shirt that had opened over hot, sensitive skin and peaked nipples.

Climbing out of bed, Laura walked out of her bedroom through the black shadow cast by the massive armoire and into the small kitchen. She poured some milk from the plastic quart jug stocked, along with a few other basic groceries, by Miss Lola in her refrigerator. No way would she risk lighting that stove to heat the stuff when clumsy with sleep and shaken by a bad dream. She could burn the place down. Taking her glass over to the French doors, Laura gazed out on Chapelle. No cars moved along Main Street. With her eyes still seeking heaven, the statue of Ste. Joan glowed near a streetlight. Laura went to her shelves and picked up the framed photo of David with his wide smile and twinkling eyes. She fixed his face firmly in her mind and went back to bed.

****

As if summer could not keep its sweaty hands off of October, Laura's first morning in Chapelle threatened to be hot and sticky again. Resolutely, she set out along Main Street to finish furnishing her apartment. The Dollar Store provided a huge petticoat fern hanging on a summer clearance rack of outdoor plants. Dot's Antiques & Used Furniture supplied a refinished solid wood table and four chairs of Depression vintage from the used furniture section of the store. The dining set did not quite have the age or elegance to command the prices of the cypress armoires and nineteenth century marble-topped washstands in the antiques section of the shop. Miss Dot, herself, promised her man would deliver the furniture that same day, nothing being too good for the new librarian.

Laura's status bought her a bargain at the Cajun Corner, a local crafts shop brimming with cornhusk dolls, oil paintings of live oaks and orange nutria tooth necklaces. She selected two large, handmade rag rugs in muted earthy tones and got a twenty percent discount and two overdue library books to return by the proprietor. A boy from the Penny Saver grocery carried two boxes of food and cleaning supplies up the stairs and into her kitchen and refused a tip. By then, the kitchen table had been delivered as promised.

Laura hung her fern from a hook where, undoubtedly, similar plants had hung in front of the French doors. The doors opened on to a small balcony of wrought iron, much like those at the rear of Chateau Camille but infinitely more rusted, not a place to stand on even momentarily. The rag rugs made circles of color on the old flooring as she laid them down.

She unearthed the carton of framed art prints, remnants of cheap interior decorating from her college days, and placed more color on her bare plaster walls. Once, the walls must have been papered, but now they were stripped bare, patched and painted in what Laura thought of as "apartment beige." Their blankness enhanced the sunny impressionist garden scene over the sofa, the waggish Toulouse Latrec above the table, and the delicate Japanese landscape by the bookshelves. The picture of her and David locked together on their wedding day she placed in her bedroom.

Laura settled in more quickly than she could have imagined, and a long unfilled weekend stretched ahead. The rugs and furniture absorbed only some of the echoes of emptiness in the new apartment. She gazed out her front window. Below, on the green, her companion of the night, Ste. Joan, looked up at her as if Laura had found the paradise she sought. The benign St. Francis, who had dined with Laura on the day of her interview, was hidden by the wide leafy arms of the live oaks. If the black kitten still lived beneath the church,

Laura had a promise to keep.

Wrapping some of the cold, barbecued chicken Mrs. Domengeaux had thrust on her at lunchtime, she went to visit St. Francis. "Thanks for the job, Frank. I hope I don't regret this later."

Laura lay a bit of chicken near the feet of the statue. The ivy rustled, and the black kitten slithered from the fist-sized hole in the foundation of the church. He ran his rough tongue over the meat, scooping it into his mouth as fast as he could. When he came to give Laura thanks in the way of cats, coiling around her ankles and sniffing for more food, she scooped up the small feline and felt his small bones beneath the velvet of his fur.

"Shall I call you Snake in honor of the scare you gave me?" asked Laura. Snake remained indifferent to everything except the last of the cold chicken. Placidly full and purring, he allowed Laura to carry him to their home.

Snake filled Laura's weekend with a trip to a veterinarian who worked on Saturdays and pronounced Snake healthy, but thin, and pumped the kitten full of vaccines for various cat-killing diseases. She obtained permission from Miss Lola who understood about promises to saints, purchased cat food and litter, and accomplished the general orientation between pet and mistress. Snake, far from being either finicky or aloof, ate everything ravenously and absorbed and returned affection in equal amounts. When Monday morning arrived, Laura faced the library with at least one small ally behind her.

Chapter Seven

Incarcerated in the glass-walled office with Miss Lilliane and released only for coffee and lunch, Laura learned the basics of operating a parish library on Monday and on Tuesday and on Wednesday until another weekend gradually crept into view. Miss Lilliane refused any suggestions for change from Laura, always citing her Bible of library practices, a thick volume issued by the State Library in 1945. The yellowed pages crumbled at the edges when the retiring librarian pounded on them to make a point.

"But we could save time in cataloging by using the CIP information on the reverse of the title page. The clerks could do it."

"Then what do you have? Someone else's cataloging—totally inappropriate to this library! Lazy person's cataloging!" Miss Lilliane pounded more paper fragments to dust.

"I believe it would be a good investment to hire a part-time secretary to do the bookkeeping and payroll. We could have more time to develop new library programs and services."

"I've been doing my own books for fifty years. You can, too."

The office offered too confined an area for Laura to scream, not to mention all the second-hand smoke she'd inhale if she did. In this library, the books stayed in perfect order on the old wooden shelves and old men slept in the periodical area during the afternoon. Housewives came in for their weekly quota of romances, but no one under thirty entered except for the students forced into coming for homework assignments.

"I wondered if we could have some sort of Halloween party for the children and maybe for their parents, too."

"We've never had anything before, and no one complained. You'll just bring the Fundamentalists down on us for celebrating witchcraft."

Laura grew more stubborn by Friday. She filed away most of her innovations for the time when Miss Lilliane finally relinquished her place behind the large desk and overflowing ashtrays, and she could remove herself from the straight-backed chair in the corner where she'd been put to learn her lessons. Feeling the need to do something—anything—Laura stuck to her point. "It's time we had a program just for fun. I'll handle the arrangements and the Fundamentalists. Maybe, we could have a bonfire on the green and call in some local storytellers. Father Ardoin told me about an old black woman with some fabulous tales only the other day. I'll bet he would like to tell one himself. Catholics don't have anything against Halloween, do they?"

She rushed on. "I know a few good stories, too, though I didn't get to practice them at the university library."

Admitting to herself her idea might be only an excuse to play hooky on a lovely Friday afternoon and escape Miss Lilliane's smoky den, Laura left immediately after lunch to begin arrangements. Miss

LeBlanc let her go with the encouraging comment, "No one will come!"

The volunteer fire department chief was amenable. He and his crew policed the annual homecoming bonfires for both the Catholic and public high schools. It meant a little overtime pay close to the holidays for Chief Fontenot, one of two paid members on the force. Father Ardoin lent his enthusiastic support. After being assured the storytelling activities would not conflict with the religious observances for All Saints Day, he volunteered himself and got halfway through the story of the Devil and the black preacher when Laura interrupted to get directions to the house of Tante Lu.

"Ah, Tante Lu! A good choice. Didn't I tell you she lives in the old Segura cabin? Alma Segura's land is still in the family after two centuries, but I imagine all that will end when Tante Lu passes on. That old woman must be nearing one hundred, and she's still as sharp as they come. Two generations separate her and the last of the Seguras. One of them works at your library, Ruby Senegal, a Segura that was. And then, there's Pearl, a maid out at the LeBlanc place, but that one never married. Might be another one, Opal, I believe, who lives in California, but I can't see any of them staying on in a country cottage. Senegal has done very well in sanitation, has his own company, lots of garbage trucks, two sons in the business with him, but of course, the old Segura family name is gone. The place should be declared a landmark when the old lady dies. I'll have to look into that."

"The directions?"

"Yes, oh yes. Take Bridge Road out by the cemetery. You'll pass through a little town called Nebo, an African-American Baptist church on the right and a country store on the left. About five miles beyond that, the old Segura place sits in a grove of oaks on the bank of Little Black Bayou. What a lovely day for a drive. Unfortunately, I must prepare for Mass. Tante Lu will probably be out on the porch in her rocker on such a nice day. Send her my blessing."

Laura took the blessing to Tante Lu along Bridge Road. The Deep South autumn put on a display more suitable for spring. The drainage ditches, free at last of summer's overflow, stood deep in goldenrod, purple with wild asters and blue with mistflower. She drove through Nebo, noting that all of the faces watching her pause at the single stop sign just past the Mount Zion Baptist Church possessed the color of coffee, black or light with varying amounts of cream.

Laura nearly missed the old raised cottage with its screen of live oaks grown so large and impressive they should have been guarding a palace instead of hiding the shabby Segura place. The low interlocking branches partially concealed a battered pickup truck, its tailgate showing a familiar pattern of rusty dents. Laura turned her car into the rutted dirt lane leading to the house and tried to place the ownership of the pickup truck, about as easy as trying to distinguish among the live oaks in Chapelle. Most nights, Main Street provided a parade route for an endless procession of such vehicles.

The deep porch of the cottage held a rocking chair and a swing on rusty chains, but no elderly woman sat on them. After Laura parked by the pickup and turned off the car's engine, she located Tante Lu by the scratch of a broom on the weathered cypress planks over in the shaded corner where a flight of short and steeply angled stairs led to the garconniere. Laura's eyes followed the stairs to the trap door and the loft where Alma Segura's sons must have slept so long ago, then quickly returned to the wizened woman vigorously sweeping dust and the leaves of October from her porch.

The old lady, so tiny the broom seemed oversized in her knotty hands, gave it a few more forceful strokes. As age shrunk Tante Lu from the inside, the skin of her younger self settled over her frame in myriad yellow folds and wrinkles. Barely covering her ancient skull, a few puffs of hair like white fleece were gathered into a small knot on the top of her head. The bright bird-like eyes in their nest of wrinkles took in Laura as she climbed the two steps to the porch. In a voice much louder than such a small body should own, Tante Lu called out, "Pearl, we have a visitor! Bring some tea."

Laura began her introduction. "I'm…"

"Yes, the new library lady. *Pere* Ardoin told me. Sit, sit." Tante Lu took her place in the rocker and gestured to the swing.

Laura obeyed. The rusty chains rattled but held. "Father Ardoin told me you are quite a raconteur, Mrs. Segura."

"Tante Lu. Even my own great-grandchildren call me Tante Lu. It's true. I know all the stories, told and untold, far back in time. Me, I never was a slave. I'm too young for that, but the children ask me just the same, all the time. My great-grandmama, born into slavery, lived nearly as long as me. I have her stories, and those from before her, stories that belong to this house and this parish."

An aluminum screen door, set like an anachronism in the walls of crossed timbers, mud and moss bousillage and flaking whitewash, slammed behind Pearl Segura as she maneuvered a tray of tall glasses and a sweating pitcher of iced tea across the porch. Pearl, out of uniform, was simply dressed in gray and white seersucker. As she set the tray on a small plastic table and poured the tea into three glasses filled with ice and crushed mint leaves, she glanced at Laura defiantly.

"I'm on my own time, and I have Mister Bob's permission to use the truck. Ruby and me and my daughter, we keep an eye on the old woman."

"Certainly," said Laura, taken aback by the challenge. Except for suddenly remembering the truck as the one she had ridden in with Robert LeBlanc and being a bit surprised that the unmarried Pearl had a daughter, she did not intend to upbraid Miss Leblanc's servant. A quick change of subject appeared wise.

"I came to ask Tante Lu to tell some of her stories at a bonfire we're planning for Halloween Eve."

"You don't want her stories. None of the white folks do, especially the LeBlancs."

"If you mean the one about the statue, I found it fascinating, if long, but I had something in the line of ghost stories in mind for the public."

"Tante Lu doesn't want—"

"Hush, Pearl," the old woman interrupted, her rocker teetering with annoyance. "I know all those stories about the *loup-garou* and the *feu-follet*. I can go on all night, but there is much more to the story of the statue than I told *Pere* Ardoin." Lowering her voice and pausing dramatically at the end of the sentence, Tante Lu revealed herself as a practiced teller of tales. She held Laura's gaze with her bright eyes and took a small sip of tea.

"I'd love to hear it," Laura encouraged. Even Pearl took a seat on the swing and silently drank her tea as Tante Lu began.

"No, I never was a slave, but great-grandmama, only a very young woman when the war ended, got freed with them that needed freeing. Those were good times and bad times 'cause no one knew where to go or what to do, black and white alike. My great-grandmama did fine because she had a special skill. She'd been apprenticed to an old midwife out on the LeBlanc place. Inez was that woman's name, and they called my great-grandmama Celie. Being slaves, they didn't have no last names before the war." The old lady bobbed her head a few times after imparting this knowledge.

"Young Celie went to learn her trade and was supposed go back to her master, one of the DeVilles, to help bring more slaves into the world. Inez knew her trade the best, so good she even birthed the white LeBlanc babies, though none of them lived. Camille LeBlanc had something bad wrong with her. All her babies except the first and the last come cold and blue into the world. *Pere* Ardoin thinks maybe that Rh factor killed them infants. Don't know about that. The first healthy child caught a fever at a year old and died. Still, Tante Inez got credit for seeing her mistress survived all those stillborns until at last in her old age, Miss Camille had a live son to hold. Some of that miracle rubbed off on Tante Inez. Even after the war, she had lots of clients, white and black, and my great-grandmama stayed on with her and inherited the trade when old Inez passed on. I'm coming to the good part now." Tante Lu stopped to sip her tea and add a dramatic pause. Waiting for her next words, Laura bent forward on the swing.

"On her deathbed, Inez told great-grandmama this story, sort of a confession I guess, because Inez would not let Celie go for a priest. The midwife figured she had brought off as many babies for those who didn't want them as she had birthed for those that did, and she said no priest would shrive her. She wanted to go to hell in peace.

"Well, it seemed it sort of hurt Tante Inez's pride that she never could get a live child out of Camille LeBlanc, and her mistress was getting too old to try again. A pity, too, that just a few miles away, a young woman lay dying of birthing a LeBlanc baby. I bet you see where I'm going here." Tante Lu pointed a finger at Laura who nodded.

"Old Inez claimed Marie Segura had a beauty like those high-yellow gals men kept in New Orleans, but she was so young and built like a china doll, a brittle toy for men to play with, but not like a real woman who had to give birth. Her baby turned out fine, a huge boy with more white blood in him than black. Inez did what she could, but with all the tearing and bleeding, the childbed fever took root in Marie Segura. Then, they called Inez home to attend another one of her own mistress's tragedies.

"Inez, a wise woman, even *canaille*, sly, some said, saw a chance to set her reputation aright. At the big house, she sent away all the servants, saying the mistress needed quiet, and then she gave Miss Camille a sleeping potion and took the dead baby from her, wrapped it in linens from the Segura cradle and returned it to Marie's bedside. Clearly, the girl would die, and if she didn't, she could have other children while Miss Camille would not." Again the dramatic pause or maybe the old woman simply needed to catch her breath. Laura drank her tea and waited for the rest of the story.

"Alma Segura was there tending her daughter, knowing she had helped to cause her death and fearing the wrath of the fiery Celestin, Marie's brother, who had opposed the liaison—impractical dreamer that he was—with Aurelien LeBlanc. Inez said Alma did not even speak when the babies were switched, one cold and blue for one screaming with life. The midwife said she had to give Marie's child a few drops of the sleeping potion just to get him into the big house, and there she had an awful surprise. The master sat by his wife, looking not at Camille with her hair going white and the wrinkles beginning to show, but at the empty cradle by the fire. He took his bastard son with the black blood, never saying a word, and laid the child on the silk sheets. Only three living persons knew of the switch, and none ever acknowledged it to the other.

"Old Tante Inez said she knew how her mistress prayed nightly to the Virgin for a living son, and she felt maybe the Holy Mother had put the whole idea into her head. Just maybe the Virgin Mary would see Inez went to purgatory instead of hell for her services.

"And so Marie Segura went to her grave with Camille's stillborn child in her arms. Then comes the story of the statue and Celestin's revenge, but you already heard that one from *Pere* Ardoin." The old tale spinner settled back in her rocker and took a long drink of cold sweet tea.

Pearl, who had heard the story often but kept a respectful silence, now remarked wryly, "Only three knew of the exchange, but the whole town suspected it. To this day, the LeBlanc men marry out of the parish. No white mothers encourage their daughters to chase after the LeBlancs, rich and good looking as they are, because there just might be that little drop of black blood in the line. Adrien brought his bride from near New Orleans, and the next one, Charles, married a Yankee. When the World Wars came, both those LeBlancs found real French women to bring home, no matter who waited here. T-Bob married Vivien Montleon out of New Orleans to make a real disaster. You'd think a little black blood would have given him some common sense, but I suppose with Angelle on the way he had no choice but to marry her, even though they were relations way back."

Laura was startled by this outburst from the usually taciturn Pearl, who on her own ground seemed to have forgotten the race of her guest and the distance she always maintained between white people and herself. Was she trying to make the liberal Yankee feel awkward, or merely spitting at the spiteful Miss Lilliane? How could the servant not resent taking orders from someone who shared the same blood? As Laura stared at her, Pearl's mouth clamped shut into a line that make her lips look as if they were sealed forever. Laura pretended to overlook the outburst and turned again to Tante Lu.

"Yes, I know the story of the statue from Father Ardoin, but tell me, who kept it all those years?"

Tante Lu gave her the answer. "Ah, Celestin Segura watched the dedication of the shrine from the back of the church loft. He reclaimed his carving when they shut the statue out of the holy place and brought it to his mother. He set it in her bedroom and forbade her or any other Segura to remove it. The statue was their shrine to sin he said, and Alma must look on it every day until she died. She did. She honored Celestin's last wish before he took his own life. Buried somewhere out here, he is. Sometimes, I think I see him wandering in these here trees, a poor lost soul who cannot rest in peace.

"The house and the statue passed to Celestin's brother, Antoine, and then to his son and grandson, my man, my Joseph. I was not born a slave or a Segura. When the last man of the name, my own grandson, passed away, I took the statue and gave it back to the church. I asked *Pere* Ardoin to pray for the soul of Celestin Segura. I see his spirit less often now. These things must end somewhere. *C'est finis.*"

The end, yes. The afternoon faded and the shadows beneath the oaks deepened. A little unnerved by the talk of ghosts, Laura hurried to conclude her business. "Can we count on you then, to do two or three stories on Halloween Eve? I could come for you before seven. Father Ardoin and I will do a story apiece to warm up the audience, and then they are yours for as long as you wish."

"I could talk all night." Tante Lu raised herself out of the rocker.

"And I could listen to you all evening," replied Laura as she moved toward her car, "But now, I must be going. Good evening, Tante Lu. This has been a pleasure. Pearl, good evening."

Pearl barely nodded, but Tante Lu waved one arthritic hand in parting.

Chapter Eight

Laura sat by her open French doors and hemmed the new skirts she suddenly had the urge to buy this morning from Helen's Boutique. Deep into October, Louisiana offered its most clement weather free of humidity and insects. She watched the Saturday afternoon procession of pickup trucks on Main Street from her chair placed a safe distance from the fragile balcony Mrs. Domengeaux kept assuring her was absolutely safe. Now and again, its rusty wrought iron creaked in the autumn breeze.

The new skirts were not merely an impulse buy. They had become a necessity because of Mrs. Domengeaux's persistent and generous feeding. As Laura cut through the shop each evening after work, her landlady thrust bowls of potato salad heavy on the mayonnaise and wedges of outrageously rich pecan pie into her hands.

"You can't get a man if you stay so thin," the robust Mrs. D. would say, slipping a praline into Laura's purse. The older woman nodded approvingly as Laura's cleavage deepened.

To her own disgust, Laura gobbled up the offerings. Her appetite after the months of depression had returned begging, pleading and urging to be fed. Now the gray V-necked sweater Jay Geiger had ogled, spanned tight across her breasts, and her casual jeans fit snug in the bottom. Laura bemoaned her loss of fashionable thinness and the return of what her mother called an old-fashioned figure with its wealth of curves—like Marilyn Monroe. Ha! Back to her old dress size and determined to diet before she went beyond it.

The skirts were to be an incentive to remain no more than a size eight. Besides, their fabric swayed when she walked, such a good feeling for a change. She wanted them shorter than the matronly length stocked by Miss Helen.

"I don't want a man," she'd sworn to Mrs. D., but gradually, it became important to have men to look at her again. This disgusted Laura more than her craving for pecan pie. David had been gone for five months, only five months.

She had to get her mind off David. Laura's eyes turned toward the Main Street parade. Two farmers in overalls got out of their vehicles to chat while the stoplight on the corner remained red. Behind them in a familiar truck, Angelle LeBlanc waved enthusiastically and called, "Come see, Miss Laura, come see!"

Laura set her sewing aside. A playful Snake, plunging from a covert spot under the sofa, immediately attacked her spool of thread. The kitten had grown as fast as Laura's appetite. She stood in the French doors holding on to both sides of the frame as she leaned out toward Angelle. The child frequently came to the library after school and rode home with her great-aunt. Though she was supposed to do her homework while waiting for five o'clock, the little girl dogged Laura's steps, straightening shelves and putting up magazines. The child had a touching hunger for a woman to emulate. Obviously, neither Pearl nor Tante Lil satisfied her need.

Behind the dusty windshield, Robert LeBlanc spoke to his daughter and continued to show no impatience when the light turned green and the two farmers kept up their conversation in the middle of the street.

"Can you come with us for some ice cream, Miss Laura? Please come!" shouted Angelle.

Hungry again, all resolutions vanished, Laura returned the shout, "Sure, why not?"

She bolted down the stairs, over to the idling truck and slipped into the cab just as the overall-clad men finally returned to their vehicles and drove on. From the balcony, Snake, switching his tail, watched their departure.

Thoroughly ashamed of herself, Laura studied Robert LeBlanc's features while his eyes stayed on the road. Ever since she heard Tante Lu's tale, she'd secretly studied his physique for signs of a black heritage. He had none as far as she could tell, even when applying old wives tales about the whites of the eyes and other nonsense. Swarthy and tanned with the dark hair and eyes of most of the men in town with a French or Cajun heritage, in her opinion he was considerably better looking than the majority.

She hated to admit the folk tale made T-Bob a more romantic figure in her eyes. That probably applied to most of the young women in town. One svelte blonde coming out of Helen's Boutique directed a wave at him now. Her green eyes distinctly excluded Laura and Angelle, although the child waved back. Of course nothing showed. No black blood had been added to the

French and Spanish since 1830, if then, if at all. Along with her dieting, Laura resolved to stop studying Robert LeBlanc.

With fine weather and good company, the conversation flowed easily that afternoon. All in the small party agreed on chocolate as the best flavor, and chocolate ice cream dipped in a chocolate shell even better. Strolling along the sidewalk with their cones in hand, Robert remained as lightly amusing as he had been while guiding his facetious tour of Chateau Camille. He pointed out the town fossil, Aldus Thibodeaux, deep asleep in a lawn chair in front of his gas station.

"Even older than Tante Lil," he whispered to Angelle with awe in his voice. "Probably as old as the bayou itself."

They stopped in front of Purdue's Bed & Breakfast. Previously, the old frame house with its odd tower room had been a boarding house, but the owner, Miss Lula, decided to go upscale, redecorating with antiques and advertising in slick travel magazines.

"She started a rumor the place had once been a fancy bordello." Robert glanced at Angelle to see if she had picked up on the strange word, but the child stayed busy trying to keep the chocolate shell from sliding off her ice cream, her face a happy mess.

"To draw tourists. As a child, Tante Lil knew the Widow Purdue who first opened the boarding house. She said that straight-laced old woman was probably spinning in her grave."

Pausing, he wiped Angelle's face free of chocolate with a paper napkin and scrubbed at a spot on Laura's sweater just below her chin. Shame on her for wishing the ice cream had dripped lower down her chest. The heat rising inside her felt fiery enough to melt the remainder of the scoop in her cone.

"You're looking good—better than when we first met you," he said, smiling into her gray eyes.

"Fatter, you mean." Laura rejected the compliment. "But at least I'm not covered in mosquito bites now, though I still do have stains on my clothes."

He looked her up and down. "If that's fat, it went to all the right places. No, I meant more alive, inside and out."

"You didn't even notice me at Miss Lola's place my first day in town, just clomped right by me with a nod and a ma'am."

"I noticed you. You stared at my backside, but there we were with Miss Lola in the kitchen and not a bed in sight. What was a man to do, sweep the hot sauce bottles off a table and go at it right there? I, being the perfect gentleman, got the hell out without coming on to you."

Laura noticed the heat moving up her neck and into her cheeks. Some of that warmth went the other way and kindled between her thighs. She turned aside, pretending to attend to her dripping dessert, and leaned over the curb away from him. Both forgot about the presence of the child, but Angelle would not be ignored. "Why don't you come stay with us again?"

"I have my own place now, Angelle."

"Well," said the child with a petulant ring. "I could make you come stay with us."

"Oh?"

"Yes, I could. I know a *traiteur* who could put a spell on you so that you would come stay with us and

93

never go away."

"Angelle! That's about enough nonsense for the day." Her father cut into a conversation rapidly getting out of hand. Laura tried to assist him, adult helping adult.

"Tell me, what's *traiteur*?"

"A faith healer, a sort of white witch, I guess you could say. They claim to cure warts and drive snakes from your yard, using the power of God of course." Robert dismissed such claims with a wave of his hand.

"Well, I lack warts, a yard, and my only snake is really a cat. Would you like to see him, Angelle?"

"Madame Leleux could make you come if I had enough money for a charm," replied Angelle, who seemed to have a stubborn streak beneath her black curls. "Pearl said she went to a *traiteur* once to get a man to love her, and it worked so well she can't even talk about it."

"Look, let's go to my place. Angelle can see my cat, and I'd like to show you an old armoire that I think is very valuable."

"Antiques, despite my residence in a place full of them, are not my strong point. Now if you had a sick cow up there…"

Angelle laughed, and the tension dwindled away.

The child charged up the old staircase when they reached Domengeaux's store. Mrs. D, busy behind the counter, nodded her blessing on Robert LeBlanc as he followed his daughter up the stairs. She called Laura aside and put three pralines in her hand.

"For dat child. Now you could do worse den Bob LeBlanc. You being a Yankee and a Protestant, you won't mind about the divorce and dem other t'ings.

Invite him for dinner. If you can't cook, I'll bring you up somet'ing nice from da store."

"They can't stay, Miss Lola. I'm sure about that."

Laura escaped into her apartment finding she had forgotten to lock it in her haste to join the LeBlancs. Even the French doors stood open as if an invitation for ice cream addled her brain. Snake had made a mess of the sewing basket and scrap cloth and as if evading a scolding, tried to ingratiate himself by winding around Angelle's legs. The girl threw an empty spool for the kitten and became engrossed in play, the grown-up world fading for her.

"Since we have become dispensable, the armoire is in here."

Laura moved to her bedroom. David's old shirt lay draped on the bed, and she knew Robert LeBlanc had taken notice of it. She threw open the doors of the armoire quickly.

"Look, 'C.S.' I am sure this is a genuine Celestin Segura cabinet." She ran her fingers over the initials carved in the honey-colored wood.

"I think you're right. Despite what I said about antiques, I did take an interest in the black Seguras at one time in my life. This is fine work. Should be in a museum, or at least out at my place."

"Mrs. Domengeaux doesn't want to sell. I just thought you would be interested."

"Because of old stories?"

Deciding not to be a total hypocrite and feign, "A story? What story?" Laura replied, "No, not at all. Something that happened so long ago should have no bearing on the present or the future."

"But it does. Was this your husband?" Robert

pointed to the wedding picture. The man was becoming dangerously serious. Laura sat on the edge of her bed and tried to break his gaze.

"Yes," she answered without elaboration.

"What you do about your life from now on will always be affected by a man who is as dead and gone as Celestin Segura. Whether you marry or not, have children or not, will depend on how much he influences your future."

"I think that is very cold and uncalled for." Laura's hand stroked the comfortable, soft texture of David's old shirt.

"Listen, I have a point to make. I first heard the story of Marie Segura and Aurelien LeBlanc when I turned thirteen. Maybe Pearl told me, but it might have been before she came back from California. Funny, I can't recall who told me. Everyone in Chapelle knew the story except for me, it seemed, and talked about it behind my back. I kept thinking if the babies had not been switched, I might have been out there in the fields planting cane, watching my own relative, the great Judge LeBlanc surveying his arpents on horseback.

"I know it isn't likely. The black Seguras were craftsmen, and nearly white. They say Pearl's sister went to California and married a white man. That's why no one ever hears of her. Now days, it wouldn't matter much, but in her youth, passing meant giving up your family. As for myself, I would have been a member of the black elite, the high yellows, the almost white. But at thirteen, all I could see were the cane workers, their sweat for my profit, their shacks for my big white mansion. That old story became an obsession for me."

"I refused to honor family tradition and study law

at Tulane. To my father's horror, I took agricultural courses at the state university. After he died, I switched our land from cane to cattle. There is more dignity in raising cattle, but much less money.

"I followed in my family's footsteps in only one way. I married out of the parish. I really believed no one in Chapelle would have me and never tried to find out. I brought home a girl from New Orleans who turned out to be my very distant cousin. We met at a fraternity party and found out we had Caroline Montleon in common." Robert smiled ruefully and studied the picture of David with his sandy hair and light eyes.

"That gave me my pickup line, 'Vivien Montleon, I have a Montleon somewhere in my family tree—we must be kissing cousins.' Clever opening, don't you think? I neglected to tell her about Marie Segura. When Vivien became thoroughly enchanted with my big plantation, my waving stands of cane and my father, the judge, I got her pregnant. Not exactly an accident on either side. I thought this way she'd be mine forever and would never leave me, even when she heard what people said about the LeBlancs of Chapelle. Later, much later, I found out she thought *she* had tricked *me* into marriage and deeply regretted her success. So did I. Would you, knowing the stories?"

Laura, listening intently, aware he had shut the bedroom door to prevent Angelle from hearing, found herself unprepared for the question and mistook his meaning.

"I don't know. I'm not ready to make that kind of a decision yet." She clutched David's shirt to her chest.

"That was a rhetorical question, not a proposal.

97

Perhaps I should have gone into law. I have just made my point. The past does matter. You cannot escape it. It can ruin lives."

Laura wanted to offer this bitter man, who usually covered his feelings with a smile and a joke, some comfort, some hope, but the right words would not come. Dropping David's shirt, she reached out a hand to him, but he turned before she could touch his arm and opened the door.

They spotted Angelle playing with Snake on the old balcony. The child's father crossed the room in three strides and pulled his daughter to his side.

"That's a poor place to play, Angelle."

Laura, just behind him, murmured, "I'm sorry. I'm so sorry. I should have locked the door."

"She's not your problem, Mrs. Dickinson. Come on, Angelle. It's too late. We'll catch it from Tante Lil if we aren't home for dinner."

As they moved to leave, Angelle returned to her old theme. "I could make you come to stay with us. I could." Her father pushed her ahead to the doorway. The group collided with Lola Domengeaux carrying a large enameled pot up the narrow stairs.

"Leaving so soon? I was bringing up dis nice gumbo for dinner. Stay a while, why don't you?"

"It's too late, Mrs. D," Laura said. "They need to get back to their place."

Chapter Nine

Devoid even of students in panicked search of report material this late Friday afternoon, the Ste. Jeanne Parish Library might as well have closed an hour early. Ruby Senegal conscientiously entered new titles into the computer while Laura made work for herself weeding shelves of forty-year-old Avalon romances with laughably dated cover art of nurses in old-fashioned caps and horror stricken maidens teetering on the brink of a cliff.

This make-work gave Miss Lilliane the freedom to nap in the office—as she often did without Laura's aggravating presence to keep her aroused. The new librarian noticed the rusted pickup truck parked in the bookmobile drive. Angelle, who had been absent from the library all week, wiggled restlessly in her father's shadow in the cab. Inhaling in preparation for the uncomfortable moment that had to come someday, Laura went out through the garage.

Smiling, she hoped not woodenly, she went directly to the driver's side of the truck to confront the man who had confided in her and received nothing in return. She began the conversation as casually as possible.

"Hello there. We've missed Angelle this week. Will you be bringing her to the bonfire and storytelling tomorrow night?"

"No. She's going to spend the weekend with her grandparents in New Orleans. Her mother is home from the spa again and should be by to pick her up any time now."

"I'm sick," Angelle interrupted, kicking at the dashboard of her father's truck with one sneakered foot.

"You got away with that story this morning with Pearl, young lady, but not with me. Now put your feet back where they belong."

"It's hot in here," the child whined.

"Come inside, please. Angelle can wait with me and have a cold drink. There's coffee, too," Laura offered, finding herself in the conspiracy of adults against a difficult child again.

"I want to get back to the ranch. Thanks anyway. Angelle, get out and wait with Miss Laura."

When the child made no move to open the door, her father leaned over and opened it for her, giving the little girl a slight shove that dislodged her in Laura's direction.

Laura caught the child's hand and reached up for an overnight bag almost as scratched and battered as the pickup truck.

"I appreciate this," Robert Leblanc said as he handed over the suitcase.

Laura waited for one of his characteristic smiles and received none. Looking grim, he backed from the drive as soon as Laura and Angelle stood clear.

"I'll tell you what, Angelle. Why don't you run over to Domengeaux's and buy a sack of Miss Lola's pralines for your trip. I'll bet your mother would like some."

"No way. She never eats candy because she's

afraid she'll get fat. But I'll get some for us."

"Look, I'll give you my apartment key, too. Would you run upstairs and see if Snake has enough water? It's such a hot day for October." Laura led the child inside and managed to retrieve her purse from a desk drawer in the office without disturbing Miss Lilliane's nap.

"It's always this hot in October," Angelle commented as her babysitter rummaged for the apartment key and spare change.

"Not where I come from. Up north, we'd be getting ready for snow."

"You don't want to go back there, do you?"

Laura looked up from her search. Tears wet Angelle's dark eyes. "Not for a long time, honey. Are you really sick?"

"No, ma'am. It's just that it's okay when Thurston comes in Grandpa's car and takes me to New Orleans. He lets me sit in the front seat, and we stop for barbecue at this place only black people know about, and then we have purple snow cones for dessert. But when Mama comes, we have to go straight to the city. I'm not allowed to talk to Thurston or have anything sticky, and Mama only talks about herself and her diets and her headaches and her hairdresser. I hate her!"

"No, you don't." Laura rushed to refute this blasphemy of motherhood. "Maybe you just like being with your father better."

"I do hate her. She didn't want me, and I don't want her. I want you." The tears in Angelle's eyes overflowed. She hugged Laura's waist like a python suffocating its prey.

Laura, feeling as helpless as any woman unused to children, removed and caged Angelle's hands around

101

the door key and two dollar bills, then gave her a hug to send her on her way.

"Go get the candy and check on Snake. We'll have a little party before your mother arrives, and you can pick out some books to read in the car."

Angelle went, head hanging, her long, dark hair plastered against her pale cheeks with tears. Laura reheated some of the strong Cajun coffee, thinking she needed something more bracing, a drink or a tranquilizer, to cope with the LeBlanc family. Fortunately, the library offered none of these alternatives. In a while Angelle and her troubles would be on the way to New Orleans and a calmer weekend lay ahead.

When she moved to the window again to see if Angelle was on her way back, she noticed the silver Mercedes parked in the place Robert's old truck had vacated. A uniformed chauffeur, a black man, lean and gray-headed, held the door for his mistress.

Vivien LeBlanc projected the epitome of elegance, slim to the point of emaciation, and pale to the extreme of ill-health. Her short, champagne blonde hair lay in feathered layers cut by some exclusive and overpriced hairdresser unknown to librarians, teachers, and other women who had to work for a living. The lady actually seemed to require assistance to exit from the car. She swung her long legs in model fashion, knees together, over the side of the seat and glided upwards with the help of the driver's arm. Once he had his passenger on her feet, the chauffeur ran ahead to open the door of the library. Vivien LeBlanc followed in her Italian shoes with her pencil-thin heels tapping out the message on the sidewalk that she did not have to walk if she chose to ride. She entered the converted house as grandly as if she were checking into one of her spas for the weekend.

"So you're the new librarian. About time they tossed the old witch out. I'm here for Angelle. Get her for me."

Laura, who had grown used to the almost overwhelming friendliness of the Chapelle natives, had no witty retort, only the truth. "Angelle is at Domengeaux's store. She'll be back soon."

"Thurston," snapped the mistress. "Wait in the car. I must sit down. I have such a headache from the drive."

Disliking the woman completely but determined to stay neutral, Laura offered coffee as well as a seat in the kitchenette area. The other staff members appeared to be needed at the front desk quite suddenly and vacated the area. Miss Lilliane slept on in the office.

"No coffee. We have a long drive ahead. I could use a cigarette, but I suppose librarians never smoke."

"I don't, but some do," Laura replied, treading on the edge of politeness. "I believe Miss Lilliane could spare a cigarette."

"Right. I forgot about the old bat and her nicotine habit."

As Laura quietly entered the office and pilfered the aged librarian's cache of menthol lights and matches, she gloated a little. Although clad in an expensive light blue suit and immaculately groomed, Vivien LeBlanc exhibited all the unpleasant signs of a heavy smoker. Robert's former wife, though only a few years older than Laura, had small crow's feet radiating from the corners of the pale blue eyes even the suit failed to color enough to make attractive. Hard lines surrounded her thin, pink-tinted lips. Yellow stained the teeth behind those lips. Her expensive clothes had a saturated odor of smoke about them Laura found repugnant. Feeling slightly superior, she surrendered the pack and matches into Vivien's nervous, nicotine-stained fingers with their pearly manicured nails.

After she lit and drew deeply on a cigarette, Vivien slid the pack and the matches into the pocket of her suit and resumed tapping her enameled nails on the Formica of the table. "Where is that child? As I said, we have a long drive. I suppose I'll have to go after her myself."

She sent Laura an imperial look implying the younger woman should volunteer to fetch the girl, but Laura gave herself another surge of satisfaction by saying, "I'm sorry you have to leave so soon. Domengeaux's is just up the street on the corner."

"I know. I used to live in this godforsaken place. Say good-bye and thanks for smokes to the old hag and give all my love to Robert." Vivien waved a pallid hand toward the office and stalked on her sharp heels toward the front of the building. Laura did not rush to hold the door for her.

A half hour later, Laura turned the key in the front lock, the last act of the library closing ritual. Sirens blasted the air, startling her. A few moments ago, this had been a routine Friday afternoon with the new librarian slamming doors and files with sufficient force to awaken the old librarian and tell her time to go. Without so much as a pleasant farewell, Miss Lilliane wheeled to her parking space shouting to the janitor for assistance. Closing duties, the one chore Miss Lilliane had relinquished without a fight. Half smiling at the abrupt departure of their old boss, the rest of the staff wished Laura a nice weekend and went on their way speculating about the location of the fire. The young librarian finished checking the stacks for loitering students or slumbering senior citizens, locked the rear doors behind her, and turned toward the shriek of the sirens.

With the volunteer fire department only a few doors from the library, the noise continued outrageously loud. Chief Fontenot's chair in the shade where he spent most of his afternoons toppled as the fire chief heaved his large belly upwards, adjusted his suspenders and lumbered toward his red truck with the flashing light attached to the cab. His assistant, an agile man of forty who waited patiently through long boring days for the chief's retirement, backed the small fire engine from the garage. Volunteers swarmed from neighborhood businesses, the earliest arrivals grabbing heavy slickers, boots and helmets from the hooks in the garage and leaping on to the side of the engine like fleas attacking a large red dog. Pickup trucks began congesting the streets and clusters of excited children clogged the sidewalks. No one had far to go for the show.

The smoke billowed from Domengeaux's store. For a moment, Laura leaned against the library door for support. Had she left the stove on at lunch time? What did it matter now! She made herself move up the block to where Mrs. D stood wringing her white apron with her large hands.

"I don't know what happened. I smelled smoke and called da chief. Myrtle Hill's ringing da rest of da volunteers now. I..." Mrs. Domengeaux stopped talking abruptly as if the wind had been kicked from her belly.

In fact, the entire crowd from overwrought small children to oldsters, who had been recounting the history of fires they'd witnessed in Chapelle, fell silent.

On the small balcony over the store's awning stood Angelle LeBlanc clutching the black kitten. The cat clawed at the long sleeves of her white cotton blouse in its panic, but Angelle seemed frozen in the furnace of the fire. She stared with large dilated eyes into the fiery heart of the apartment through the closed French doors. The heat popped a pane of glass from the window frame. A flying shard slashed through the child's thin blouse and drew blood. Angelle jerked but did not move. The frantic cat struggled free in the brief second the child's grip loosened. Snake bounded from the balcony onto the awning beginning to smolder as cinders from the roof bit into the fabric. He leapt, landed on all four feet and shot toward his cool, remembered sanctuary beneath the church.

At last, the fire company acted. The earliest of the volunteers connected the hoses to a nearby hydrant, braced and sent spraying streams of water onto the roof and awning. Angelle's white blouse clung to her small back and her black curls turned into wet snaky ringlets against the fabric. She stood completely still.

Chief Fontenot called to her, "Be right there, sugar. Now don't you move," as if Angelle had been thrashing in terror. The chief hoisted his bulk on to the second rung of a ladder resting against the building and steadied by his slimmer assistant. He moved slow, so slow that Laura wanted to tear him from the ladder and save the child by herself. She took a step forward, but Mrs. Domengeaux held her arm and a volunteer fireman pushed her back into the crowd. The hot bricks began to lose their grip on the rusted bolts of the old balcony. The metal bent and dropped a foot from the wall. Angelle fell with her back pressed against the ornate grillwork, but she did not move of her own accord.

Someone with the yellow slicker of a volunteer thrown over blue jeans and a work shirt pulled Chief Fontenot from the ladder. The fireman shouted, "I'm the chief! This is my job. Get out the way, Bob."

"That's my child, you old fart!" Robert LeBlanc climbed the ladder two rungs at a time. Angelle did not turn or reach out for her father, but he grasped her beneath her arms and slung his child over his shoulder. The balcony yawed again and crashed through the awning. The ladder swayed but held to the wall with the weight of Chief Fontenot on its bottom rung. Father and child descended to safety. Lola Domengeaux cried, "Praise be to God" and crossed herself with the rapidity of constant practice. The crowd cheered.

"Just like an old time movie," murmured Laura. Just like a movie, except her life had gone up in flames, burning all that remained of David out of existence. Nothing would be left, not a picture or a piece of shared bed linen, nothing old or new, borrowed or blue, simply nothing.

At the edge of the crowd, a medic covered Angelle LeBlanc's small body with a blanket and strapped her to a stretcher to be lifted into an ambulance dispatched from the funeral home. Laura wanted to move toward the ambulance and yet she felt—nothing. The blankness following David's death settled over her like an old well-loved blanket, a warm safe blanket.

"Miss Lola, Miss Laura, come to da ambulance

now." A volunteer, who appeared to be old Thibodeaux from the Canal gas station beneath his outsized fireman's hat, took their arms. "Doc Bourgeois wants y'all." He led them from the multitude across the open space cleared by the firemen to the ambulance with its doors open wide as a tomb and its black lettering reading "Duchamp's Funeral Home" on the side.

"David," Laura said softly. Her knees wobbled and she steadied herself on the side of the vehicle.

Robert bore down on her. "What the hell was Angelle doing in your apartment? She's supposed to be on her way to New Orleans. She can't be left alone like that! Do you hear me?"

Laura jerked back sure Angelle's father would strike her with his powerful fists. She lost her balance as her window on the world went dark.

Dr. Bourgeois caught her on the way down and helped place Laura on a second stretcher.

"Bob, get into the ambulance with Miss Lola and be quiet. This young woman has had a shock and doesn't need you bellowing in her face. I'll meet you at the hospital."

The medic slammed the doors of the emergency vehicle behind patients and passengers. The ambulance siren flashed and whined, clearing the way toward the clinic.

Chapter Ten

David's comfortable old shirt felt strangely starchy and her wide brass bed so hard and narrow. Reluctantly, Laura opened her eyes to white curtains separating her bed from others in the clinic. Beyond the flimsy partition, she heard a childish voice.

"I wish I could have seen it. You were a real hero, Daddy."

"But you were there, Angelle. You were very smart and brave not to jump and to shut the doors to escape from the smoke," a deep male voice answered.

"Yes, I shut the doors to keep the flames away from me and Snake."

"You see, you do remember."

"No, I don't after that. I hid in the old closet from Mama, but I was sure she would find me. There aren't many good places to hide in Miss Laura's apartment, but Mama went away without looking inside. When I came out, the stairs were on fire. I picked up Snake and went to the balcony to wait for help like you told me to do if our house ever burned while I was upstairs. After that I don't remember. Is Snake okay, too? I want to go look for him."

"We can go after Dr. Bourgeois checks you out."

Laura shifted in her bed and wondered desperately how she could make her way to the bathroom in the hospital gown with the two inadequate ties in the rear.

"Sounds like Miss Laura is awake. Should we visit, Angelle?"

Laura wanted to cover her face with the pillow. No, don't come in here, don't come!

One glimpse of Robert LeBlanc's face as he parted the curtains reminded Laura her own face must be puffy with sleep and grotesque with smeared makeup. Beyond him, Angelle, full of the recuperative powers of the seven-year-old, slid out of her bed. Her long-sleeved flowered cotton nightie, obviously delivered by her caring father, swept across the hospital tiles. The child giggled, full of anticipation as she stood by Laura's bed.

"You look like you passed a bad night." LeBlanc gave her a wicked smile.

"You have no tact," Laura retorted, feeling as irritable as her bowels. She shifted her hips in discomfort.

"If you accept my apology for that scene by the ambulance, I'll leave and let you get cleaned up. If not, I'll stay and embarrass you until the nurse comes with the bed pan."

"Like Angelle, I have very little memory of last evening. You're forgiven for being an overwrought parent, and you were entirely correct. She should not have been alone in my apartment. Domengeaux's store was an old and dangerous building. A fire inspector never set foot in the place, I'm sure. I suppose nothing is left of it?" Only the lightness of the banter kept her from screaming the question.

"Nothing." Her visitor sobered, then returned to his former tone with determination. "I didn't expect to be forgiven this easily, so I brought something to make peace."

He presented the patient with a large pink dress box tied with silver ribbon. A silver seal stuck on one corner advertised Helen's Dress Shoppe.

"It's from Helen's Boutique. Miss Helen changed the name to boutique when boutiques came into vogue. She said it sounded so French, but she didn't want to waste her old seals. Now that boutiques are passé, she's thinking of becoming a shoppe again, or so she said this morning. She remembered your dress size and took a guess on the lingerie."

Laura opened the box, took a quick glance at the labels on the black lace bra and panties discreetly buried in tissue paper and replied, "Good guess."

She recognized some of the contents, a trim gray skirt with matching slacks and jacket she had rejected a week ago as too expensive and a blouse of wine red silk she would not have chosen for herself in a million years—along with black lace underwear. Those kinds of garments were simply too much hassle to wash by hand.

"The gray for your eyes, the red to brighten your face. My mother had coloring like yours, and that is what she would say in her very French way. She came from Paris, and Miss Helen always stocked the latest fashions for her. Of course, *ma belle mama* accounted for a good share of her business. You have no idea how that old lady glowed when she got to bill another LeBlanc."

"Your wife never shopped there?"

"Ex-wife. *Mon Dieu*, no! Only New Orleans is good enough for the Montleons."

"I should have known. We met yesterday."

"You mean collided. Vivien meets no one. She mows people down and walks over the bodies. I avoid her when I can get an unsuspecting victim to take my place. I'm sorry about that, too."

"Well, she didn't mow me down, but I understand what you mean. Speaking of bodies, please get out of here so I can put on this incredibly expensive gift— which I am accepting only until my next pay check comes through."

"No repayment necessary. I want you in my debt." He disappeared in back of the curtain, leaving behind the impression of a grin like the Cheshire cat.

Angelle, who witnessed the whole scene with delight, left after giving a hug and whispering, "Now you must come to stay at our house." Chateau Camille appeared to be the only place she could go—after the bathroom of course.

A nurse's aide intercepted Laura as she backed toward the toilet. She covered her rear without comment, helped her into the shower after she'd used the facilities and guarded the door while Laura restored herself. When the aide brought her purse, which had been locked in the clinic office overnight, Laura seized the handbag as if it were full of gold coins. The purse did contain a compact of power, a lipstick and comb, two barrettes that had sunken to the bottom of the accumulation and the credit cards and checkbook she could use to restore her wardrobe without becoming a charity case.

Looking into the bathroom mirror, Laura hated the childish look the barrettes gave to her damp brown hair, but without a hairdryer or curling iron, they kept the wet strands out of her face. The lipstick and red blouse did brighten her complexion, giving her enough confidence to face the world once more. She took a seat in the visitor's chair next to the bed she'd occupied and clutched her soiled clothes in a plastic bag a nurse had given her. Dr. Bourgeois checked on Angelle in the next compartment.

"All functions go, Angelle. Nurse Anders has some juice and ham biscuits for you in the office. Go on now. I want to talk to your daddy." The child's footsteps skipped down the hall.

"Keep an eye on her, Bob. You were right about her reactions being abnormal. Two traumas like this in her life aren't good. She might have nightmares and behavioral problems over the next few weeks when this all catches up with her."

"I remember. I'll be there when she needs me."

"Good. You might do the same for Mrs. Dickinson. This hasn't been an easy year for her either."

"I will if she'll let me."

"Fine."

When Dr. Bourgeois pulled back the curtain, he seemed surprised to find Laura dressed and ready to be discharged.

"You certainly get out of a bathroom faster than my wife and daughters, Laura." Exuding his best bedside manner, Dr. Bourgeois checked her pupils, pulse and respiration.

"I didn't have to linger deciding what to wear."

"Bob always did have good taste. You look superb, and you can go home now."

"I look barely passable, and I have no home to go to." The brittleness of her answer made Dr. Bourgeois pause.

"Laura, I'm sorry for your loss. I am sure it was no joy to wake up in a hospital, but I felt the situation called for a little sedation and observation. One minute, I was telling you to get in the ambulance because Angelle had asked for you—but you didn't seem to hear me—and then you collapsed. Physically, you are fine. However, I would suggest you talk to someone about this tragedy. Chapelle doesn't have much to offer in the way of mental health facilities, but I've written a few names on this card of people in Lafayette who can help you. In the meantime, I'll give you some pills to get you through the worst of this trouble."

"I don't need or want them! I will do fine on my own." Laura's voice overflowed with sudden anger. She rose from her chair and, clutching her purse and the plastic bag containing all she owned in the world, went into the hall, leaving the bewildered doctor behind.

Robert LeBlanc awaited her. "Pearl has the guest room ready for you at the Chateau. You're coming home with us."

"Of course. I have nowhere else to go now, do I?" Laura looked around the empty clinic. "Mrs. Domengeaux. How is she?"

"Miss Lola went home last night. She said it would kill her husband if he heard about the fire from anyone but her. Louie has a bad heart, you know. He gave up the business after an attack and a triple by-pass several years ago, but Miss Lola kept on until now. She said this was God's way of telling her to retire, but she is mighty sorry about your things. She implied God sent you a message, too, and she would pray to the Holy Mother about it to be sure after she called the insurance company. Don't worry about Miss Lola. God is always on her side—even if He was a little drastic this time."

Laura smiled, and the little knot of tension inside of her loosened. That same visceral knot tightened like a noose a half hour later when the pickup truck stopped at the light by the ruins of Domengeaux's store. Laura recognized nothing in the rubble except the twisted remains of her brass bedstead. Someone had pushed her car across the street to the Canal station where Old Thibodeaux had washed and waxed it. If the residents of Chapelle had known where she was going to stay, the kitchen at Chateau Camille would have been overflowing with Magnalite pots of hot gumbo and bowls of gelatin salad by now

"I'd like to get my car. Please let me out, Robert."

"You can do that later."

"No. Now!" Laura felt as stubborn as Angelle at her worst.

"Let her out, Angelle." The child, her face cloudy for the first time that day, reluctantly allowed Laura to pass from the cab.

Robert, leaning across his daughter, spoke to her from the open door of the truck. "We'll see you for lunch then."

Using the changing light as a pretext for escape, Laura hurried to the sidewalk and waved as the father and daughter passed. She did not cross the street to her car. Instead, she entered the brick façade where the front door of Domengeaux's store once opened. She sought something, anything, from her past, but the fire had obscured that completely. Here lay a charred plank, perhaps from the Segura armoire. No one could tell. It nestled near the bedstead, contorted beyond salvage in the frame part of the building that had been over the storeroom. The internal noose would strangle her soon if she did not find something of David to preserve. She jumped when someone spoke behind her.

"I been at da church, *cher*, and seen you come in. Believe me, dere ain't not'ing left. Even my beautiful Virgin is gone." Mrs. Domengeaux poked at a black sticky mass of melted plastic flowers.

"You know I been t'inking just before da fire my votive candle went out. I t'aught it was a bad sign, you know. But when I went over dere, da cup and da candle, and everyt'ing, it was gone. I t'ink maybe dat little girl took it up to your place, and she don't want to tell her daddy what she done, no. I started to go up, but den Mrs. LeBlanc, who was looking for Angelle, come down and said dat child must have sneaked out just to aggravate her.

"I get busy behind da counter and can't keep a good eye on everyt'ing, you know. When I saw dat child on da balcony, I t'aught it's my fault if she die. But da Virgin answered my prayers again. I tell you, she is da best saint dere is. I prayed on it dis morning, and I'm not telling the insurance company about dat candle, no. Dis was meant to be, I'm certain. Believe you me, I'll give you your share when dat check come in. What for I paid all dose years if dey can't pay me back now?" Miss Lola said with great certainty.

Laura did not try to refute Lola Domengeaux's logic. She thought instead of a willful child, used to getting her own way, helping herself to a votive candle in a red glass holder and letting herself into Laura's apartment with the librarian's own keys. Maybe, she had set Laura's clothes on fire accidentally when she went to hide in the armoire and took the candle with her to ward off the dark. Could be, Angelle had set the fire intentionally to get her own way about Laura's coming to live at Chateau Camille. Laura closed her eyes and leaned against a sooty refrigerator case.

"You got somewhere to stay, *cher*? My daughter and her kids is coming up from Baton Rouge to help out, so we'll be a little crowded, but we can always fit one more in da house."

"Thank you. I'll be staying out at the LeBlanc place for a while," Laura replied, though the thought suddenly gave her chills. She shuddered slightly.

"If you need anyt'ing, you call me, *cher*." Miss Lola brushed some soot off Laura's blouse. "You look real pretty in red."

"Thanks."

After she got the second toothbrush and sack of necessaries she had purchased in Chapelle that fall, Laura could no longer delay the inevitable. She drove the road to Chateau Camille ten miles under the speed limit and arrived at the front door at twenty past noon. Angelle waited on the porch. Her new pink going-home dress rumpled beneath her as if she had sat there all morning, the little girl sat in one of the verandah rockers.

"I've been waiting for you all day!" Angelle bounded off the porch and seized Laura's paper bags. "Lunch is ready. Better hurry."

The child dumped the sacks on the four-poster in the guestroom and hurried Laura to the dining room where her father and great-aunt were seated and already eating cold crab salad served in half an avocado. The ever-present iced tea and a bread pudding frosted with meringue sat on the sideboard.

"We gave up on you a little while ago."

The host held a chair for Laura. Tante Lil continued to eat in silence. Angelle attacked the crab salad after moving her place closer to Laura's chair. Robert LeBlanc watched both of them carefully as if making mental notes for a report to Dr. Bourgeois. Laura ignored his eyes and chattered to Miss Lilliane as if they were the best of friends. She picked at the shreds of crab, ate one or two forkfuls and drained her iced tea, then excused herself to make telephone calls before the dessert was served.

She knew her voice sounded overly vibrant to the family in the dining room and to her own mother on the other end of the line who kept saying, "Are you sure you are all right?"

"Certainly, Mother. I just wanted you to know where I'll be staying. Miss Lola says this was a sign from God telling her to retire." Laura tried for a little levity, though in the back of her mind the words "Gone, all gone" repeated liked a scratched record.

"Well, it might be a sign from God for you to come home. You've said that bitchy old lady still comes into work every day. What do they need you for?"

"She's training me. I need to learn the ropes. I've only been here a few weeks."

"And already a disaster." Her mother sighed. "I'll send some of the clothes you left behind."

"No, don't send those old things. I'll buy new down here. Besides, I might go on a diet again. Yes, yes, I'll keep in touch. So long."

She phoned Father Ardoin. "No, don't cancel the bonfire and the folktales. I feel fine, and so many people would be disappointed. You'll pick up Tante

Lu? See you tonight."

When Laura turned, she saw the master of the chateau standing in the hallway and still watching her with concern. Robert LeBlanc did not need one more thing to worry about, she thought. Passing the unsmiling portraits of Aurelien and Camille LeBlanc, she placed one hand on the shoulder of their descendant, looked into those bittersweet brown eyes and said, "I do love this outfit, and you were right about the color. Thank you for your kindness. I have been very ungracious."

She kissed him lightly on the cheek and before his reaction could register, she turned and called over her shoulder, "But I do need more clothes. I am off to buy out Helen's Boutique." She sailed out the door certain she had acted perfectly normal even if her life was falling apart.

Only later, when she placed her purchases in Caroline LeBlanc's massive armoire did the void threaten to engulf her again. The large house sat as quiet as a creaky old place could. Dinner had been rushed, really just leftovers from lunch, as Miss Lilliane wanted to attend six o'clock Mass and Angelle agitated to go trick-or-treating. No costume had been planned since the child was supposed to be in New Orleans with her mother. At last, Pearl took the girl to her own room and decked her in ropes of cheap beads, tied scarves around her small waist and black curls and made up her pale face as a gypsy dancer with bright red lipstick, black penciled eyebrows and thick mascara. Satisfied and toting a huge shopping bag donated by Laura, Angelle went to wait in the truck for her father to begin the night of Halloween.

"You'll be all right alone, Laura?" Robert asked.

"Pearl is here. She'll come into town with me for the bonfire. Tell Dr. Bourgeois I don't need a babysitter if you see him."

"Now that sounds like Laura Dickinson, liberated woman." He blessed her with a grin well worth receiving.

"Oh, go trick-or-treating and save a chocolate bar for me."

She shut him out of her room, but she could hear his deep laughter in the hall. When the masculine sound of him vanished and the new clothes hung in closet, she began to cry, a night and day's worth of accumulated tears sinking into the lovely cathedral window quilt on the antique bed.

Chapter Eleven

Laura arrived just before the starting time of the program. She could not quite face the sympathy and curiosity of half of Chapelle. The bonfire blazed on the green under the careful supervision of Chief Fontenot and his assistant. Its scent covered the charred odor from the ruins of Domengeaux's store, and its light drew youngsters like moths. Some arrived still swathed in homemade costumes of bed sheets and old shirts stuffed with straw. Others came encased in plastic cartoon characters bought at the Dollar Store. The crackle of the fire and of candy wrappers filled the tepid night air.

Oldsters in light sweaters had moved aluminum lawn chairs under the oaks after Mass ended. Black parents shoved their small children toward good seats on the grass before the fire then faded back into the shadows to listen at a distance to tales they already knew.

Laura introduced herself and opened the program with the story of Will-o-the-wisp, the blacksmith so mean the Devil gave him a coal to start a little Hell of his own. She felt as if she glowed like the flames at her back, the aura of the fire and the color of her blouse reflecting redly on her face and hands. She set the stage and gave way to Father Ardoin, a contrast of black and white, his face like the full moon in the October sky, his glasses small shining stars in the flickering light. With relish, the priest told the one about the traveling preacher in the haunted house. Hands trembling and familiar face grotesque with imaginary fright, he evoked laughter from the children and smiles from the parents. The little ones clapped when he ended.

All fell silent as Tante Lu made her way to the fire. Its diminishing flames yellowed her face to the hue of old ivory. Father Ardoin placed a rocking chair and seated the old woman who had wrapped her sparse white hair in a red bandanna as if recreating a scene from another time—black woman, red tignon, yellow firelight. Rocking slowly and beginning softly, she told the tale of the *loup-garou*, the werewolf. This story, it happened right here in this parish about seventy years ago—for true.

"There was this rich planter, name of Grayson Darby, who loved a black girl, name of Mary. Each night she came to him along the cane field road and each night returned the same way to her cabin. Now, Grayson Darby warned her not to come to him on nights with a full moon because a full moon brought out the evil in men. Mary, she thought he was just ashamed 'cause she wasn't a white, and he thought the nightriders might come and make an example of them both. Or maybe, Grayson feared his beloved sister would see her walking the road in the bright moonlight and figure out that they was meeting. That girl, Mary, though, had lots of spirit, and she was determined to go to her lover whenever she wanted. So, one full moon night, she set out along the cane field road."

Tante Lu threw back her head and howled over and over. Small children fled back into the crowd to hug their parents' legs, and older children shivered with anticipation. Adolescent boys took advantage of the howls to place their arms around their dates and pull them tight against their sides.

"The field hands found Mary's body in the morning, savaged, the throat torn open by a wild animal. Crazy with grief, her lover took his dogs out the next evening to track the beast." Tante Lu sent another series of howls ululating off the church walls.

"When they didn't return, a search party organized to find Grayson's body. They found Darby unconscious among the torn bodies of his hounds, blood in puddles everywhere. He could not remember what had attacked him.

"On the next rainy night with the still nearly full moon peeking in and out of the clouds, Mary's brother, who had tried to keep the lovers apart, died in his own cabin, bitten all over by big fangs. There were no footprints in the mud by the open window, just the pad marks of a huge dog, a *loup-garou* everyone said. A werewolf had done the deed. Well, pretty soon everyone who had any silver was melting it down to make bullets against the *loup-garou* since that is the only way you can kill one—in the heart with a silver bullet. Grayson Darby made some himself to hunt the critter down. Now his sister was a mighty religious woman and said God would protect them, but Grayson locked her in the house the night he went to kill the *loup-garou.*"

Tante Lu howled again, but this time, it came out long and sad. "Grayson's sister heard only one shot late that night, and in the morning when the servants came and let her out, she found her brother dead on the cane road. He had put a silver bullet through his own heart. After that, no one else was killed by the *loup-garou*. That family is gone now. The sister entered a convent to pray for Grayson's soul. I nursed her on her deathbed, and it's she who told me the story—but me, I remember those murders well."

The crowd thinned slowly as children became sleepy or scared and were carried home by their parents, but the adolescents drew closer to the fire and waited for more. Tante Lu began a second story.

Leaning against an oak on the green, Laura could see the ruins of her apartment. She had lived there such a short time and yet impressions of the place stayed in her mind—of sitting by the window on these autumn nights listening to the low whispers of boys, the nervous laughter of girls beneath the trees. These old live oaks were made for lovers with low-slung branches to recline against and thick evergreen canopies touching the ground to form private nooks in their shadows. Over by the fire, Tante Lu spun a tale of supernatural love.

Laura half listened to the old woman, half listened to her own body, so empty, so bereft. She recognized him, despite the darkness, as soon as he stepped from the crowd and came toward her. "What are you doing way back here?" he asked. "Tante Lil took Pearl and Angelle home a little while ago, but Pearl asked me to watch out for you. She didn't like the look in your eyes when you drove here."

"I'm fine." Laura's voice quavered and she turned her face deeper into the shadows.

"You're crying."

With a touch of his hand, Robert LeBlanc turned her face back toward a sliver of moonlight coming through the branches. "Don't do this. Be the woman who took a tough job in a strange place despite Tante Lil. Be the one who Vivien can't grind into the dirt. I want that woman. I'd give her back all she lost and more."

He placed his lips against her partly open mouth, licked the salty tears from the rim and deepened the kiss. He pressed her pliant body between the hardness of his and the rough bark of the tree. Tonight with the rush of the festivities, the man who should shave twice a day hadn't, and the abrasive texture of his beard rasped seductively against the skin of her cheek. So male, so close, for a moment she could not recall her dead husband's name or face. When she did, he felt the change—the stiffness of her body pulling away from the trunk of the tree, the turning of her head, the closing of her lips.

"I'll wait until that woman comes back," he said and left her alone beneath the tree in that little sliver of moonlight. She recognized the sound of the engine when he started his old truck and returned to Chateau Camille.

Out on the green, the fire died to embers. Other elderly folks had taken Tante Lu's place by the coals and swapped yarns. Father Ardoin helped the old woman to his car for the drive back to Nebo. The youth of Chapelle, paired off, lay together beneath low slung branches. Laura tripped over one couple as she stumbled toward the fire.

"Hey, lady, watch where you're going," the annoyed boy shouted in a voice that cracked at the end of the sentence.

Back on the green, Chief Fontenot and his assistant

killed the embers of the bonfire with a fire hose. She thanked them and the remnants of the crowd for coming and drove out to the Chateau, alone and chilled by the night air.

Chapter Twelve

Even though wide awake and glad she had bought the modest blue cotton nightgown instead of sleeping in the nude, Laura had no desire to rise and get dressed when Angelle tiptoed into her room at seven a.m. to invite the houseguest to attend Mass. Her head throbbed against the old down pillows, and she wanted nothing more than to put one over her face and spend the rest of day hiding from Robert LeBlanc and his attention, a difficult trick since she lived in the man's home.

Angelle, who had taken her first communion not too long ago and still took her religion seriously, appeared to ponder the state of Laura's eternal soul before capitulating. "I guess it's okay. My daddy never goes to Mass, and he's not going to hell, he says."

Between Angelle's farewell benediction and the sound of the Lincoln heading down the drive toward Chapelle, Laura dozed. When the old house stood quiet on Sunday morning, she rose and slipped on the matching blue robe that buttoned securely beneath her chin and tied tightly around her waist and made her way toward the kitchen to brew some coffee as an antidote for her headache. She ran straight into Pearl.

The sideboard held a pitcher of orange juice, croissants in a basket and a caddy of butter and jelly. The housekeeper plugged in a hotplate holding a carafe of the strong and bitter coffee that made all other coffees taste like dishwater after one developed an immunity to—or an addiction for—it.

"We'll have eggs and grits when Miss Lilliane and the child get back from Mass. Mr. Bob is out in the barn checking on the cattle," the housekeeper said.

"Please." Laura snatched the full cup of liquid caffeine Pearl held out to her. Sadly it was too hot to gulp. She took one cautious sip and asked, "Mr. LeBlanc never goes to Mass?"

"Never. There isn't much place in the Church for a divorced man. He can't take the sacraments, you know, and Mr. Bob, he refused to get an annulment. Said he wasn't paying the Church to declare his daughter illegitimate."

The screen door on the kitchen entrance slammed. Laura seized an unbuttered croissant and the cup of black coffee and fled the dining area, saying to Pearl as she passed through the doorway that she felt ill and would eat the roll in bed. Then, she worried her excuse would bring Robert LeBlanc into her bedroom to check on her condition.

As she heard the master of the house ask Pearl for coffee, Laura bypassed her own room. She slipped quietly up the wide stairs at the front of the hall and entered the old library, the only place offering sanctuary on a floor of deserted rooms. At first, she sat on the edge of the antique desk and sipped the coffee. Then, nibbling on the croissant, she paced the bookshelves. They held mostly old legal texts, some in cracked brown leather bindings as old as the desk, others dating back only half a dozen years in a cheaper modern paper format.

She crossed the room to where the books shifted

from non-fiction to novels. Nearer to the sunny gallery a few pieces of wicker furniture gathered dust and aging novels crammed the shelves, some true collector's items like the improbable romances of Emma Southworth, others, like the original Nancy Drew books, of great nostalgic value, no better or worse than the pop fiction being written for young girls today, but certainly more innocent. Clearly, the LeBlanc women of several generations had claimed this corner of the library for their own, escaping into novels from their trying, or boring, everyday lives.

The topmost shelves of this corner, well beyond the reach of small children and the view of the casual browser, held perhaps twenty small tan leather volumes without author or title on their spines. With stained covers the books looked much handled. Laura tipped the first of the set off the shelf. A small metal clasp with a tiny keyhole guarded the contents, but either broken or aged beyond use, the lock opened easily when Laura nudged it with a fingernail.

A fine feminine hand had embossed the first yellowed page in brown ink—*The Diary of Caroline Montleon LeBlanc, 1851, Written in hope of informing future generations about the customs of our times*. The volume did exactly that. The words chattered gaily about wedding plans: lengths of sprigged silk purchased and lists of nuptial gifts received, each with a small check beside it to indicate that a "gracious note of appreciation" had been sent by the bride.

Laura pulled the wicker chair toward the window and settled into the musty cushions to retreat for a while into a more untroubled time. The diary read like a travel guide to the antebellum homes along the Mississippi and the Teche, although many of these were gone now, lost to war, decay and fire. But in those times, the mansions had held the relatives and friends of the Montleons and the LeBlancs. The bridal couple lingered six weeks with the most congenial company and two weeks or less at the homes of those presumably less cordial. No hint of what had shortened some of the visits ever crept into the descriptions of endless evening balls, daily picnics and afternoons of horse racing.

Laura skimmed through the diary, skipping over passages that seemed repetitious or where the ink had faded enough to make reading a strain. She contrasted the contents to her own simple chapel wedding and brief honeymoon. She and David had been so eager to get on with the real things in life, creating careers, establishing a home and family. If Laura had kept a diary of those brief months, David's name would have been on each page and the contents too personal to be used to inform future generations.

Caroline mentioned her husband only occasionally. "Adrien seems to be always the victor at the horse races, both on and off the race course," or "Adrien danced with each and every lady, charming even those matrons who watch from their chairs aside the dance floor." At the end of the volume, the bride adopted a more personal tone, describing her triumphal entry into Chateau Camille upon the newlyweds' return from a year of post-nuptial visiting.

With the LeBlanc field hands and servants lining the roadside for several miles, a holiday having been declared by their master, Caroline entered the mansion "where I was immediately taken to the chamber of Mama LeBlanc who has not been well. I confided to her that I believed myself to be with child and have suffered so little indisposition that I may still be of use to her and Papa LeBlanc in running the plantation despite my condition. Indeed, I feel full of well-being and do not fear what is to come in the least. Mama Leblanc assures me the same midwife who brought Adrien safely into the world after so many fruitless deliveries is still among the servants and will assist me in ways known only to her. Above all things, Mama LeBlanc wishes for many grandchildren and does not want to burden me with duties in my delicate condition. Above all things, I have told her, I wish to be of use to Chateau Camille where already I feel quite secure."

Laura closed the first volume and repositioned her chair in order to stretch for another. She suspected the bride was about to experience some mother-in-law trouble. At the same time, Laura wished she felt secure beneath the roof of Chateau Camille, peopled as it was with a hostile aunt, a distant servant, an impetuous child and a sexually attractive man. She could hear his heavy tread in the hall below. The sound of his presence and the memory of his kiss last evening made her want to both hide behind the library draperies and rush down the stairs to be near him. She chose to remain hidden with the diary still in her hands and recently stirred memories of David still in her heart.

Robert LeBlanc's deep voice penetrated to her hideout. Anger made it echo in the stairwell.

"Why wasn't Angelle with you in New Orleans?...Couldn't find her! Why the hell didn't you send Thurston, Vivien?...Didn't like Laura's attitude. Yes, Laura. She's staying with us since Domengeaux's burnt to the ground and almost took Angelle with it.

Well, how could you know when you were on your way back to New Orleans? Go to hell Vivien! I only called to say that you can tell your parents if they want to see their grandchild they must come in person." He slammed the receiver so hard its bell rang once in protest. Then, he left in a rage of slamming doors.

Leaning over the antique desk and peering through the window with its tiny ornamental balcony overlooking the rear gardens, Laura watched the angry man cut through the flower beds, taking a direct line to the barns as if he could not tolerate the convoluted pathways. Laura returned to the bookshelves. She wanted to select a second volume of the diaries to steady herself after being caught in the reverberations of Robert's explosion. She desired a retreat into the past when life was lived with grace and the demands made upon women were predictable and preordained, but through the French doors on the other side of the room, she saw the black Lincoln nose like a turning whale into the drive. Reluctantly, she shelved the first volume, replaced her chair and went down to dress for breakfast.

Chapter Thirteen

From the beginning of Laura's stay at Chateau Camille, Robert LeBlanc appeared as uneasy in Laura's presence as she was in his. Meals provided safe periods with light conversation about the weather, livestock and library happenings under the chaperonage of Tante Lil, Pearl and Angelle. Since Robert sat opposite his aunt, and she across from Angelle, the two of them were able to avoid any direct eye contact. She filled her days with work at the library, he with hours at the ranch, as he called the cattle barns, having abandoned the word "plantation."

They spent evenings together more awkwardly. Laura usually read in her room after dinner, but Angelle often forced her out to join the group in the parlor. Angelle bedeviled her with requests to play games, often lengthy ones like Monopoly, which the child drew out even further by needing help with her play money and property cards from both adults. The little girl shrewdly chose to sit between them forcing her father's eyes to meet Laura's many times over a throw of the dice or a purchase of Park Place or Reading Railroad. When tensions became too high, Laura retreated to bed early, knowing Angelle would insist on resuming the game exactly where they left off the next evening. Tante Lil complained about the clutter left on the floor, but the child's father told her to let it be. Often enough, he left the game first on pretext of having work to be done in his office/bedroom.

Going to bed early provided no defense against Angelle, however. If Laura allowed her bedside light to burn too long after retiring, she soon had a companion as the girl perched at the foot of the bed like a small black-haired succubus. The child was wearingly inquisitive and seemed always to be scheming to make her a permanent part of the household whether she could get her father to cooperate or not. Whatever Bob LeBlanc thought or felt he held back hard since that night under the oaks.

When a box of unwanted and unrequested clothing arrived from Pennsylvania, Angelle appeared to assist with the opening. She pawed over each one of Laura's sister's discards, her mother's bargain finds and her own old junk: jeans too small, dresses too frilly, blouses too tight in the bust, sweaters too warm for the climate. Laura, standing before the mirror inside the armoire, selected a few of the more classic items that did not span across her chest or bind in the rear. The rest she repacked, including one lingerie box containing a white lace nightgown and filmy peignoir still in their original wrappings. Angelle retrieved the nightie before Laura could hide the garments beneath the next layer of rejects destined for Father Ardoin's charities.

"It's so beautiful," exclaimed the child. "Did you wear this on your honeymoon?"

Not at ease with this precocious conversation, Laura said shortly, "No, I never wore it at all. One of my mother's friends gave it to me as a shower gift, but it's too fancy for me, okay?"

"Then what did you wear on your wedding night?"

The child held the peignoir before her face like a bridal veil.

"Nothing." Laura changed course in mid-sentence. "Nothing that I have now. It burned in the fire."

"Oh. Then you could wear this when your other nightie is in the wash. You could wear it when we play Monopoly. I could ask Daddy to wear his robe and pajamas like he did at night before you came to stay with us. We'd be like a family in the evening."

"We're not a family, Angelle. I'll be leaving as soon as I can find a furnished apartment."

"Please keep the nightie anyhow. See, it doesn't take up much room, and it's so beautiful."

Angelle gently folded the set into a square and placed it in one of the small drawers in the base of the armoire. With a quixotic change of subject, she said to Laura, "I hope I get some money for Christmas. I sure need it in a hurry."

"It's not even Thanksgiving yet, Angelle. Now go to bed—please!"

For a change, the little girl responded to Laura's suggestion, but the child came back early the next morning, double checking the box of discards Laura intended to drop off at the church that day to make sure the peignoir had not been included.

****

Folding his hands, Father Ardoin prepared to listen or to talk, whichever seemed applicable to the situation. He sat quietly waiting to help after Laura donated the box of used clothing and thanked him once again for looking after Snake these last few weeks.

The cat, literally landing on all fours, disappeared briefly after the fire. Laura, checking the fist-sized hole beneath the church each day, finally found her pet in his original refuge. How he could squeeze his maturing body though the kitten-sized hole remained a mystery of the animal world, though he was thinner because of his ordeal. Laura wanted to bundle him off for a good feeding, but she settled for asking Father Ardoin to give the cat a can of food each day rather than burden Pearl with more work or raise the wrath of Miss Lilliane who loathed pets along with everything else. Angelle had been disappointed that Snake remained at the church. Laura placed a small sack of cat food on his desk beside the box of clothing and began to talk.

"I really must find my own place and give Snake a home before he gets too wild. Have you heard of anything available at all?"

"Several persons are willing to rent rooms but of course, the situation would be similar to what you have at the LeBlancs. Things aren't working out over there? Is Miss Lilliane giving you a hard time?"

"No, not exactly. In fact, she barely acknowledges I'm there. She rarely follows me to work anymore. Her lungs seem to be bothering her more in the cool weather. I can hear her coughing several doors down. And Angelle suffers from nightmares. She's in the next room and cries out in the middle of the night."

Laura paused, confessing only to herself what really disturbed her about Angelle's dreams, the proximity of Angelle's father in the next room, holding the terrified child and talking softly to her until she rested. Often, Laura fell asleep listening to that low, strong voice on the other side of the thin partition. She did not care to tell the priest about her own dreams where her David turned darker and darker until he became Robert LeBlanc—who did all the things she'd done with David and more.

"And Mr. LeBlanc is a problem, too," she added with sudden honesty.

"Oh now, I'm sure Bob LeBlanc would never take advantage of the situation. I know about those unsavory stories passed around after his divorce, but I am positive the whole thing was staged." Seeing Laura's look of surprise, the old priest stopped. "I need to do penance for my babbling mouth."

"I thought they divorced because of incompatibility."

"Extreme incompatibility, but the lawyer cited adultery as the principal grounds. Now I've added the sin of gossip." Father Ardoin bit his tongue.

"His or hers?" Laura probed.

"His, so they say. But as I said, I am positive the actual carnal act was staged. It could not have been coincidence that the incident involved Pearl's daughter."

"Pearl's daughter!"

"You see, Pearl's daughter is a working girl."

"I'm a working girl," countered Laura.

"But not exactly in the same profession. You don't do most of your work at night!"

"You mean she's a prostitute."

"Well, yes. Oh, worse and worse! These things should only be discussed in the confessional." A blush heated the priest's soft, round cheeks. "I suppose I have to tell you the whole story to clear Robert LeBlanc's reputation, though he certainly never sought absolution from me. You see, my dear, not that many years ago, divorce in Louisiana was very involved. Blame the

Church if you must. Grounds of incompatibility required a much longer separation period before the marriage could be ended. In cases of adultery, the termination could be executed quickly. Bob was in a hurry and did not want to leave the child with Vivien. To make the story short, a photographer, ostensibly his wife's private investigator, caught him in flagrante delicto with Pearl's daughter. I personally believe old Judge LeBlanc, his father, set up the whole affair. Not too fond of his daughter-in-law, the judge, but then, no one was."

The priest steepled his fingers making a little church of his hands. "The divorce proceedings concluded with remarkable speed thanks to a very good friend of the judge. Afterward, Vivien went to one of her spas to recover from the affront. Once the whole disgusting matter concluded, Bob had custody of the child. Now, I doubt even Judge LeBlanc would have condoned his keeping Angelle if a real affair with a dark lady of the evening had taken place. Puzzling to all the gossips, though, that Vivien did not protest the disposal of the child. In fact, she didn't even visit her daughter for well over a year after the divorce. Of course, I wouldn't describe Vivien as a loving mother at any time."

Realizing he had now besmirched another reputation, Father Ardoin hastened to say a good word about the woman. "Although she wasn't well liked in Chapelle, Vivien Montleon did have some good qualities. I mean the people here felt she put on airs, hauteur, if you know what I mean. Still, she served as president of the genealogical society and spent many hours here transcribing the old records and searching family histories. Every day, she lit a candle at the grotto shrine and contemplated the statue of the Virgin at length. She also donated generously to the restoration of the church. Every Sunday, Vivien brought them all to Mass, even the baby, marching the LeBlancs to the family pew past windows and woodwork she paid to restore. You see, despite her regrettable personality, Vivien did care about some things."

Laura's attention wandered during his praise of Vivien. She ran her hand over the spines of the thick baptismal registers lining the walls of his office. Happy with her distraction, Father Ardoin quickly dropped his subject and took down one of the old volumes.

"See here, the baptismal record of Adrien LeBlanc, the one I spoke of on your first visit to Chapelle. The LeBlancs lost so many babies at birth they baptized the infant the day he was born rather than wait the traditional six weeks."

He took another volume, a register of internments, from a different shelf. "And here, the burial of Marie Segura and infant son on the same day. What a coincidence. No wonder legends arise from things like these." As he closed the heavy book, a piece of the brittle paper flaked off in his hands.

"Really, Father Ardoin, these records are extremely valuable and deteriorating rapidly. I'd like to help the church and the library by having these microfilmed, or even digitized, at the university with your consent. I could hand-carry them a few at a time. We'd place the microfilm in our library and let the university make a set as well. No one would have to handle these fragile originals to get their information. I know I could get the board to fund the project. Then, anyone could make copies without transcribing from the originals."

Pleased to be free of the previous subject matter and caught in the wave of Laura's enthusiasm, the priest agreed whole-heartedly. "Of course, I must get the consent of the archbishop, but I'm sure there will be no problem."

"Good. Look, I'll call the university to make arrangements."

Discussion of their new project had carried them both from the office into the church as Laura sought the shortest way back to the library. In her haste, she tripped on the edge of a marble inset in the floor covering the tomb of one of the early fathers of Ste. Jeanne d'Arc. Catching herself on the rail of the LeBlanc pew with its brass nameplate, she muttered, "Why do Catholics do things like this?"

"Oh, no one is buried there now. It is a special honor, of course, to be granted burial within the sanctuary. Father Blaise founded Ste. Jeanne d'Arc. I think that as well as being an honor, there is a superstitious belief those buried here will continue to watch over the church. Unfortunately, Father Blaise had to be removed when the foundations were reinforced recently. We left the stone though, as his memorial. It is due to my neglect the slab hasn't been properly cemented into place yet. I must see to it one of these days."

"Before someone breaks an ankle or worse," joked Laura, hurrying off too intent on her new idea to mind a stubbed toe.

Chapter Fourteen

Work, the solution to all her problems, work to forget the death of David, heavy work to weight down a rising passion for a new man far too soon after the death of her husband. Laura single-handedly hewed out a children's corner in the old library by moving the stacks and hundreds of adult books with the help of the janitor to create a sunny nook where she read stories to a small, but steadily growing group of preschoolers once a week.

She recorded the stories of Tante Lu in both French and English and sought out other elders with tales to tell. With Father Ardoin's permission, she began transporting the Ste. Jeanne church records, volume by volume, thirty miles to the local university for microfilming. In exchange for copies for their archives, the university supplied the film, equipment and the expertise of their archivist whose slow methodical ways often irritated Laura into laboriously turning and photographing each page herself when the work bogged down in his hands.

Now and then, an entry arrested her attention, like those recording the births of Caroline Montleon LeBlanc's children. "Baptized August 12, 1852, Charles Adrien LeBlanc, son of Adrien LeBlanc and Caroline (Montleon)", "Baptized January 14, 1854, Catherine Castille LeBlanc," "Baptized May 5, 1856,

Aurelien August LeBlanc," "Baptized September 16, 1859, Felice Camille LeBlanc."

The entries supplied the bare facts to trace a lineage. The diaries of Caroline LeBlanc which Laura had taken to her room and read one by one, fleshed out these facts. At first, the diaries provided a quaint diversion, a mild escape. Caroline barely mentioned her pregnancy throughout the volume for 1852. Instead, she filled the pages with rambling commentaries on household management with an occasional recipe or housewifely hint thrown in for posterity.

A gap occurred in the entries for August after which the diarist wrote, "Two days ago, I was delivered of a healthy son after a long and arduous travail made easier by the skills and potions of Tante Inez." Caroline described the baptismal ceremony in detail, followed shortly by the affecting scene so loved by Miss Lilliane when Camille LeBlanc on her deathbed handed the young woman the keys to the plantation.

Naturally, the diaries provided Miss Lilliane's source of information, though the old librarian neglected to mention the keys Caroline received opened not only the larders and wine stores, but the safe and cash boxes as well. The massive iron safe still stood in a corner of Robert LeBlanc's bedroom, open now and crammed with old ledgers, agricultural magazines and new bills, the large key long lost. Laura had seen it herself when Angelle dragged her into Robert's room to coax her father into yet another game of Monopoly. The diary also recorded the dying woman's parting advice, "Give Adrien enough money to allow him to be a man, but not enough to ruin the plantation—for Mama LeBlanc realized she had indulged her son terribly."

The diary for 1853 revealed a young woman blossoming with motherhood and responsibility, a woman who redecorated, planned entertainments, revived the gardens, oversaw the preservation of the plantation bounty by the cooks, ministered to the health of the slaves and fulfilled "so many duties I fear I have neglected this diary."

Laura entirely understood this burst of energy. Since Tante Lil had retired at last to brood in her mansion, Laura cleaned, discarded and rearranged, making the library her own. The story-telling evening had been only the first of many programs to lure the citizens of Chapelle.

One feeling she could not share with Caroline LeBlanc was the young wife's mild surprise "that I am with child again so quickly, which only proves that I perform my wifely duties as joyously as I perform all others." Laura laughed over that coy remark one evening as she thought about her earlier comment to Miss Lilliane. Perhaps, Caroline had enjoyed sex very much indeed.

Still troubled by her own longings in the night when Robert LeBlanc came to chase away his daughter's night terrors in the next room, Laura lay still in Caroline's marriage bed convincing herself that Bob had inherited his ancestor's animal magnetism along with the ole plantation. Perhaps, she only yearned for what she had lost, David. Whichever, she had no intention of acting on the attraction. Plenty of projects to keep her busy and involved, really.

In their depiction of domestic life, the diaries had historic value. Laura planned to ask Miss Lilliane for permission to film them once she'd completed the church project. She wondered why the old woman with her family pride had not published the manuscripts long ago. She hadn't found any deadly secrets in the diaries, at least not up to 1856 when Caroline gave birth to her third child and second son. The young mother could be forgiven, perhaps, because of her times and circumstances for a slight disappointment expressed at the earlier birth of her daughter for: "I have perceived that to have only one son is a hazard and having been reared in a family with over many daughters, I do no desire to repeat that pattern either." Regarding their publication, she would have to catch Miss Lilliane in a good mood—if she had any.

Laura joined the local genealogy club meeting once a week to intertwine their collateral lines. While she still maintained her antecedents had no bearing on her own life, she did recognize ancestor hunting as a major obsession in Chapelle, and therefore, she had to know more about it. Besides, the weekly get-togethers removed her from Chateau Camille every Thursday evening. By the time the elderly women who composed ninety percent of the membership finished their tea and scones, repacked their notebooks and asked Laura for a ride home because they disliked driving in the dark, all the residents of the Chateau had adjourned to their rooms: Angelle asleep, Miss Lilliane coughing into her pillow and Robert working on his accounts or reading. Laura always tried to slip soundlessly through the spill of light from the transom over his door. Occasionally, he caught her, or they collided by accident in the hallway, Laura could never decide which, the game they played being as complicated as Monopoly.

One evening, he mocked her, standing in the

doorway of his room with the light and shadows making alluring patterns across the dark, curly hair on his chest only half-covered by a deep burgundy-colored robe. "So you have discovered the importance of the past. Have you joined the DAR, too?"

Laura felt up to the challenge as her independence returned with each successful project she completed. "No, Mr. LeBlanc, I'm simply making inexpensive Christmas gifts."

She showed him two ornate family trees, gilded and embossed, that she'd filled in with calligraphic script. The twisting roots held the names of Josef Schumann and his wife Hannah born in the early nineteenth century. Laura's own name, and that of her sister and her sister's children, rested in the outermost leafy tendrils of the tree's canopy.

"Unfortunately, Josef Schumann arrived in Pennsylvania in 1830 during the great German immigration along with several million other anonymous farmers. However, Mrs. DeVille assures me if I trace all my female lines, I am bound to find someone who will make me eligible for the DAR. I think I'll quit after I have these framed for my mother and sister. My nephew and niece are getting voodoo dolls, which I'm sure they'll find more interesting, especially if they dress them like each other."

"Yes." He smiled and said, "Angelle is fascinated by that sort of thing, too. At her age, she still believes a person can use magic to get what they want."

To avoid his direct, dark gaze, Laura slid her eyes across his shoulder and stared into his bedroom dominated by a massively carved half-tester bed fit for a French king. "Well, I'm feeling a little tired. Guess

I'll turn on. Turn in, I mean."

"A good night kiss, then."

Robert leaned over and brushed his lips softly over her forehead as if she were Angelle, then placed another gentle kiss on her cheek. Turning his head, slightly prickling her skin with his stubble, his mouth moved toward hers. Laura bolted for her room. She heard him laughing at her retreat all the way down the hall. "Coward," he called after her. "In any battle, you should stand your ground."

The kiss hadn't been as potent as the one under the oak tree, but it disturbed her enough to keep her awake and reading Caroline's diaries because she could not rest. That night, she found the first inkling Caroline Montleon was not a paragon of virtue. The now mature mistress of the Chateau, nearing Laura's own age, wrote, "Without joy, I have discovered I carry a fourth child. Papa Aurelien is failing and Adrien is so often gone that more and more of the burden of the plantation is thrust upon me. I cannot carry two such heavy loads."

Two weeks later, the diarist noted, "I have lost the child but am recuperating at good pace. The tragedy brought Adrien to my side. Perhaps now, he will share more of the responsibility of the plantation. Tomorrow, we go together to light candles at the church for the soul of our lost child."

If the previous passage about not wanting the child were omitted, then the second was quite affecting. Laura, her tired mind full of ancestors, Montleons and LeBlancs, and Christmas gifts for her own family, thought what strong stuff the past could be if it were as well-known as this family's history. If she could convince Miss Lilliane to allow the diaries to be printed, what a contribution they would make to the local history of the area, perhaps to the history of the South. Caroline Montleon had been far more candid about her sexuality and bearing children than most women of her era. The diaries went from being a charming discourse on manners and customs to a personal outlet for the writer, and so would speak directly to the concerns of modern women.

Thanksgiving waddled into view next week. Yes, if she began now, she could have the first diary typed, printed out and bound at the university bookstore by the holidays. That would surely please the old librarian and soften her up for having all of the volumes published. Pleased to have another project on the way and another gift out of the way, Laura slept unusually well that night after all.

Chapter Fifteen

Thanksgiving Day arrived coated in frost. Cajun snow, Pearl called it. This token of northern weather buoyed Laura's spirits. She could trace Robert's footsteps through the garden to the cattle barns where he had gone early to tend the stock. She had a childish urge to follow his dark path through the crisp rime but saw Angelle already doing that, heavily clad in a brilliant red wool jacket and cap for the first time that winter. Laura turned from the kitchen window where she'd come to offer a contribution to the Thanksgiving dinner and any other help that would be acceptable in Pearl's domain. Even Miss Lilliane congregated there adding her one culinary accomplishment to the meal—her perfect pralines.

Unusually cordial today, the old curmudgeon sat dropping the brown sugar and pecan mixture by the spoonful on to a marble slab sitting on a low table the height of her wheelchair. "I've always been a career girl, you know. Never learned to cook. We had servants for that," Miss Lilliane went on to Laura as if Pearl were not standing by the stove working on the rice and oyster dressing.

"But my old black mammy taught me how to do pralines the right way. That Lola Domengeaux knows nothing about the perfect praline. Always use a marble slab, never waxed paper like she does. Why, this is

perfect praline weather. Keeps the slab good and cold."
Miss Lilliane had stationed her slab as far from Pearl's
stove as possible.

"Now watch, Laura. I might as well pass this along
to you since Angelle is too young. Though being a
Yankee, you probably won't catch on to praline
making."

Laura watched, laughing on the inside. At home,
her family considered her a good cook. Not having
"servants" her mother taught her at an early age, but
she'd already learned this morning that Pennsylvania
German recipes were not exactly to the Cajun taste.
Earlier, she had baked a corn pudding made with dried
sweet corn mailed from Lost Spring by a mother
determined that her daughter would be able to have one
traditional family dish on this holiday spent in a strange
land where people ate frog legs and crawfish. Both
Miss Lilliane and Pearl tasted a small bite and
pronounced the corn too bland. Pearl remedied that by
vigorously dousing the pudding with hot sauce, stirring
it up and then rebrowning the top. The adulterated corn
pudding now sat on the sideboard, awaiting reheating
once the mammoth turkey came out of the oven.

Pearl's fresh coconut cake and a pan of glossy
candied yams sat beside Laura's offering. Pots on the
stovetop held green beans with salt meat, the rice
dressing and a chicken and sausage gumbo to serve as a
first course, enough to serve a horde, let alone five
people. As far as Laura knew, no one else had been
invited.

In this assumption, she proved wrong.
Experiencing a wonderful sense of family among the
women in the kitchen, Laura reveled in the holiday,

even though Miss Lilliane cursed each time a praline shattered while being removed from the slab and Pearl remained taciturn as usual. Simply warding off Robert with a cup of gumbo and bribing Angelle with pralines to keep the man and child out from underfoot brought back memories of her own childhood—her dad pinching a piece of crisp, greasy skin from the bird, her sister begging for a serving of the green gelatin-marshmallow-pineapple fluff before dinner. For a brief moment, she pretended the people in the kitchen belonged to her, complete with flaws and idiosyncrasies—until the chauffeured Mercedes glided up the shell drive.

Thurston in his livery opened the car door. As Vivien LeBlanc swung gracefully outward, Laura had the urge to retreat to her room, but she stood her ground as someone in the household had told her not too long ago. Happily, she wore the expensive ruby blouse, a snug sweater-vest and the gray skirt Robert had given her, an outfit every bit as good as Vivien's couture. Well, maybe not quite, but she certainly did not look dowdy today. Since the fire, she'd allowed his gift to hang in the armoire like clothes too good to discard but too unsuitable to be worn.

Today, she'd decided to call a truce with the man as she dressed for dinner. No more avoiding Robert or becoming upset about a few stolen kisses. For Thanksgiving, they would be like family—not kissing cousins—more like distant relatives together for the holidays, jovial and tolerant of each other for a short period of time.

Seeing Laura's choice in clothing, Angelle shed her jeans of the morning for a gray jumper and red ruffled blouse. She'd begged Laura to tie the scarlet ribbons in her thick black braids, rejecting help from her Tante Lil or Pearl. Now they stood, clad like mother and daughter, waiting for Vivien to assault the verandah. Her ex-husband stayed in the parlor seemingly entranced by a football game on television in which he had shown little interest until now. Talk about cowards!

Vivien paused at the foot of the steps and waited in a model's slouch with her hips thrust forward in a straight skirt of muted heather plaid so tight her pelvic bones protruded under the fine wool. Thomas aided an elegant older woman and a distinguished gentleman from the automobile. Angelle, frozen to Laura's side, suddenly thawed and dashed to the car.

"PawPaw! MiMaw!" She gave the older couple a vast hug. "Why don't you come see me more?"

Although the regal Mrs. Montleon frowned at the grammar, she returned the child's affection. Robert roused himself to shake hands with his child's grandparents. During the greetings, Thurston, the chauffeur, slipped quietly into the kitchen to greet Pearl.

In a marvel of timing that precluded awkward conversation, Pearl announced dinner. The gold-rimmed antique Parisian china, amber Bohemian crystal and heavy silverware graced a tablecloth said to have been embroidered by Caroline Montleon herself. Honey-colored beeswax candles burned brightly in heirloom candelabra ringed with silk autumn leaves. The heavy-breasted turkey browned to perfection and awaiting carving served as the centerpiece surrounded by side dishes. Hmmm, not exactly Thanksgiving in

Lost Spring after all. Robert quickly seated his mother-in-law at his side and urged Laura into a chair at his other elbow. Lastly, he placed Vivien on the far side of Laura across from her father. Miss Lilliane reigned at the other end of the table while Angelle sat ensconced happily between her grandparents.

With the aid of Thurston, Pearl placed a small cup of gumbo at each place except Vivien's, that guest having waved the soup aside. Robert engaged his ex-mother-in-law on his right in constant conversation throughout the dinner leaving Laura on the host's left locked in silent combat with Vivien LeBlanc. Occasionally, the battle slipped into words.

Vivien picked at a thin slice of white meat and played with a few carrot sticks from the relish tray. She ate with the air of one accustomed to dining on hummingbird tongues and nectar. Although her dinner companion killed her appetite, Laura accepted a bit of everything, curious about the difference in Thanksgiving dinners, north and south. Here, the gravy had the sting of pepper sauce, and her own corn casserole bit her back. Still, a delicious meal. Making an effort, she turned toward Vivien.

"Aren't you feeling well? I see you have no appetite."

"I never have cared for Pearl's cooking. I did try to teach her something better, but these colored women are impossible."

"Try the corn casserole. I made that."

"I never touch starch." Vivien fixed Laura with her cold gaze and pulled a cigarette from her small mauve leather bag exactly matching a pale lavender thread in her jacket. Thurston sprang from some hidden recess of the dining room and lit it for the mistress.

"I must say you have grown quite fat and happy since the last time we met." Vivien blew a stream of smoke in Laura's direction.

"Really?" countered Laura. "I've heard heavy smoking kills hunger and causes premature wrinkles in women with fair, dry skin." Laura plunged her fork into a plump oyster and ate it with all the sensuality she could muster, running her tongue over her lips as she finished. When she glanced up, Robert LeBlanc watched her with amused, dark eyes.

Laura reached down the table and seized one of his brown and calloused hands. "What a wonderful dinner, Robert. I feel like part of the family."

None of the dinner guests missed the gesture. Angelle smiled happily. The Montleons appeared startled, but pleased. Miss Lilliane coughed in disapproval while Vivien smiled sourly at the intimacy. Only Robert saw the "I'll-get-back-to-*you*-later" stare Laura forced on him.

Regret set in after the dessert, a choice of yam pie or coconut cake or a small serving of both. After all, Robert LeBlanc was *not* her sweetheart. She had given everyone a false impression in a petty urge to slight Vivien whom he already loathed. While they sipped sherry or brandy in the parlor and sampled the perfect pralines, Laura made an extra attempt to be civil to the woman. She took a place next to her on the uncomfortable horsehair and rosewood Victorian love seat where Vivien sat alone as she smoked another cigarette.

"I heard you are interested in genealogy. I've been working with the Ste. Jeanne parish records and…"

"They are full of errors. Robert and I are not co-descendants of Caroline Montleon. Caroline had many sisters, and one of her favorites was named Felice. I am quite sure she named her youngest daughter after her favorite sister, and this is where the confusion begins." Vivien's thin fingers with their manicured French nails fluttered in agitation.

Mrs. Montleon, seated in a chair near the fireplace with Angelle at her feet, inclined a head as blonde and tastefully arranged as her daughter's toward her husband and grasped his wrist as he stood beside her drinking his brandy. The lines in the distinguished gentleman's face deepened into concern. Both watched their daughter as closely as they would an approaching hurricane.

Vivien continued her lecture. "Caroline was the eldest of nine girls, and Felice—my Felice, my ancestress, not Robert's—would have been young enough to seem to be her daughter. Of course, the war left so many girls spinsters with no one to marry, all those young men dead in heroic battle, but I am sure it was my Felice, not Robert's, who married a cousin in New Orleans in 1876. I am still looking for those marriage records. It shouldn't have been allowed in any case, the marriage of relatives. Inbreeding produces aberrations, terrible aberrations. They could not be blamed back then because they did not know. I know. I thought that common lineage set Robert and I apart from the crowd, that we were ordained to meet and marry and produce children with a fine pedigree. But, the aberrations can be terrible."

The normally icy woman blazed with denials. Her fingers raked the air, and ash from the cigarette lit by her father's slim gold lighter fell unheeded onto her wool skirt. The cigarette loosened by Vivien's frantic gestures toppled into her lap. Laura quickly slapped at the burning butt and removed it to an ashtray, but it still burnt a small hole in the lovely muted plaid of the material. Vivien LeBlanc appeared oblivious to the damage as she tried to prove her point.

When Laura sought help from the occupants of the room, she saw them fixed in a tableau beyond her understanding. The two men, brandy glasses still in hand, stood immobile and wordless by the mantel of the fireplace, its grate dark and empty. Mrs. Montleon cradled Angelle protectively against her black linen skirt, the weight of the child disheveling the fabric. Tante Lil poured herself a double sherry, dripping some of the liquor on her sleeve because of her haste.

Robert reacted first. "I think Vivien has had enough entertainment for today, Edward." Calmly, he sat his snifter on a small table and called for Thurston to escort the ladies to the car.

Now Vivien, totally rambling, wanted to know why no fire burned in the grate when the air was so frigid outside. "We should have a fire on Thanksgiving Day," she asserted, standing and waving her hands in agitation. Her parents caged her between them, each one taking a flailing arm. Thurston brought up the rear as they left Chateau Camille. Robert followed them out, and Laura bobbed along in his wake with Angelle trailing her. Miss Lilliane stayed behind and made no effort to say farewell. Once the women were seated in the Mercedes, Edward Montleon paused.

"Robert, you know we wanted to see Angelle, but it was inadvisable to bring Vivien. Still, we felt we couldn't leave her on a holiday. She has been so self-contained lately, not even upset about Angelle and the fire. I suppose that was a bad sign after all, but parents always want to think the best. Laura seems like a fine woman. Try to give Angelle a normal home life. That's what we want for her." The men shook hands gravely and parted company.

With the departure of her grandmother, Angelle attached herself to Laura's side again. Laura knelt beside her. "Angelle, honey, bring me my drink from the parlor."

As soon as the child left, she descended on Robert LeBlanc still standing in the drive. "Why didn't you warn me Vivien is unbalanced? No, you hid at your end of the table and stood at the other end of the parlor and let us duke it out over someone not worth the trouble, you bastard!"

"Maybe I'm not worth the trouble, but Angelle is. As many people as I can put between her and Vivien, the better. You are a strong woman, Laura. Help me, please!"

Laura chose not to understand. These were not her people. These were not her problems. She had her own, and so she just repeated, "You bastard!" as Angelle opened the door.

Laura seized the sherry and consumed it with a gulp. Patting the child in passing, she went to the kitchen to help Pearl with the dishes. If Pearl had troubles, she kept them to herself. As Laura brushed past Angelle, the child began begging her father for gifts again.

"Daddy, I really, really need money for Christmas."

Odd, the child had more concern with what she would find under the tree on Christmas day than with the disturbing scene her mad mother created. How many times had Angelle witnessed such outbursts or heard such words that she appeared immune to them? Again, Laura reminded herself, not her problem.

Chapter Sixteen

The interval between Christmas and Thanksgiving is simply too brief when everything must be put in order before a vacation. Laura worked frantically at the library completing the vacation schedules and leaving instructions with the staff on how to conduct the children's Christmas party, her own inspiration that she felt guilty about abandoning to others. Determined not to spend this holiday among strangers, she planned to head home to be with her nice, normal family back in Pennsylvania.

At night, she wrapped gifts in her room. Really, the presents were only tokens since she'd stretched her finances to replace her wardrobe and make the rent she insisted on paying to the LeBlancs over Robert's protests. She did not want to owe him anything. Bad enough he still looked at her with those longing, bedroom eyes despite their quarrel. Mrs. Domengeaux's insurance settlement seemed a very long time in coming. That good woman had promised Laura a share for her lost furnishings. Perhaps, the adjuster had heard rumors about the source of the fire.

So, Dad and her brother-in-law got the alligator tooth keychains from the Cajun Corner, and her nephew and niece would have to make do with the voodoo dolls stuffed with Spanish moss and supplied with thorns for sticking. Undoubtedly, they'd name the dolls after a teacher or each other and try them out. At least, the framed family trees for Cissy and Mom looked impressive. She begged a few of Pearl's best recipes, the ones not calling for too much seafood or pepper sauce, in order to have something else to share.

Actually, she'd spent more on the LeBlanc family than on her own. The binding of the typed diary had been more expensive than she'd reckoned. Since Angelle incessantly asked for money, she put twenty dollars inside a hollow Victorian Christmas ornament for the child. Twenty dollars, too much to be giving a seven-year-old who would have been content with five, but Laura recognized it as guilt money, hating to leave the child in case her deranged mother decided to visit again.

For Pearl who, although quiet and sometimes hostile, often put flowers in her room or snatched up laundry before Laura could do it for herself, a gold-plated stickpin with a small cultured pearl on the end seemed appropriate. She'd gotten Robert LeBlanc the most impersonal gift she could conjure, a year's subscription to *American Cattleman* magazine. Hopefully, the postcard announcing the present wouldn't arrive until she was long on her way to Pennsylvania.

When she completed her wrapping, Laura curled up with the Montleon diaries, which increased in relevancy and became less quaint in tone with each passing year. The year 1858 brought a cholera epidemic to the hot, low-lying plantation lands. The disease took many of the slaves, Caroline's youngest son, and an unborn child aborted with the cramping symptoms of the illness.

In a hand still shaking with weakness, the mistress wrote, "In many ways we are still blessed. Papa Aurelien lives though he is very weak. My strength is returning, and I am able to conduct business from my bed. Charles and Catherine seem free of permanent damage, and my husband, who is away visiting in a healthier clime, is entirely untouched. Still, I wonder if the taking of little Gus and the unborn one, also a male child, is a punishment for my past sin. Tante Inez says my illness has rendered me foolish. Women have always done what must be done, and Mother Mary forgives them, says she. I pray that is so."

In 1859, Caroline wrote with irritation of the impending birth of her next child. "Although I am in my eighth month and the heat of the summer weighs on me, I am expected to tend to those in the quarters, though Tante Inez and her apprentices can do as well without me. The women who come to sit with me know Adrien came home for the holiday season, but where is he now? I wish I had the courage to deny this birth, but I fear for my immortal soul. God help me."

Of the actual birth of her second daughter, the diarist said, "The child was small and the labor easy. I was able to return to my duties rapidly. This daughter is sweet and fair and unlike her quarrelsome dark brother and sister. I will call her Felice in hope that joy will come to her and that she absorbed none of my bitterness in the womb." Caroline mentioned no favorite sister by that same name.

The year 1861 brought the war to Chateau Camille. Caroline commented acidly, "All the talk is of war, but Adrien merely paints. His obsession is to complete an informal portrait of myself and the children before he leaves. Hardly can I see my husband as a soldier. He has always been as he is now, an artist and a lover of women. As he paints, he says he will take no side in a war over slavery. I understand the evil of our peculiar institution, but how will we plant the cane that makes our fortune without their labor, I ask him. Do not plant he says and paints on."

Again avoiding the LeBlanc family, Laura kept to her room and continued reading the diary for 1861, completing it on the same evening she finished her packing for her holiday trip back north. Lying in Caroline's marriage bed with the cathedral window quilt pulled up to her chin, Laura gazed at the metal bar once used to draw the now vanished mosquito netting over the occupant and contemplated the timelessness of anger and revenge. She thumbed the diary to pages underscoring her thoughts.

"Adrien has taken ship, not with the grand Confederate navy, but to Paris, the one thing denied him by his adoring mama. Says he, let the Confederacy pursue its dreams while I pursue mine. I asked if he ever considered the dreams of his wife. Adrien replied that I already had my dream and should continue to live it. Less glibly, he made the expected protestations of the trip being too dangerous for a woman and young children. He is taking our portrait with him so we will be with him always.

"I preferred his more honest first statement. Chateau Camille is my dream. Even at that age when a new silk gown meant more to me than the slavery question, I knew I married Adrien not for love, but for this plantation. What could be more ideal, I felt, than a husband who cared nothing for his land, an only child with aged parents who would leave the running of the place to me most gladly. At last, I would no longer be secondary to my three brothers or at the beck and call of a demanding mother and eight younger sisters whose ranks Mama added to with each passing year. Adrien, of course, wanted to be relieved of his responsibilities by a strong woman like old Camille and found her in me. I have relieved him for so long in so many ways it should not amaze me that he feels no responsibility toward myself or the children."

Bitter passage followed bitter passage. "And now I find that Adrien has left another souvenir of his lust beneath my skirts. I called for Tante Inez and demanded her special services again. She brought her elixir once more. This time my partner in sin rolled her yellowed eyes and said she is not sure Mother Mary forgives the taking of a life in anger but only those taken out of necessity. I sent that pandering old darkie from the room and drank my wine of gall, a last toast to Adrien LeBlanc. I drank it to the final drop, far more than Tante Inez prescribed, but it will be, as is my hope, doubly effective. I feel intensely ill."

The diary did not resume for nearly a month. Then, a chastened Caroline wrote, "I shall never act out of anger and revenge again. I am thankful I was too weak to confess when the priest came to administer last rites. As he did so, my thoughts dwelt on how to avoid the Kingdom of Heaven or the eternity of Hell and stay on this earth to rear my living children. Papa Aurelien, meaning well, made Charles and Catherine watch by my 'deathbed.' He spared only Felice due to her tender years. Poor children, having to sit in a room reeking from the bloody rags that staunched my hemorrhage in the heat of midsummer. Hearing their prayers kept me on this earth. For them, I recovered."

Caroline's serenity proved momentary. "What is this folly!" I asked Papa Aurelien. He replied he felt compelled by his honor to take Adrien's place at the front defending our homeland. I told him honor is nearly as worthless as revenge, but he looked upon me sternly and said women know nothing of honor. He commended Chateau Camille and his grandchildren into my care and rode off to die.

"Christmas—1861. No gifts for the children. The package of luxuries promised in Adrien's letter has not arrived, but I place no blame, both the war and my esteemed husband being equally unreliable. How I wish my prediction regarding Papa Aurelien had not come true. It erred only in the cause of his passing. Old and feeble as he was, camp fever took him quickly and he never saw a day of battle. Is the Confederacy so desperate they would retain a soldier who needed aid to dismount his horse? Neighbors have come to express their sympathy but do not linger at the home of a man who fled to France. I face the New Year alone."

Laura, unable to sleep before her trip, delved into the year 1862. The entries were far spaced and sketchy as if Caroline LeBlanc had become too exhausted to write in the evenings. Her energies consumed by her labors, the diary read like a chronicle of the times rather than an outlet for her emotions. "I have erected looms and found an ancient Acadian woman to instruct both the servants and myself in the craft of weaving. We must prove to be apt students, or the Negroes will be in rags shortly. Imagine half a state growing cotton with no mills to spin it, and you will be able to envision a

Confederacy at war with no means to make boots for their soldiers. *Mon Dieu*, men are so impractical!

"New Orleans has fallen, and Yankee gunboats are on the river. The Negroes are beginning to disappear in the night, going down river to join their saviors, no doubt. Well, that makes only 299 pairs of trousers to cut and sew as there are no able-bodied men to bring back the runaways. The Conscription Act has snapped up even Charles' tutor, weak-eyed and knock-kneed though he was. How desperate the Confederacy has become! I will have to undertake my son's education—though I do not know when I will find the time.

"I have managed wheaten loaves for Christmas dinner, a true triumph from a small amount of home-raised and milled grain. We are in no danger of starvation but are worn down by the monotony of cornbread, morning, noon, and night. As yet, we have not suffered the depredations of my family along the Mississippi. The Yankees are slow in coming to our little bayou. I have offered my kin sanctuary at the Chateau, but they decline to take hospitality at the home of one who has shirked his duty. Their sporadic letters come by the irregular mail boat or overland and bring naught but bad news. Brother Regis is dead in some skirmish that will be forgotten within months. Brother Armand is captured by the Yankees at Vicksburg. My foolish sisters, Lizette and Helene, have married in haste to soldiers who fill a uniform well—which seems to be their only criterion, though one, a Lieutenant James Wallace is said to have a plantation in Alabama. The youngest, Anne and Suzette, protest that by the time they are grown there will be no more men left in the Confederacy to marry. I believe they are right. All will be dead and buried in foreign places. Regis will never lie next to Felicite, Marguerite, and Marie, those barely remembered sisters lost in their infancy. Such morbid thoughts, but I know what 1863 will bring to Chateau Camille—the Union Army."

Laura reached beneath the bed for another volume and pressed the catch, but this single book remained locked. The clasp appeared to be newer than the rest, its brass untarnished, its lock more sturdy than the usual diary security. Ah well, the hour grew late. She intended to rise before dawn and be on the road before the rest of the family woke up. Laura cushioned the old leather diary with underwear and packed it in her borrowed luggage in case the holiday offered some leisure reading time.

Restless all night, she rose in the dark and washed her face at the kitchen sink rather than use the bathroom at Robert's end of the hall. She applied minimal makeup, tied her hair back and slipped into the comfortable slacks and shirt she liked to wear for traveling. Silently and almost furtively, she passed out of the front door and cursed the suitcase that bumped softly against the frame and the winter coat slung over one arm that caught on the knob.

As Laura eased the trunk of her car closed over her belongings, Pearl in a worn pink robe materialized on the front porch. Bearing a thermos and a lunch bag, the housekeeper silently placed her offerings next to the driver's seat and before Laura could say her thank-yous, retreated into the house. Driving slowly toward the rising sun, she gazed at Chateau Camille framed in her rearview mirror. Another dark figure stood on the gallery. He raised a hand as if to catch her attention.

The early light reflected off of a bit of red foil wrapping paper covering the small box he held. Laura did not stop. She turned her eyes to the road, followed the bayou, and then veered for the interstate and headed east.

Chapter Seventeen

Christmas in the bosom of her family turned out not to be as Laura pictured it fifteen-hundred miles away in Louisiana. Her mother escorted her relentlessly from relative to relative, even seeking out one decrepit great-aunt in a nursing home. The old woman blinked repeatedly while trying to place Laura in the family genealogy and finally wished "Lulu" all the best. More cognizant kin listened politely to Laura's account of her new job and locale and redoubled their expressions of regret over David's death. Everyone, including her own mother, said how nice that Laura had found something interesting to do until she remarried.

At least Sister Cynthia had a different attitude. She teased Laura about the mysterious man who owned Chateau Camille and answered the phone sometimes when her mother called. "He sounds tall, dark and handsome, Mom says."

Laura tried to deny this. "I wouldn't call my landlord mysterious exactly. Okay, maybe he is. I certainly don't understand him. He is dark and possibly handsome in a swarthy sort of way, but definitely not tall. We aren't together in any way at all." Laura stepped unheeding into her sister's trap.

"Well then, if you're not involved with this southern gentleman, you should go to the New Year's Eve party Don's boss is giving. We'll fix you up with this really fun salesman who recently got divorced. You'll have a great time with Benny."

Laura consoled herself by thinking she still had Christmas and a week after that to come up with an excuse not to go out with Benny, but Christmas day held its own little horrors. She warned everyone not to expect much from her and asked for nothing in return. Naturally, she received gifts costing twice as much as usual. Her parents had purchased a new set of luggage for her and enclosed a note hoping she would use the bags to come home more often. A present claiming to come from "Your Niece and Nephew, Jennifer and Jason," contained dark brown leather driving gloves purchased from the best department store in the mall. The box from Cynthia and Don held a matching shoulder bag, soft, capacious and almost jet-set in quality. The most dreadful gift of all came in an envelope and brought out all the tears of obligation, embarrassment and anger Laura had been stifling—a check for $100,000, David's death benefits.

"It's been here for a while, but I just couldn't risk mailing the check to you. Why don't you put the money in the bank up here and let it draw interest until you decide what to do, Laura? More cash will come when the helicopter company settles. There, there, everything is going to be fine now." Amazing how her mother could misinterpret emotions when she chose.

Laura endured the rest of the morning, accepting thanks for her inadequate gifts and helping to clean up of mounds of torn paper and discarded boxes. She pleaded a headache and went upstairs to lie down before dinner. Wanting desperately to escape into another life, she tried to open Caroline Montleon's diary with a hairpin. It held its secrets tight.

Her brother-in-law, Don, the selected ambassador to summon Laura to dinner, found her still struggling with the lock on the diary. "I could smash that for you with a hammer," he volunteered.

"No thanks, it's not mine to smash," Laura confessed.

"Hot stuff?"

"No, historical papers I want to have reprinted for the library."

"Look, Sis, you came here to get away from work for a while. This New Year's Eve party is exactly what you need to cheer you up. Now come to dinner and get some real home cooking. I'll bet that foreign food is giving you ulcers." Don laid an arm around her shoulders and led her to the table with all the finesse of a hungry grizzly bear.

****

This New Year's Eve party is definitely *not* what I needed, thought Laura from her corner of the overstuffed couch.

She watched her "date" Benny Schweitzer gyrate his paunch around the store manager's wife. On Benny's long frame, his belly looked like a basketball shoved beneath his black silk shirt. Or maybe he is six months pregnant, Laura speculated, smiling into the ruby surface of another cosmopolitan. He shouldn't be drinking then, no, no, no. She could have as much liquor as she wanted. A series of cosmos had carried her beyond the point of being kind to or even amused by with her escort. She wondered if the fur on his chest where the gold chains nested was real or glued on like the hairpiece whose base showed when he tossed his head in the dance. Benny threw her a supernaturally green glance just to let Laura know he hadn't forgotten her while doing his duty by the old bag—his own words. Funny how the tinted contact lenses made his eyes appear almost opaque, completely depthless.

"Eyes are the mirror of the soul," Laura mumbled to herself. She poked the lemon slice floating in the cocktail glass like a huge yellow eyeball. David's eyes had sparkled, embracing her and the rest of the world. Robert's eyes drew you into their dark, troubled depths until you swam without direction, not knowing up from down. She tried to avoid Robert's eyes, but could not. She wanted to drown in them. Yes, an excess of vodka was making her honest.

Definitely time to leave. She scanned the room for Cynthia and Don who had brought her to the party, introduced her to Benny, then melded themselves into the group they called "the old married folks." Apparently, the old married folks had gone home to pay off the babysitter.

Benny slithered toward her as if his tight pants made it impossible for him to walk normally. "Dance?" He held out his arms.

"No thanks." To dance with Benny meant keeping time to the music while he circumnavigated the room, now appearing to dance alone, then seeming to have two partners at once as he bisected other couples. Laura felt the greatest urge to fall asleep.

"I think I need shome—some—fresh air."

She pushed for the door. Benny slid along behind and dropped a coat not belonging to her around Laura's shoulders. The frigid air hit her near naked chest and made her gasp. What was she doing in borrowed, low-cut black spandex? Oh yes, the dress belonged to Cynthia, long lean Cynthia, her sister. Mother had done some emergency hemming, but not let out the bodice. Laura looked down at her breasts packaged like two prize winning honeydews wrapped in black tissue. At least, they made her mother happy.

"I'm so glad you decided not to diet. You look your old self again," Mom said. Merry Christmas, Mom, and a Happy New Year. My boobs are back, my gift to you. They made Benny happy, too, if his stare was any indication. "It's cold out here. What say we go to my car, turn up the heat and enjoy a little privacy?"

Laura pulled the coat a little closer, but it failed to cover her. Too small—someone else's jacket. Benny guided her down the icy drive to a vintage black Camaro painted with gold racing stripes. The inside seemed to be swathed in gold fur much like Benny's chest. Even the steering wheel needed a shave. Laura giggled. Benny eased her on to the reclining passenger seat, turned on the heat and the stereo, making many fine adjustments to the tuning.

Laura dozed off and dreamed the upholstery had been stripped from the hides of many teddy bears. She woke abruptly when Benny's hand began to grope along her hemline as he sought an entryway under the tight, rubbery material of her skirt.

"I am not a spandex person," Laura announced.

"What?" Benny, intent on making a hickey on one white breast, barely paused in his suction.

"Home, James," she commanded, too numb to feel.

"It's Benny." She upset her date enough to force him up for air.

"Home, Benny. Why should I let you touch me

when I've got a man down south so hot he makes you look like a cartoon character? Twice—he's kissed me twice, and I can't put him out of my mind, those kisses were so fine."

"What the hell!"

"Home!" she shouted over the stereo. Another couple emerging from the party stared toward the parked car.

Squealing his wheels around every corner, Benny drove Laura home. He made no effort to open the car door for her. Laura did that for herself.

"You know Laura, you're a real cold fish," he shouted after her. "I bet that guy down in Lou-siana gets the chills every time he touches you!"

"No Benny, I think I give him a fever." Laura skittered safely up the icy walk to the house. *In vino veritas.* In wine, truth.

Chapter Eighteen

Though her memory remained hazy, her headache terrific and her annoyance intense at the round and ugly bruise on her breast Laura embraced the thought of a new year in Chapelle with eagerness. She left a day sooner than planned after assuring her family that only some important unfinished business pulled her away from their loving arms. She forged through the ice and snow of the northeast to the rain of Georgia, was delayed by detours outside of Mobile, but at last turned off the interstate at the gas station that had become her landmark showing the road to Chapelle.

With the cane harvested, wide new vistas opened between the windbreaks of skeletal pecan trees and long-needled pines. Just a bit of white furred the roadside weeds and frosted the grass, but this vanished by noon when Laura turned her car up the shell drive of Chateau Camille.

Angelle, lightly covered with a sweater, small hands buried in a black muff on her lap, sat on the steps. Before Laura could park the car, the child's father stood on the gallery again as if he'd never left the spot where she'd seen him last. Laura caught a glimpse of Pearl's white uniform in the open doorway behind Robert. The entire household lay in wait for her, and she could not escape them by arriving early as she had with her dawn departure.

Robert came off the gallery taking two steps at a time, took her keys from the ignition and busied himself removing the new luggage and borrowed suitcase from the trunk. The muff held by Angelle materialized into the black cat, Snake, grown fuller with his winter coat and overfeeding. Her pet twined around Laura's legs as if tying her with invisible bonds of love. Angelle hugged her waist in a grip of iron.

"We're so glad you're back." Angelle sighed and chattered faster than Laura could take it all in while Robert said not a single word of greeting.

"You and Daddy gave me money for Christmas. Madame said that was a good sign. Tante Lil asked me what I wanted, and I said for Snake to come to live with us, too. Tante Lil said no and gave me a book called *Little Women* instead, and I said I didn't want her old book, I wanted Snake. So Tante Lil said yes, but he couldn't come in the house unless he got fixed. I said he didn't look broken to me. Then Daddy said we couldn't fix Snake until you came home and gave permission. Permission for what, I asked. Daddy said he'd tell me later. Snake and me have been waiting out here for you for two days. I knew you'd come early because I bought lots of red candles on sale after Christmas at the drug store."

When Angelle paused to take a breath, her father handed her Laura's new carry-on bag. "Take that to Miss Laura's room. Leave the cat outside."

The child protested, but Pearl's firm hand grasped her elbow. The housekeeper picked up one of the suitcases Robert had deposited on the front door sill and steered bag and baggage into the house. Robert blocked Laura's entrance.

"There's something I want to show you." Using Pearl's guidance technique, he took Laura around the chateau by the same side path she'd followed to her embarrassing encounter with T-Bob in the cattle barn. Intensely aware of his strong hand on her elbow, Laura prayed they would not have another awkward moment. She dearly wanted things to be better between them now.

Robert stopped by a large camellia bush protected from the winter by the bulk of the house. Laura smiled her appreciation of its beauty. Large open blooms like wild red roses with golden centers festooned the small tree. She had never seen anything like this in the dead days of a northern January. He broke a blossom from a branch, brushed back her hair and placed the flower by Laura's ear.

"The Christmas camellia. It blooms earlier than all the others. Sometimes the frost kills the buds, but this one bush always blossoms in the shelter of Chateau Camille."

"It's lovely. And so good to be home—I mean back here in a warmer climate." Forgetting David only for a moment but remembering Benny, Laura allowed herself to sink in the unfathomable black depths of Robert LeBlanc's eyes.

He smiled, not one of his ravishing smiles, but just a small tender curving of the lips. "They say once you've tasted bayou water, you'll always return."

Struggling to resurface, Laura babbled, "Heaven forbid anyone would drink from the bayou. You know, I often go to stand on the bridge near the library and watch the water flow by on a nice day, and I've never been able to see the bottom of it for all the silt and heaven knows what else. Who knows what's in there? Sewage, snapping turtles…"

He pressed a finger to her lips as if he were silencing Angelle during one of her talking sprees. "Not now. I have something for you. I hoped you would accept this before you went away, but you left us so quickly and without looking back, I feared the bayou hadn't worked its magic."

With the same hand that plucked the camellia, he offered her a small box. Laura took it, and let the bit of red foil wrapping and golden cord drop to the ground among the petals of fallen Christmas camellias. The red velvet of the jewelry box was worn bald around the edges, and its satin interior gone yellow, but the ring inside had aged with grace. The central garnet in its antique setting shone clear and sparkling as newly poured burgundy.

"Vivien never wore it. She had no taste for Caroline Montleon's heirlooms. My father did not offer it to my wife, but my mother wore it often. She said only a French woman whose own family had lived through World War II in Paris could understand the things Caroline had done. This was Caroline's engagement ring given to her by her second husband. I want you to wear it."

Laura did not look at the ring. She gazed again at Robert, waiting for his explanation to end, waiting for his hand, toying with the collar of the pale blue flannel shirt she had partly unbuttoned as the warmth of the day increased, to move around her and pull her close. Her reason tried to tell her this came too soon—she wasn't ready—they hardly knew each other—but she did not want listen to reason.

The setting and the man all perfect—the surrounding garden, its camellias green and heavy with bud, sable-haired Robert with his back to the one bush flowering in blood red splendor. The many windows of the mansion shone down on them in the winter sunlight like the eyes of approving ancestors as his face moved closer to Laura's to claim a kiss. She would remember this moment forever, but only with regret.

The kitchen door crashed open. Tante Lil bounced her wheelchair down two concrete steps and mired the wheels in the gravel of the garden path. Her immobility only increased her fury as she tried to reach Laura. Instead, she pitched the vermilion-bound reproduction of the diary Laura had given her for Christmas as hard as she could. The falling book broke a small branch off the camellia bush and sent a shower of spent crimson blossoms to the ground.

"I'd sooner burn them than have you expose my family to shame. Do you hear, you goddamned Yankee! Traitor under my roof!" A fit of violent coughing interrupted the old woman's shrieks, but her liver-spotted hands, clawing the air, left no doubt of what she wanted to do if she reached Laura.

Laura snapped the ring box shut and thrust it at Robert, but his hands still clutched her collar as if he would never release her. The box dropped to the ground—ring, book, camellias, all fallen, the raucous coughs of Tante Lil making background music for the interrupted romantic interlude. Laura pushed away and popped the button holding her shirt closed across her chest in her attempt to escape. He saw it instantly, the nasty bruise applied by Benny Schweitzer's flabby lips, an ugly purple stain low on her breast. Robert released her, smiling tightly as if he had been the victim of some tasteless practical joke.

"I thought I was giving you time and space to accept your husband's death before I asked you to marry to me. My mistake, I figured you wanted me, not some guy back in Pennsylvania. God dammit, must I pay for my stupidity with women for the rest of my life?" He turned his broad back on Laura and went to his aunt, removed her body doubled over in spasm from the wheelchair and carried her inside the mansion.

Laura, alone, looked up at the house that had so suddenly withdrawn its blessing and saw Angelle framed like a portrait of tragedy in the second story window of Miss Lilliane's old room, not a memory she would cherish. Pearl, not Robert or Angelle, came from the house and gathered up the book and ring box and the crumpled wrapping paper. She led Laura inside through the kitchen to the housekeeper's room, a space bearing no resemblance to the austere personality of Pearl.

The iron bedstead, pink chenille spread and dresser thickly painted with white enamel obviously had been in place before Pearl's coming. She'd obscured these fixtures with personal mementoes, gaudy and diverse. Small pillows smothered the bed: a red satin heart, a fringed souvenir of Los Angeles, one of lace resembling a ring bearer's cushion. A large traveling trunk, battered and bestickered in a way to be envied by stay-at-homes, took up most of the space between bed and dresser. The lid bulged open over the hoard of bright beads and costume jewelry that had turned Angelle into a gypsy on Halloween. Wedged into a corner by the dresser sat an old black sewing machine and a small stool, both buried in swaths of fabric, chains of sequins and small bunches of artificial flowers.

Framed show posters of famous black performers mostly from the forties and fifties, their hair straightened and slicked, dressed in tuxedos and glittering gowns, obliterated the cabbage roses of the wallpaper. Along with the famous, she'd hung more personal photos. Laura recognized one of Tante Lu, who seemed old even in her youth, and another of Pearl and her sisters with arms linked. Short, slightly plump Ruby had frizzy hair setting her apart from the other girls, tall, ever-lean Pearl with just that hint of color betraying her race and the long ago decamped Opal, a young woman with features so sharp and skin so pale and eyes so light, she could have passed for white in any other grouping.

More fascinating still, a shot showed a row of chorus girls, all leggy, all black, all with more feathers in their headdresses than covering their bodies. Given the makeup, costumes and passage of time, Laura wondered if the one just off center could be Pearl. A fuchsia plume thrust behind the frame seemed to confirm the fact.

The intriguing clutter of Pearl's room distracted Laura from the confrontation in the garden until she turned and noticed the housekeeper still in the doorway, her thin body neatly enshrouded in the white uniform with the stickpin Laura had given her for Christmas thrust through the collar. Laura squinted trying to imagine Pearl dancing in fuchsia plumes when the woman looked as if she never took her hair down from its tight twisted bun even at night. Did the LeBlancs know of about Pearl's past? None of them came to this room except the child.

"Sit down, girl, and do something with those hands." Pearl pushed Laura to a seat on the bed and handed her a pile of gauzy material. "Men, think they own a person."

Laura unclenched her fists. Her knuckles had turned white, and her fingers tingled as she tried to relax them enough to accept the needle that Pearl threaded. "I don't sew well."

"Anyone can tack on a few rosebuds. This is Angelle's dress for Mardi Gras. Comes early this year, so we need all the help we can get. Just sit and talk with me a while." Pearl picked up a small bodice, mostly complete except for the handwork, and seated herself on the stool by the sewing machine.

"I won't be here for Mardi Gras, Pearl, not after what happened out there in the garden. You know, I thought I learned something up north. I thought I knew what I wanted. I could hardly wait to come back here and start again. The ring came a little too soon, but you know, I almost accepted it." Laura pricked her fingertip with the needle and quickly sucked on the wound to prevent the pinpoint of blood from staining the fabric. "Saved by fate from a big mistake, I guess."

"No, just bad luck and Miss Lil. We tried, me and Angelle, to keep that old woman in the house. She been stewing about you since Christmas, but that one's so *canaille*, she sent me off for a sweater. Angelle went upstairs and got too busy watching from the window to pay attention. Miss Lilliane won't live forever, remember, and that child needs mothering. I can't give it to her. I tried being a mother once and did a poor job of it. Mr. Bob, he needs you, too, and he knows that. A good man, T-Bob."

"But now he doesn't want me. He thinks I have another man."

"Well, do you?"

"No, no one but David. I've finally accepted that he's gone, and it's natural to be attracted to someone else. I went to a party back home with a blind date and had a little too much to drink. He put a mark on me before I realized what was happening, but believe me, that mark is as superficial as the man who put it there. All the way here, I thanked Benny Schweitzer for helping me to make up my mind. Now, I hope he chokes himself to death with one of his gold chains!"

"We all been there, girl. Explain. Go to Mr. Bob's room and tell him. A man don't get that upset unless he cares a bunch."

"Why should I have to explain? You said it. Robert LeBlanc doesn't own me or tell me what to do. If I did sleep with someone back home, he'd just have to live with it. He never tried to take more than a kiss!" Laura tugged the thread too tightly and puckered the material.

"Besides, Miss Lilliane is right. I am an outsider. I have no business here. I'm going to call Miss Lola and see if she can put me up for a few weeks. David's settlement came. I was going to invest the money, but now I can use it to put a down payment on a small house and buy some furniture. In a year or two after I prove myself here, I can sell and move back where I came from, find an administrative job at a library up north. Isn't it convenient that I haven't unpacked yet?" Laura desperately smoothed the material with both hands.

"Now you sit there for a while until you thinking better! He's gonna get over this." Pearl tried to reach over the lengths of material separating them, but Laura had discarded her work and gotten to the door. Pearl did not follow her beyond the threshold.

Consumed by an immediate urge to act on her words, Laura rushed to her bedroom. She opened the door into Caroline Montleon's suite so abruptly she caught Angelle entirely by surprise. The child balanced on a chair by the massive dresser. She held a wooden match to the second of two red candles set in holders on either side of the mirror over the chest. The air of the closed room stank of the odor of burnt hair underlaid with the essence of less familiar herbal scents. Startled, Angelle dropped the lit match on to the crocheted runner covering the dresser top. The match flared briefly, adding the smell of singed cotton to the atmosphere.

Laura rushed to the dresser, knocked Angelle out of the way and crushed the small flame with the heel of her hand. The little girl did not cry out as she hit the hardwood floor with force. Instead, making herself as small as possible, she crawled to the door while Laura remained preoccupied with the fire. Once out in the hall, the child got up and ran.

Resting her head briefly on the dresser, Laura examined the small charred area burnt into the lacquer. Any competent furniture refinisher could remove the slight damage done to the antique, she supposed. Pearl or Miss Lilliane would repair the runner or make a new one. That was hardly the point. Angelle might have burnt the house down. The other red candle still glowed, spilling wax messily down it sides and on to a ring of dust at its base. She had to tell Robert about the incident and her suspicions. Directly after that, she resolved, she would call Lola Domengeaux, put her bags in the car and leave Chateau Camille behind her. Laura wet her fingertips and pinched out the flame of the red candle.

She went to search for T-Bob. Not finding him in the house, she entered the garden, averted her eyes from the Christmas camellia and the ruts made in the gravel by Miss Lilliane's wheelchair, crossed the yard quickly and found him in the same cattle barn where they met on her first day in Chapelle. Robert LeBlanc stood ankle deep in fresh straw in the holding pen where the calves were put for weaning. He leaned against the partition with his back toward her, just leaning, not working, and staring out the far side of the barn as if he strained to see something out of his range of vision. Laura had not intended to come up behind him so quietly.

She rapped formally on the side of the barn. He turned his dark eyes and sad mouth toward her.

"Is Miss Lilliane all right?" she asked.

"She'll live if she can keep her temper under control. I gave her a large dose of her cough medicine. She'll be out for hours." Still leaning against the stall but facing her now, he made no move to come closer.

"Look, I have to talk to you about Angelle. Then, I'll go."

"Talk."

"I found her lighting candles in my room just now. She could have destroyed the house."

"But you caught her, so no harm done. I'll talk to her about it."

183

"There's more. Mrs. Domengeaux noticed her votive candle missing right before the fire in her store. I believe Angelle took it. Look, I've read that pyromania can start at a very early age. You have to admit Angelle's reaction to the fire at Domengeaux's was hardly normal. And there have been other fires. I saw the marks when we toured the house. How old was Angelle when she set Miss Lilliane's room on fire?"

"There's nothing wrong with Angelle!" he bellowed like one of his injured bulls and stepped toward her.

"Your ex-wife is mentally ill, Robert. She could have affected Angelle. If the child gets help now, she might grow up normally."

"There's nothing wrong with my daughter! Or me. But what about you, Laura?" He moved swiftly and caught her collar again, roughly this time.

She fell into the straw when Robert hooked one foot behind her leg and toppled them together, his full weight on top of her body. He tore at her buttons and pushed the bra from her shoulders without unhooking it. The straps pinned her arms at the elbows, but Laura did not fight him. He rubbed his heavy beard against her naked breasts abrading them in a way both painful yet exciting, as if he wanted to put his own mark on her and obliterate any sign of the other man.

"Did the family legend repel you the way it did Vivien? We share the same blood, Vivien and me." His fury ebbed. He kissed her lips more tenderly than he had her breasts. Perhaps, he noticed the tears forming in the corners of her eyes and mistook them as a sign of fear.

Laura cried for herself. She had pictured them

joining together at last on her long drive, but not like this. If her arms had not been pinned by the shirt and bra shoved from her shoulders, she would have put them around him and shown him all he said had no truth. When he bent to kiss her a second time, very gently, Laura opened her mouth to respond, but another hand knocked against the barn door.

"Mr. Bob, you want that bull moved to the north pasture?" Tony, the black stockman, swung his eyes from the scene in the straw back to the other side of the barn. He retreated a step as if to go away, as if he had seen nothing.

Robert stood protectively in front of Laura while she sat up and buttoned her shirt. "Yes, move the bull," he ordered, calmly brushing straw from his sleeves.

"Yessir." Tony retraced his steps energetically and with a great deal of noise.

Robert offered Laura a hand up from the straw. She took it, but he dropped hers as soon as she stood.

"Don't worry," he said with a pained smile. "It's an old southern tradition not to tell who you saw rolling in the hay with the boss man. It's my shame that I've spent the last few minutes proving I'm not worth having instead of apologizing. I couldn't stand the thought of you going with another man because I'd held back giving you time, Laura. I'm sorry."

She would have reached out to him if he had not walked away so swiftly and without looking back. She doubted if he heard her say, "There is no other man."

Chapter Nineteen

Laura called Lola Domengeaux within the hour. She wanted and needed to leave the influence of Chateau Camille, both past and present, and go somewhere more neutral to collect her thoughts. The phone rang repeatedly in the Domengeaux home, and then Myrtle Hill, the operator, interceded.

"I expect they're still at the hospital, honey. Why don't you try after eight?"

"Hospital?"

"You been out of town of course. They took Louie Domengeaux in for chest pains right after Christmas. It don't look good, if you know what I mean."

"Thanks, Myrtle."

"Any time, hon."

The town talked of replacing Miss Hill after her retirement with a computerized phone system, but no computer could ever do the job along with gossip the way old Myrtle did. "Telephone, telegraph, tell-a-woman," the all male parish council joked, but they dialed her up regularly to keep abreast of the news.

Late that evening, Laura did reach the Domengeaux residence, but the daughter, not the mother, answered. Yes, Mama was fine but tired. Yes, she'd tell her Laura Dickinson had called. Click. Because she had no place else to go, Laura went to the guestroom and unpacked.

In the morning, Robert and Laura initiated another beautifully coordinated program of mutual avoidance. He had his early coffee in the kitchen, slammed the rear door loudly in signal of departure, and as soon as the crunch of his steps on the gravel pathway sounded far enough away, Laura emerged fully dressed from her room, used the bathroom, grabbed her coffee and a hot biscuit from Pearl and hurried off to work.

In the late afternoon, she politely phoned Pearl to say she would be late for dinner, please not to wait for her or set anything aside. Laura stayed at the library, sometimes actually working, cataloging a truck of books or playing with the budget to make room for a new project, sometimes merely reading a suspense novel or a piece of light non-fiction, but never a romance. When the clock reached an hour when Laura could be certain Robert and Angelle were safely in the parlor of the Chateau, she drove back to the mansion, parked in the front, but entered through the kitchen. Pearl had a tray of food waiting for her.

Laura insisted on reheating the meal herself. Afterwards, she usually joined Pearl to work on the Mardi Gras costumes in the housekeeper's room. Sympathy had not made Pearl more talkative, but she could be drawn out by a continuous string of questions as Laura discovered when she found sewing in silence did not take her mind off Robert LeBlanc sitting nearby in another room.

"Where did you learn to sew, Pearl?"

"My mama taught me. I used to make my own costumes to save on the money."

"Costumes?" Laura's eyes went to the picture of the nearly nude chorus girls.

"Yeah. I danced when I was young. Tap, ballet, everything, at Miss Starr's School of Dance. Miss Starr was kind of a hippie, still is. She had classes separate for the black kids to keep the white mamas happy, but she always told us we had more *joie de vivre* than her other students. *Joie de vivre*, that's Miss Starr. That old lady is still dancing to this day. My mama paid for the lessons. I sewed my own costumes. Sure came in handy later."

"Would that be you in the first row, just off center?" Laura nodded at the photo, her hands being too busy to point.

"That's me at the Cotton Club."

"Cotton Club!"

"Not the one you thinking of. I ain't that old, baby. This one's in Los Angeles, least it was."

"When were you out there?"

"Oh, thirty years ago. The times might have been a-changing, but there were still plenty of men would pay to see black women dance with nearly nothing on. Still are. That's where Beulah was born."

"Beulah?"

"My daughter. I called her after my mother, but neither of them ever thanked me for it. Children take strange revenge sometimes."

"Revenge?"

"Yeah, revenge. See, when I was young I went with a white boy for a while. Well, my folks broke that off fast because white boys only want one thing, they said. Funny, we hadn't got that far at all, but I was so mad I went out and found the blackest boy in town and gave him my all." Pearl released a sear little smile. Clearly, the revenge had backfired.

188

"I got pregnant before my parents could bust that one up, too. See, to a respectable high yellow family like the Seguras, going with a black Black is almost as bad as going with a white man. Worse probably. My folks didn't buy into the black is beautiful campaign. Always marry lighter, my granny said."

"So, you went to California."

"No, they sent me off to my sister Opal until after the baby came. What my mama didn't know—because Opal never told her—was she married a white man out there and was passing. Well, that was fine with me. With all those Mexicans and Indians and foreigners out there, I could pass, too—until Beulah came into the world. You should have seen Opal's face. Turned whiter than that guy she married when she saw my little ebony bundle of joy." Pearl smiled again, this time at her sister's pretensions. "Opal never did have any children. Maybe she was afraid they'd come out black."

"So you and Beulah stayed out there."

"Yeah. I got a job dancing at the club. We toured all over. I'd leave Beulah with a friend and go. Those were some years." Her face softened, and then tightened again. "But dancers get old fast. Even so, it was too late for Beulah. She was twelve going on twenty-one by the time we came back here."

"What happened?" Laura asked, even though she knew, to keep Pearl talking.

"Oh, she went bad on me. No parental guidance, the school said. She took money for her services, too. That's something I never did—even with the judge."

"The judge!"

"Look, Laura, you're almost family it seems to me, and the family knows all about this. When I came back,

I took the maid's job here at the Chateau. A comedown for me, you know, but I needed the work. I still had my looks then, being just over thirty. Miss Auree, T-Bob's mama, was only in her forties and dying of cancer. She'd have her good spells and her bad ones, but that lady always remained brave and wise. One day, she called me into her room and plain asks me to sleep with her husband. She said he needed the comfort she could no longer give him, and being a judge and all, he wasn't free to go out and get some, if you know what I mean. I said he had never bothered with me. She said he would, and sure enough he came to my room a few nights later."

"We never talked much except the night after his wife died. Then, we both cried together for her. Things kept on the same between us until his heart gave out. Never thought he loved me or anyone else but Miss Auree. He never considered marrying again. He didn't leave me nothing or give me nothing, but I did it for her, and I never asked for nothing either."

That night, Laura, who knew very well she was not family, felt she had pried. On other nights, Laura realized though she asked the questions, she was the one being led.

"So tell me about Mardi Gras in Chapelle."

"Well, it's not like New Orleans where the rich people dress up and go to balls and the poor people stand in the streets, get drunk and show their titties for beads. Here, the whole town works on the costumes and anyone who buys a ticket goes to the ball, but it helps to be somebody if you want to get elected to the court."

"Is that why they chose Angelle?"

"Well, the LeBlancs are old family, but I suspect

Denise DeVille had something to do with it."

"I don't think I know her."

"Oh, she comes around here plenty when you're at work, that Miss Denise. Nineteen and as foxy as they come. She's old DeVille's granddaughter, and this year's Queen Marie Antoinette the thirty-second."

"Old DeVille who always falls asleep in the library?"

"That's him. Would you believe he used to chase after Miss Lilliane years ago, but his family broke it off because of those old rumors? Well, I think little Miss Denise believes those stories are so romantic she's going to break with family tradition and marry a LeBlanc."

"Marry who?"

"Why Mr. Bob, of course. Naturally, all the DeVilles are upset, especially the mama who won't be able to have a big Catholic wedding at the church if Denise marries a divorced and very lapsed man who's made it clear he ain't paying for any annulment. And then, there's the age difference and the old stories."

"I don't think Robert is interested. He never mentions her."

"How would you know? You hardly talk to him no more. Why all month, she's been over here asking for information on the artificial insemination of cattle. Says it's for a college biology paper, my ass. Why just last week, I had to serve her lunch and listen to all that stuff over my food in the kitchen. Mr. Bob, he keeps loaning her farm magazines, and then she has to return them. While she's here, she plays Barbie dolls with Angelle since she isn't too far from the grade school herself."

Pearl gave Laura a sharp look. "You know, a man

can be put off too many times and begin to look elsewhere, especially when he wants a mother for his little girl. Me and Tony thought you and Mr. Bob had finally got together out there in the barn. Said he could see you brushing off the straw and buttoning up, even with Bob standing right there in front of you as if nothing was going on. I guess old Tony got it wrong. His eyes must be going before his mouth stops talking, but he sure was sorry to interrupt whatever might have happened."

"I thought it was an old Southern custom not to talk about things like that!" Laura blushed a red so hot she could feel beads of sweat form on her forehead and start to roll toward the fabric she bent over trying to hide her face.

"That's what white folks want to think. Just foolin'. Won't go no further than Tony and me. Sure wouldn't want Miss Lil catching on. Tony and me, we're pulling for you, not Denise."

Laura cleared her throat. What could she say to that? Thanks for being on my side? Instead she opted to steer the conversation back where it had begun.

"So, tell me how the court is chosen."

"Well, the members of the Mardi Gras Association nominate people, and they have to be pretty well off because costumes are expensive and they pay for their own. Now, I know they nominated Mr. Bob for King Louis the Sixteenth, but he backed out, so Dr. Bourgeois is going to do it. That didn't please Miss Denise at all. Before we know it, Angelle is nominated for the court, and her daddy didn't have the heart to say no."

"What's the theme this year?" Laura made another

attempt to direct the conversation far, far away from Robert, Angelle, Denise and herself.

"The Four Seasons at the Court of Queen Victoria. Old Miss DeGravelle is going to be Queen Victoria. She sure has the weight for the part. Angelle is in the Court of Spring. They asked Mr. Bob to be in the Court of Spring while you were gone, but he said he hadn't done anything so foolish as to dress in a green tuxedo since he turned seventeen, and he wasn't going to do it again." Pearl paused, waiting for a question. When none came, she went on by herself.

"But Denise talked him into being in the Court of Winter because the men are wearing black tails, and he would look so-o-o handsome, she said. He will, too."

Again Laura had no comment, so Pearl asked a question. "Who's taking you to the ball, Miss Laura?"

"I wasn't planning to go." Laura bent way over the rosebuds she tacked to Angelle's skirt as if she were entirely engrossed in the task.

"Everybody goes."

"Even the black people?"

"We have our own affair—to which I am going with Tony."

Suddenly grand, Pearl stood up and lowered the zipper on a full-length clothing bag hanging from a hook on the narrow closet door behind the sewing machine. Her gown was a startling shade of tangerine. Not a dress Laura would care to wear, but she truly believed Pearl could carry it off without any trouble and look fantastic.

"Our ball is just as fine and maybe even better than the white folks' ball, not so stuffy, you know. We got a much better band. "What are you going to wear to the ball, Madame Librarian?"

Laura smiled and answered, "Nothing."

"That might do for after the ball. But, we have to talk about beforehand."

"I'm not going."

"Black spandex?"

"Absolutely not! I've had a bad experience with black spandex."

"Silver lamé?"

"Not going."

"Let me get your measurements tonight," Pearl said, and she did.

Chapter Twenty

"Hold still, child!" Pearl lowered the completed Mardi Gras gown over Angelle's head. The little girl stood on the housekeeper's bed, arms raised but covered by her nightie because the child complained the room was too cold. On the lower half of her small frame a hoop petticoat hung over the top her granny gown. The dress settled over Angelle like an elaborate wrapping on a very small package. Pearl began zipping. Laura watched from the doorway since the child's costume seemed to fill the small room.

She and Angelle had returned gradually to their old relationship. After all, Laura reasoned, Angelle was not her child. She'd reported her suspicions to the girl's father. Let it rest there. At first, Angelle had stayed in the parlor with Robert, but as the excitement of Mardi Gras increased, she began to visit Pearl's room. When not evicted or reprimanded, she remained, sewing on scraps at Laura's feet and interrupting the adult conversation more and more until she became her old exuberant self again. Laura welcomed the child's chatter and even encouraged her when she realized Angelle's presence kept the talk away from Robert.

"It's heavy," Angelle complained, shifting her weight from foot to foot and making the bed creak with each movement. "And the sleeves are too short." The child examined her arms where her nightie protruded

Lynn Shurr

from the small puffed sleeves of the dress.

Laura moved into the room. "Well, it would look much better without the nightgown. Here, let me roll up your nightie so you can see how the dress really looks."

Angelle pushed her away. "No! The sleeves are too short. I won't wear it. I hate this dress. Get it off me!"

The child tore at the skirt, trying to raise the dress over her head, but Pearl's zipper held firm. Instead, her grappling wreaked havoc among the garlands of rosebuds hand sewn by Laura. Her hysteria grew as she tried to claw her way out of the gown. Her shrieks brought Robert running from his place in the parlor where he had been told to await Angelle's grand entrance.

With her father's arms around her, Angelle quieted. Pearl removed the gown and hoop over the child's head. The hoop caught in the flannel of the nightie, and off went the nightgown, too, leaving Angelle shivering in the cotton panties with Sunday emblazoned across the rear. The child raised her arms to accept the warmth of the nightie again. Then, Laura saw the cause of the unreasonable hysteria that made her brand Angelle a spoiled child only a moment ago.

Scars, Angelle had hideous scars on her back and upper arms. Pink, thick and shiny like an ugly growth, they contrasted with the child's porcelain complexion. Laura became aware that she had never seen Angelle without long sleeves, even on that broiling day of her interview. She assumed long sleeves were part of the required and nun-enforced parochial school uniforms Angelle wore on even the most scorching weekdays. The fact the child always dressed alone Laura assumed was due to the same overdeveloped, seven-year-old modesty her own niece had passed through. Most unforgivable of all, Laura knew she stared at flesh damaged by fire and could not move her eyes away.

Angelle's big, brown eyes watched Laura unblinkingly as the nightie lowered over her shoulders. As soon as her head came free, Angelle, tears forming, said, "Now you think I'm ugly, too. Mama thinks I'm ugly. Now you do, too."

"No, no," Laura whispered. "You couldn't help what happened to you."

Robert moved aside as she went to the child and held her. Angelle sobbed on her shoulder.

"I'm so afraid of fire, the doctor says, because I got burned as a baby. Madame Leleux said if I wanted the spell to work I had to light the two red candles, sprinkle the magic powder over them and burn some of your hair and Daddy's hair in the flames together. Then, you would love each other forevermore."

Laura's eyes met Robert's over Angelle's shaking back.

"But I was afraid, and it looked like I didn't need a spell when you were out in the garden together. Then Tante Lil ruined it all, and I had to light the candles. Had to. You came in before I could finish. Now the spell won't work, and you won't love me or Daddy. You'll go away. And I have no more Christmas money to give Madame Leleux and the Virgin Mary for another spell."

"I love you, Angelle. Truly. Even if I do go, I can still love you," Laura comforted.

"Mama went away, and she doesn't love me."

Robert interceded, taking the child and carrying her to the door. "Miss Laura won't go." He looked directly at her and formed the word, "Please," with his lips. "Tomorrow I'll see if you can be in the Court of Winter with me. You have to wear long sleeves in wintertime, and I think Dr. Bourgeois' little girl is exactly your size. Maybe you could trade dresses."

Dimly, Laura listened to more words of comfort as the father carried the child to bed.

"It was worse than that, way worse." Pearl appeared to be talking to herself as she examined the tears in the gown.

"Tell me about it, Pearl. Tell me *all* about it because I don't understand what's going on here."

For once Pearl did—without prodding or leading questions or innuendos. "You saw how crazy Miss Vivien is at Thanksgiving. Well, when she first come here, she wasn't so bad. Everybody knew the baby came way too soon after the wedding, but they pretended not to notice and fussed over Angelle like any other newborn. Angelle, so pretty just like a tiny china doll, not red like some babies, but she had this big birthmark on her back. It was black, black. Real particular about looks, Miss Vivien kept her covered up even in the summer so it wouldn't show. The child always had to be spotless clean, too. They had another maid besides me back then before Mr. Bob stopped growing cane. That woman was forever changing the child before Miss Vivien would hold her own baby.

"Then, things went really bad. Miss Vivien didn't work and wasn't much use around the house, so she took to clubs and such, got involved with tracing the family tree. She sent money to politicians with beliefs like David Duke and worked with their campaigns." Pearl snorted.

"Miss Vivien got a real shock when she found out Adrien LeBlanc was her great-great grandfather and not just some uncle by marriage way back. See, by then she'd heard all the rumors about there being black blood in the family. Don't matter much to no one anymore, but it did to Miss Vivien. After that, she wouldn't take Angelle nowheres.

"I was with the Judge the night Miss Vivien tried to burn that birthmark off Angelle. He had his room next to the library then. Mr. Bob and Miss Vivien had the front room. Then came Angelle's nursery and Miss Lilliane's room over the garden. When the judge shut his door, no one disturbed him. I'd go to him through the closets. See that little door there behind the sewing machine? Looks like a closet. Well, it's a staircase going up to the judge's bedroom, and it was built into the house long before the judge and me got together.

"So there we were doing the nasty when we heard this shrill, high-pitched scream from Angelle like isn't normal for a child. The shrieks went on and on. We ran to the nursery, the two of us barely dressed, and there Miss Vivien stood holding a burning rag on a stick against Angelle's poor little back.

"Turned out she and Mr. Bob had a fight about her not showing Angelle in public. He went outside to cool off, and Miss Vivien decided to 'purify' the child. Yes, she used that very word, to purify the child of her black blood. She accused the judge and me of, well, keeping up the family tradition, I guess.

"They took Miss Vivien away to some private crazy house. T-Bob sat by the child in the hospital, day and night, blaming himself for not being there to protect her and setting Vivien off in the first place. But you know how children bounce back. Wasn't much damage except for the scars, we thought, and that could be fixed some when she got older. Except whenever Miss Lilliane lit a match, the child pitched a fit, so the old lady had to smoke in her room after that."

"And that led to Miss Lilliane's accident and more guilt for Robert," Laura assumed.

"I have my own thoughts about that. See, Miss Vivien came back cured, we thought. They talked of reconciliation, if you know what I mean, between her and Mr. Bob and maybe another child on the way. About then, the judge started having chest pains, or maybe he thought our doing what we were doing might upset Vivien, so I slept out most nights at Tante Lu's. I wasn't around that evening, but I saw the place next day, had to help clean it up. No matter what the judge told the fire chief, there wasn't much damage to Miss Lilliane's bed. Only the quilt T-Bob used to put out the fire got burned up. The room smelled of lighter fluid like someone had splashed it on the floor."

"When Miss Lilliane woke up, all she saw was a sheet of flame between her and the door, and like she always says, she panicked and went straight out the window. Seems T-Bob is always trying to make up to her for bringing Miss Viven into this house. That's why he takes all he does from her."

Laura stayed quiet for a while, absorbing it all. "And Angelle never got over her fear of fire."

"Oh, it cleared up some. She stopped having fits if someone lit a match, but she never goes too close to a flame even now. At that Halloween bonfire, she wanted to hear the stories, but we stayed way back in the trees to make her feel safe."

"Then she couldn't have started the fire at Domengeaux's."

"Whoever said something that crazy?" Pearl mouthed her disgust.

"A stupid but well-meaning outsider, Pearl. Thanks for the explanation. I'll see you at breakfast."

Laura went to her room. Not that it did her any good to lie down in Caroline Montleon's bed. She could not sleep. In the next room, she heard Robert still calming Angelle, and farther down the hall, Miss Lilliane coughing in her own bed. The old lady had been confined since her tirade in the garden. Her lungs simply would not clear. Divine retribution, thought Laura.

She might as well know it all. Laura picked up the diary for 1863 that she hadn't returned to the private library and sprang the lock after diligent work with a metal nail file. If tonight was the night for all the LeBlanc family skeletons to come out of the closet, one more would not matter. If she was going to stay here, and it seemed she must for Angelle sake, she should know all.

The first few entries read much the same as the previous years—more hardships, more privations, more slaves running off, and no word from Adrien. Caroline wrote, "I have learned the Union Army is one day's march from Chateau Camille. I hear they take everything, even the fence posts for firewood. What shall I do?"

By the time the enemy army approached Chateau Camille, Caroline Montleon had acted. "I called Tante Inez, who stays by me, and the other servants. 'Shall we hide the silver, they asked?' 'But no,' I answered. 'Lay the table with it and the fine china. Kill the chickens, bake the pies, use the last of the wheat flour and get the wine from the storeroom. We are having guests for dinner.' They thought I had gone mad, but obeyed.

"I met the Yankee general in my best ball gown of deep green silk and gold lace, now three years out of mode, but what do men know of fashion? I welcomed him to my home and explained my husband had fled to France rather than fight against the Union, that Monsieur Le General could have respite from his dusty journey without fearing hostility. General Alexander Moore immediately posted guards around my property.

"We dined as civilized men and women do and afterwards, I had Catherine play the piano so we could dance. Ah, my child looked at me with hatred, but she did not understand my strategy. Tonight, the children and I sleep in the upper rooms, the staircase guarded by a sentry. Chateau Camille is safe. What care I for the thoughts of others?"

Laura skimmed over short entries and missing dates as the Yankee officers continued to occupy both Caroline's time and home. Finally, a longer entry slowed Laura's reading.

"The good general has asked my permission to come up the stairs to use the library. I can see he is a man of intellect and sensitivity. Poor heart! He has but a sickly wife and one homely daughter waiting for him in Pennsylvania. He showed me their tintypes, which he carries in a little leather case. He remarks on the vigor of my children. Little Felice willingly goes to his lap. She has so little memory of her father. I do wish Charles to be less aloof and Catherine less spiteful to this kind man, but then, things are seldom as we want.

Perhaps, I will join him in the library."

Caroline LeBlanc did join her good general that evening in the library and later on other evenings, invited him to her own room for further discussions. The words were not explicit. Perhaps, the mother feared her children would find the diary sooner or later. The most blatant statement followed a short paragraph about a small spate of luxuries contributed to the larder, courtesy of the United States government.

"I did not realize how I longed for freshly ground coffee in the morning or the pleasures of the marital bed at night before the Yankees came."

That sentence made Laura smile and sympathize with the woman who might as well have been a widow and lived under one roof with a desirable man. She felt Caroline's dismay when another child appeared to be on the way. This time the mistress of Chateau Camille did not rant. In resignation, she called again upon Tante Inez and her potions.

"Once more I have tasted of Tante Inez's elixir, and I write with regret as I await the start of the pains. This child would have been loved by its father and despised by society. I do what must be done reluctantly.

"Again, I have bled too freely. Tante Inez cautions that at my age, I must not do this again. I stay abed longer than necessary for my general tells me he must soon march on and return to his war.

"How ironic that as soon as I was able to sit up, the young officers, who believed me to be overcome by a fever, came to cheer me. We played at cards. From observing Adrien who taught me many things, I could have won often, but in their kindness, the young men allowed me to triumph hand after hand. My mattress is stuffed with their good greenback money and some hard and lumpy coinage, too. Sin should not be so well-rewarded. It tempts one to go on sinning as Catherine, my little nun, reminds me when she comes to my bedside to pray morning and night."

So that was it. Another dreaded LeBlanc secret revealed. The heroic Caroline had saved the family seat by sleeping with a Yankee general and aborting his child. Clearly, her gambling winnings had seen the family through the rest of the war and into Reconstruction. These funds, later entries said, were supplemented by "Letters of Regard" and additional money from the guilt-stricken General Moore. Nothing was heard from or mentioned about the silent Adrien LeBlanc.

Laura, ashamed over her intrusion, but not shocked by the revelations that must have rattled a woman of Miss Lilliane's generation, crept silently up the stairs in the night and replaced the diary in its original space in the row of little brown volumes. Only a few diaries remained, but Laura declined to take any more unless invited. Feeling pregnant with secrets, she returned to Caroline's bed.

Chapter Twenty-One

Mardi Gras obsessed the town. For the entire week before the event, the Ste. Jeanne Parish Library was devoid of business. The staff, white and black, could talk of nothing else over coffee. They took the grandeur of past costumes, the beauty of former queens, five, ten, twenty years ago, out of storage for the sake of conversation over the last crumbs of King Cake. Laura's piece of the coffee cake, gaudy with its yellow, green and purple icing, held the little plastic baby doll representing the Christ child.

"That means you bring the cake start of next year, or maybe you have a baby of your own by then." The staff chuckled and elbowed each other. Laura strongly suspected her piece of cake had been rigged, but she laughed with good humor and threatened, "If you want to eat what I can bake, you've got a deal."

Laura did not attend any of the satellite parties revolving around the great galaxy of the Mardi Gras ball, but she would attend the main event. Her trustee Jules Picard had seen to that. Oozing bonhomie, J.P. dropped by the library and thrust a ticket on his new librarian, implying that to purchase one was a civic duty. His being president of the Mardi Gras Association had nothing to do with it at all. In fact, buying two tickets would show even more community support. Laura assured J.P. that she needed only one ticket.

Though Picard came on like an ignorant country Cajun for the sake of his appliance business, Laura soon realized he was one of her most astute board members, more politically minded than even the regal lawyer, Arthur DeVille, uncle to Denise, and related to many by that name. Jules tuned into public attitudes even more than the Reverend Ramsey Polk, her black representative who seldom spoke at meetings, but nodded in dignified agreement or withheld his vote in silence. The appliance king had a more realistic view about business than either the doctor or the undertaker.

"None of our Cajun boys after a nice young lady like you? Well, that's mighty slow of them. Being a widow don't matter. Just means they don't have to break you in—like a good used appliance." He squeezed Laura with one plump hand. "Just teasing you, sugar. I hear you got other interests."

"Not really." Laura took the embrace and the comment as they were meant, all part of Jules Picard's style.

"Now, Arthur tells me his niece has been throwing little pink fits over you living out at the LeBlanc place. She says it's immoral and all, but we just don't listen to that. Besides, if something immoral is going on, I'm sure you'll get married one of these days, heh?"

He leered at Laura and pinched her arm. Knowing Jules, this could be a warning clothed in comedy or simply another of his jokes. Hard to tell.

Laura gave an evasive answer. "Believe me, with Miss Lilliane under the same roof, we are well chaperoned."

"See you at the ball for sure now." Picard hurried away in his usual state of hyperanimation, as if he were always in the midst of filming a thirty second television commercial for slightly dented washing machines at Big, Big Savings. He left Laura unsure whether he meant his last statement as a casual remark or an order.

****

Stores, schools, banks and all forms of local government, except the police department, closed on Mardi Gras day. Religion had nothing to do with it. Baptists lined the streets for the big parade, along with Catholics and those who had fallen by the wayside. Mardi Gras was the biggest party of the year, and no one, not bank teller or store clerk, teacher or student, wanted to be left out.

Laura selected a place to watch the parade on the curb near Dot's Antiques and Used Furniture, far enough from the church green and the ruins of Domengeaux's store not to stir unpleasant memories. She stood alone among the revelers, some masked, some half drunk, all wading in street gutters half-filled with beer cans. Angelle and Robert would ride the floats. Pearl, like everyone else, had the day off. Miss Lilliane stayed home under doctor's orders but vowed she would go to the ball that evening with or without his permission.

Clearing the streets with his siren, Police Chief LeDoux in his black and white patrol car led the parade. Following in the fire truck, bulky Chief Fontenot blasted the siren every few feet while his lean assistant waved intermittently at the crowds. A troop of small children, probably little Fontenots, clung to the ladders and threw sparse handfuls of peppermint candies to the less fortunate youth. Either they were gauging the length of the parade or were hopeful of keeping whatever they had left afterwards. A few teenagers booed as one peppermint arced into a crowd of twenty people. Chief Fontenot drowned them out with a prolonged, ear-splitting shriek from his horn. Laura made a mental note to enter the bookmobile in next year's parade with a more lavish supply of candy—if she stayed in Chapelle.

A National Guard unit came next bearing the flag, followed by two cheerleaders holding a banner telling everyone in ignorance this was the Mardi Gras Parade. The Chapelle High School band, the Swinging Saints, came after them, heavy on the drums and tubas. Black musicians stepped high and fancy in their worn maroon and gold uniforms. The sun refracted crazily off their dented instruments.

A group of merry Shriners, red-fezzed and red-faced, rode tiny motorcycles in small circles to please the children and keep the way clear for the small pages bearing Queen Marie Antoinette's banner. The queen's float rose, a mountain of white capped by a gilded throne, over the throngs. The queen's cape laid spread down the mountain, its intricate pattern of gold fleur-de-lis and seed pearls on display. Tiny purple-clad trainbearers sat on either side of the heavy cloth. The costumed girls waved daintily, as their mothers had shown them, from their nests of finery, while the small boys kept their plume-capped heads down and their tight-covered legs tucked beneath them in mortal fear of being seen and recognized by their peers in jeans and T-shirts along the way.

The magnificent queen's gown was a hand-me-down, altered from year to year to fit the reigning queen because of its great expense. Laura had to admit Denise

Deville filled the dress as if it were made for her alone. The low, square-cut bodice encrusted with golden beads showed just enough of the queen's small white breasts to be tantalizing. Though Denise had the dark brown eyes of the French, she had somehow achieved honey-colored hair that frothed around her shoulders like the meringue topping on a delectable slice of lemon pie. Her crown of rhinestones nestled lightly in the golden fluff without displacing a hair. Envy seized Laura whose ordinary dark brown strands snarled in the mild February breeze. She had never been a beauty, never been a queen, and was beginning to feel as if she had never been as young as Denise DeVille.

Queen Marie Antoinette waved regally and smiled artificially down upon her subjects. Now and again, her wave grew more vigorous and her smile more genuine as she sighted friends in the mob. Laura fancied for a moment when their eyes met the queen ceased to smile and wave altogether, but the float moved on, and she would never be sure.

After the formality of the queen's float passed, the real business of Mardi Gras began. The krewe floats came interspersed between the more formal ones holding the courts of Spring, Summer, Autumn and Winter. The krewe members using the summer theme strutted on an artificial beach. They'd chosen as their attire Victorian swimming gear in gaudy stripes topped by clown masks and red wigs. The clowns slung sand pails full of cheap plastic beads and Mardi Gras doubloons out at the crowd. Adults reached and grabbed, plucking necklaces and fake coins from the air. Urchins scrambled in the gutters, tussling over fallen treasure. Now and again, a foot stomped heavily on a rolling coin, or occasionally on a rival hand. One clown wearing a frilly woman's swimsuit stuffed with huge balloon breasts targeted Laura for a rain of bright purple, green and yellow beads. Though buffeted by the crowd, she seized her share and waved an armful at the obscenely funny krewe member she recognized as Jules Picard. She would save her bounty for Angelle who, riding on the float with the winter court, would be unable to gather her own lucre.

The winter krewe rode dressed as Pierrots with white-faced masks and conical caps. They cavorted in confetti snowdrifts and threw Styrofoam snowballs as well as the usual necklaces and doubloons. One Pierrot, his broad shoulders filling out the baggy costume, launched a fake snowball directly at Laura. The Styrofoam bounced harmlessly off her forehead and into her hands. A nearby child, beringed by a collar of necklaces worthy of a Ubangi, whined because he had not gotten a snowball, too.

The Court of Winter float approached. Angelle rode near the front, her thin arms covered with silver gloves to the elbow where they met the puffed sleeves of her white and silver gown. One arm waved eagerly in Laura's direction. She returned the wave with the hand clutching the snowball, a little gift from Robert, thrown as an icy symbol of frustration or, maybe, simply with the wry humor she loved in him. There were getting to be too many eithers, ors, and ifs in her life, entirely too many.

The appearance of the king's float signaled an end to the parade. Dr. Bourgeois, supposedly disguised by a black beard and wearing a cape of red velvet and gold embroidery every bit as elaborate as the queen's train, winked one eye at his librarian and tilted his scepter imperially in her direction. She returned the recognition with a mock curtsy.

"Gee, lady, do you know that dude?" said the same small boy who coveted her snowball.

"Yes, and a few clowns, too," replied Laura, suddenly feeling good about being part of Chapelle on Mardi Gras day. She tossed her snowball into the air and let the little boy catch it, then moved through the dispersing crowd to her car.

Chapter Twenty-Two

The afternoon between the Mardi Gras parade and the ball was a void of quiet between two frenetic events. Angelle and Tante Lil napped. Robert, ever conscientious, or just plain wishing to escape from the hoopla, went to check on the cattle. Pearl and Laura rested in their rooms. Restless in their rooms would have been a better description. Laura went to pass the time with Pearl but saw through a crack in the door that the housekeeper was struggling to apply false eyelashes with fingertips long out of practice. Laura retreated.

She found herself on the stairs to the second floor of Chateau Camille and continued up them. Idly, she investigated the old judge's vacant bedroom next to the library. She found the narrow door blending in with the paneling, hidden and too inconvenient to have been used by servants carrying trays or bringing basins of water in olden days. In addition to the secret stairs, the rest of the closet held cleaning supplies, old sheets to be torn for dust cloths, cans of wax and a vacuum cleaner. Laura had the urge to don a sheet, creep down the hidden stairs and give Pearl a fright, a cruel idea since Pearl labored over her makeup. Laura abandoned the prank and wandered to the library.

The hours until the ball passed too slowly, and the temptation grew too great. She seized another diary out of sequence and, curled in the old wicker chair, pried again into Caroline LeBlanc's life during the year, 1870. Here and there, the diarist had inserted yellowed letters among the pages—more "letters of regard" from the general or word at last from the errant Adrien? Laura carefully unfolded one fragile missive.

My dearest Caroline,

I fear my good wife Lucretia is in the last stages of her consumptive illness. Soon I will be a widower with a motherless daughter on the verge of young womanhood and in need of gentle guidance. Can you not pursue the whereabouts of your husband? He has been silent for so many years that unbeknownst, you may have entered the estate of being widowed that will soon be thrust upon me. It is my deepest desire that we should merge our families if such is the case. My fortune would be at your disposal for the education of your son and the restoration of your lovely home, which I would not ask you to leave. Chateau Camille holds many dear memories for me.

I remain your ardent admirer,
Alexander Moore

Judging by the following entries, Caroline had pursued Adrien's fate, sending letters with friends going abroad and inquiries to officials in France. She found his reputation everywhere, but his whereabouts remained unknown. Evidently, he had returned to the pursuits of his youth: riding and gambling with a fast set, painting the wives, daughters, and mistresses of his friends, spending months in their homes to do so, and living well. The final word came to Caroline from an unexpected source, a surprise even to her, as the year ended. Another letter, thinner and browner than the others with one side written in French, the other in English, and addressed in a feminine hand, lay between the pages. Laura struggled to read the faded ink of the translation.

My Dear Madame LeBlanc,

It is my sad duty to tell you of your husband's death. I have nursed him through an illness of many months. To be truthful, I have seen to all his needs these past five years. In seeing to these needs, he has given me two lovely daughters whom he named Aurelie, a family name, I believe, and Caroline after your own dear self.

I regret that to support my two small children, I have had to sell his remaining paintings and paints. Once I posed as an artist's model, but you, also a woman, must be aware of the ravages of time and childbirth.

One picture I have put aside for you because I am sure it holds great sentimental value. It is of yourself and your three children, the youngest so like my own Caroline, who is not so well dressed or fed. Adrien gazed at it often during his last days and only then did he smile. He begged you to see that here he could be simply Adrien LeBlanc, artist, while in your country he was only part of a family legend and no more.

You do understand, I am sure, and in your understanding will send me a generous bank draft for the portrait and its shipment. I have relied on a friend to put these words into

English so that you cannot mistake my meaning.

> *With deepest Sincerity,*
> *Martine LeBeau*

Laura sought the diary entry for the day of the extraordinary letter's arrival and found the tone jubilant.

I have laughed and cried over the letter from Martine LeBeau. She shall have her generous bank draft signed by my good general, these six months an eager widower. Oh Adrien, we were a pair! The way you ended your life has in some ways lifted the guilt of how I have lived mine. I wish you well in whatever netherworld you reside. Catherine says I am godless and vows to go to a nunnery before she will accept a Yankee for a father. I believe I shall grant her wish. In the convent, she may pray for both our souls. Adieu, my husband!

And so ended romantic Adrien LeBlanc. Laura suddenly lost interest in the remaining diaries filling out the top shelf. She could guess their contents. Caroline married her general, a staid, stable, and wealthy man. Robert had offered Laura the silver and garnet ring sealing their engagement. Certainly, they lived happily and unexcitingly ever after.

Caroline LeBlanc survived to an attenuated old age, seeing the turn of the century arrive with ease, but not living to learn the outcome of the Great War. That Laura knew, having seen her birth and death dates in the many local history books she plowed through to learn about Chapelle. How much longer those years would have seemed if Caroline had lived them alone. Once again, Laura maneuvered herself to the edge of a decision, but she stepped away from the brink and went to dress for the Mardi Gras ball.

****

There, ready or almost ready. Laura peered at herself in the long glass on the open armoire door. She wore a silver gown, not made of glittering lamé or stiff taffeta, but a lightweight silk, rich and soft. In keeping with the Victorian theme, the skirt was full, filled out by gathers and an underskirt rather than by a cumbersome hoop. The waist fit snugly, the bodice tight and strapless like an old-fashioned corset, very Vera Wang goes nineteenth century. With her dark hair upswept, a vast amount of bare flesh lay exposed between Laura's chin and cleavage. Pearl, as a good seamstress, knew how to pick out a person's best points. None of the thin chains and small pendants Laura had acquired since the fire filled the gap very well.

She raised her skirts to inspect the silver evening slippers with low heels for dancing and rosettes on each toe, an extravagant purchase considering she would probably wear them only once. The shoes complemented the gown perfectly, but she still had the problem of the neckline. Grasping her few bits of good jewelry in one hand and holding her full skirts up awkwardly with the other, Laura went to consult Pearl.

From down the hall came a muffled oath as Robert nicked himself shaving in a rush in the small bathroom. Graciously, he'd allowed the women to monopolize the facilities all afternoon and into the early evening, and now he hurried to fasten studs with clumsy fingers while Angelle urged him to move faster. The child would slip into her elaborate gown in the dressing room at the ball. At the moment, only her professionally styled hair and a touch of lipstick allowed by Tante Lil indicated she was going to participate in Chapelle's big event.

Miss Lilliane, her wheelchair turned away from Laura, waited impatiently in the hall. Pearl, who needed time for her own dressing, had attended to her earlier. The old woman wore a long, pale blue gown that glittered when her chest rose and fell in a coughing spasm. The cloth swagged across her sagging breasts and hung down like the dewlaps of her ancient neck. She'd chosen crystal drop earrings and a long rope of the same beads knotted in the middle to accent her outfit. Her hairdresser had permmed her gray hair into tight and springy smoky blue corkscrews for the special occasion. To complete the ensemble, Miss Lilliane selected a pair of silver shoes consisting of many thin straps holding high spiked heels to her feet. She sat there, the epitome of outdated elegance. For a moment, Laura pitied the old lady with her outrageous shoes going off to a ball in a wheelchair, but then caught herself, remembering that Miss Lilliane accepted pity from no one.

Laura moved into the kitchen, her wide skirts seeming to catch on every knob and chair. She passed the tray of ham biscuits and fruit salad Pearl put out to feed them while they dressed, but the food had barely been touched in all the excitement. Laura certainly couldn't bring herself to eat with her nerves jangling. The door of Pearl's room stood wide open now, and the housekeeper posed transformed before her mirror.

A turban of the same tangerine material as her gown hid the wiry gray strands of her hair. A jewel of unlikely size and color lay centered in the cloth. The folds of her matching gown draped gracefully on the long lean frame of the maid. With the shoulders of the dress slightly padded, the ball gown had a slinky Forties look that suited Pearl well. Her yellow complexion, smoothed and highlighted by makeup, took on a golden glow, and her dark eyes, disguised with fake lashes and a sparkling shadow on the lids, became exotic. She seemed taller, and Laura realized she wore high-heeled shoes as steep as Miss Lilliane's pair. Anyone entering the servant's room at this minute would know for certain that Pearl was the dancer just off center in the front row of a line of chorus girls pictured on the wall behind her.

"You look perfect!" Laura exclaimed.

"Well, you don't. You need more color on those cheeks, a brighter lipstick, and this." Pearl, still assessing her critically, shoved a worn red velvet jewelry case at Laura. She sprang the latch to reveal a necklace of heavy silver. One large red stone pendant hung in the center and at intervals, smaller graduated garnets glowed in the sterling setting. "Let me put it on you."

"Oh, no! That's too valuable." Laura backed away from the necklace far too similar to a ring she had almost accepted.

"Just a piece of costume jewelry from the old days really. Like this," Pearl said tapping the immense glass topaz in her turban.

Laura doubted that as she felt the weight of the necklace, unlike any modern costume jewelry, settle around her throat.

"And these are from Mr. Bob. With that neckline, you'll have to wear them at your waist." Pearl presented Laura with a florist's box.

"Not that you are anything special, mind. He sent me and Miss Lilliane orchids." Pearl opened her own box and looked again into the mirror to affix two small, yellow orchids to the shoulder of her dress.

"Wonder what he sent Denise DeVille?" Turning to see if her remark had scored, she caught Laura with tears gathering in her eyes as she stared into the corsage box holding two blood red camellias.

"Here now, you'll ruin your makeup and go to the ball looking like a raccoon." Pearl took the box of flowers and fastened the camellias at Laura's waist, then briskly turned her toward her own room.

"Look, I have to go now, honey. Remember, more blusher and brighter lipstick." Pearl seized an evening bag and a light wrap and left by the kitchen door where Tony waited in a rented tux and the truck Robert had loaned him for the evening.

The front door slammed, too, as Angelle hurried her father and great-aunt into the black Lincoln, reminding them shrilly that members of the pageant had to be there early to dress.

Laura was alone in her room, alone in the house, all alone. She studied herself again in the mirror. The necklace filled the white expanse between her throat and breasts magnificently. The red camellias nestled intimately against her waist. Again, she felt the urge to cry, fought down the tears, made the changes in makeup Pearl had urged and calmly sat on the bed reading a book until departure time with her silver skirt outspread to avoid wrinkles.

At the appointed time, she got into her own car and took herself to the ball like some neglected Cinderella. Not being part of the pageant, she'd been reluctant to invite herself to go with Robert and Angelle and wished desperately he would have asked her if she wanted to ride with them. Never would she interfere with Pearl's one night of glory by cramming into the truck with her and Tony.

As she passed along the dark country roads toward the town's recreation center where they held the ball, she suddenly yearned for David who had been pushed from her thoughts these last few weeks. She imagined him with her now, laughing and joking, treating her with the exaggerated courtesy their costumes and the occasion demanded, then dancing and dancing, slightly high on champagne and each other. They would stop on the way home in their formal attire at some absurd place like an all-night diner, and then home to bed, to bed with each other. This fantasy grew so real Laura reached across the seat to touch the space where David should have been, but the lights and traffic surrounding the recreation center lay just ahead. She withdrew her hand, and whispering good-bye to her husband, went to present her single ticket at the door.

Chapter Twenty-Three

Laura wandered the recreation hall trying to find a table with a free chair and a few acquaintances where she might sit for the pageant. She gave up and resigned herself to a solitary seat along the wall where many of her elderly library patrons gathered in dresses as crepey as their skin. Some wore real jewels on their spreading bosoms and others outmoded tiaras bobby-pinned to their sparse white hair. They welcomed Laura among them, reaching out withered hands to feel the fabric of her gown and nodding approvingly at her necklace. Miss Lilliane sat in the group among the wallflowers, but gave Laura only one venomous glance before the pageant began.

A skillful decorator had dressed the recreation center for the event. The basketball hoops were raised and obscured by a dropped ceiling of gold painted latticework from which hung the royal banners of purple, green and gold. Regal red runners covered the boundary lines on the gymnasium floor except for the area reserved for dancing. Every other inch of space held tables and chairs packed with local citizenry. The curtain on the stage in the rear of the gym rose to reveal three golden thrones.

The center throne held Queen Victoria, alias Iola DeGravelle, whose sheer bulk made her the obvious choice for the part. The matronly queen, dressed in

221

purple and gold, and crowned with a reasonable facsimile of the imperial jewels, stood and welcomed her subjects to the presentation of her honored guests, King Louis and Queen Marie Antoinette. The royal couple appeared opposite each other, paced toward the center of the ballroom and crossed so that everyone in the audience could view the magnificence of their capes held up by two small pages each. Then, ascending ramps on either side of the stage, radiant Denise DeVille and courtly Dr. Bourgeois took seats on their thrones with the pages clustered at their feet.

From her space on the sidelines where it seemed Queen Marie Antoinette had thrown an especially vivid smile on seeing her among the old ladies, Laura observed the entrance of the Court of Spring, two young women decked in capes and voluminous ball gowns portraying the flowers of the season. Each wore a towering headdress of stylized cherry blossoms and carried a staff wrapped in ribbons like a small maypole and topped with a nosegay. Following each princess, a little girl came holding the edge of the heavy cape off the runners and displaying its embroidered pattern of pink and green flowers to the crowd. Laura had pricked her fingers over one of those children's gowns swagged with rosebuds, but she did not recognize the girl wearing it.

As the Maidens of Spring came from opposite doors and progressed slowly toward the center of the room, young men in pale green tuxedos, pink rosebuds in their lapels, appeared beside them and took their arm, a gesture more practical than romantic. The young women needed more help in balancing their enormous headdresses and heavy capes than the staves and little girls could offer. Still, the gorgeous couples made an excellent show.

Jules Picard, his tubby body enclosed in his own tuxedo, served as captain and announced the members of each court as they appeared, giving not only real names but royal titles and elaborate histories to each princess. He proclaimed the Maidens of Spring to be the fair flowers of the Netherlands, the Princesses Helga and Beatrix, portrayed by Renee Landry and Louise Theriot.

Summer's princesses came from Spain with headdresses like radiant suns and gowns of red and gold. Their escorts wore pale yellow dress suits with small white daises in the buttonholes. Autumn's ladies arrived clad in yellow and orange with rustling headdresses of colored leaves, each supported by men in dark brown tuxedos decorated with one yellow mum. All were purported to be from Italy. Lastly, arrived the Court of Winter, the royalty of Germany.

Laura craned from her seat to see Angelle's entrance, but the rotund Princess of Winter obscured the child who carried her cape. Up until now, the magnificence of the regalia covered up any physical flaws the princesses might have had. No one really looked at the small oval faces beneath the headdresses or at the bodies dutifully dragging the weighty capes and gowns about for display, but there was no hiding the fact this princess of winter was fat. Her small eyes, sunk in a doughy face, blinked incessantly, betraying the fact she had gotten contact lenses just for this occasion. Beads of sweat on her temple reflected the light as if they were a planned part of her lofty tiara of silver snowflakes.

The girl trudged along hopelessly, leaning heavily on her white staff with its garland of silver holly and willing the eyes of the audience elsewhere. Without warning, the stout princess tripped on the red runner. The cape matching her silver and white gown and carried by Angelle who had only now appeared within the doorway ripped from the child's hands. Small gasps from the onlookers predicted a disaster for the pageant, but Robert LeBlanc caught her arm and steadied his maiden, smiling and whispering to reassure her no harm done. The Princess of Winter turned red, but smiled timidly. Angelle, at a nod from her father, picked up the cape, and all three resumed their march across the hall.

Near Laura, a fleshy matron in a red dress with a spangled bodice suitable for a circus performer announced loudly, "That's my little grandbaby, T-Michelle. We proud of you, honey, and you got the best lookin' man, too."

Little Michelle on Robert's arm paced well past their group, but the back of her neck between her headdress and gown blazed crimson. Miss Lilliane, offended by the woman's lack of decorum, replied in an equally loud voice, "T-Michelle looks exactly like her *memere*."

In a lower voice she told Laura, "Emilie Boudreaux's daughter married up, you know. Roger Maturin was so homely no one else would have him. Poor Michelle has her father's face and her grandmother's figure."

The two old women began a match of shooting each other poisonous glances while Laura sat between them and concentrated on the stage where Robert bent as solicitously over T-Michelle as the younger escorts did over their more willowy princesses. As the lights came up, the overheated crowd made their way to the restrooms or the punch bowls and refreshments set up in an adjoining room. Family photographers flocked to the stage where a professional attempted to take the official pageant pictures while flashes from small cameras went off all around him.

Laura found herself alone when Miss Lilliane wheeled off in search of a restroom and the heavyset grandmother sought some punch and sandwiches. Waiters with trays of champagne glasses began to serve those preserving their places at the tables. Laura seized a glass and wandered out to the lobby to stand in the long line of women forming at the ladies' room door. As usual, the men's room had no queue. Laura speculated over why this was always the case—larger bladders, greater fluid retention, less to take off, who knew?

By the time she accomplished her mission, not so easy in a wide gown, and returned, the court had left the stage. A band tuned up in their place. One by one, the princesses reappeared minus their headdresses, capes, and staves. The wisest maidens had looped their hair into tiny, uncrushable displays of braids. Michelle Maturin's head, whose close cut style brought out the pumpkin-like roundness of her head, was still damp with sweat where the headpiece rested. Robert did not escort her. Instead, her portly grandmother chaperoned. A tall gaunt man with small eyes set close to a large beaked nose and ears that would have flapped in the breeze had there been a breath of air in the hall trailed them. This gentleman, no doubt, must be the homely father, here in a rented tuxedo to do right by his equally homely child.

When the music began, the hall filled again. King Louis and Queen Marie Antoinette led the dance and were joined by Queen Victoria and Jules Picard. In pairs, the princesses and their escorts came out on the floor. Robert appeared in time to guide the stout Michelle around the other couples. Gradually, the onlookers entered the dance.

Laura, who had lost her seat, found herself holding up a section of the wall and trying to avoid the crushing footsteps of small pages rampaging around the gym like normal children, free at last from all the restrictions of the pageant. She wondered irritably if Robert had to spend the whole evening with his princess. It looked that way as he began another dance with the ecstatic Michelle in his arms. Even Angelle found a partner, a little Bourgeois boy imitating his father.

The dancing continued. Wedged in by the proud grandmother and on her third glass of champagne, Laura watched as Robert turned Michelle over to Jules Picard and claimed Denise DeVille. They made a handsome couple, he so dark, she so fair. Resolutely, Laura struck up a conversation with Emilie Boudreaux, complimenting her on how bravely her granddaughter had handled that little stumble. Mrs. Boudreaux gave credit where it was due.

"My little Michelle is blind as a bat without her glasses. Good thing her escort caught her, or she would have gone splat. That T-Bob is a nice boy—unlike some of his family I could mention. But, you know they got crazy people and all kinds of bad blood in those LeBlancs. In some, it comes out." She stared at the back of Miss Lilliane's head while her victim obliviously supervised Angelle from the edge of the dance floor.

"Maybe I shouldn't be saying this to you, but you got to live with her, poor heart, so I'm just warning. Things must be real serious between you and T-Bob for you to be wearing his mama's heirloom necklace. I ain't seen that out the box since way before Auree LeBlanc died. You got her coloring. It suits you. But Auree was only a slip of a woman. That's why the cancer took her so quick. No meat on her bones like you and me."

Mrs. Boudreaux pinched Laura's bare arm, but she barely felt it. She wanted to shove through the throng, take off the necklace and offer it to Denise DeVille. She wanted to create a big scene. She wanted to get Robert's attention.

Before Laura could move and carry out her champagne inspired act, Robert began dancing with Iola DeGravelle. She settled back into her place and learned the true meaning of the word "wallflower" as he chose Angelle for his next partner, then several elderly women, Michelle again, and then Angelle once more.

Finally, Laura said goodnight to Mrs. Boudreaux. The waiters had not passed her way for quite some time, and her champagne-fueled impulses faded. Though still before midnight, she thought she would return to Chateau Camille, leave the necklace in Pearl's room and go to bed. That seemed safe and sensible. As she pushed near the dance floor to tell Miss Lilliane her intentions, a man seized her from behind and whirled her around in time to the music.

Jules Picard, a short man, breathed heavily into her

cleavage and questioned her as they danced. "Why you hiding out with all the old ladies way back in the corner where no one can get at you? Did Robert make you promise not to dance with anyone but him? Well, you dance with me while he does his duty. I done mine!"

Laura wondered if she really had been hiding, waiting for Robert to make some grand gesture. Jules Picard exercised her vigorously, then took her to his table for more champagne and handed her off to another member of the Mardi Gras Association. After that, she had no chance to escape and go home. The array of partners seemed endless, thanks to Jules. They ranged from young members of the court, who disguised their age with slim moustaches and slight beards, to her undertaker trustee whose hands were not at all cold this evening. Laura lost track of dances danced and champagne consumed. She waved gaily to Angelle when the child departed with Tante Lilliane and laughed at everything Jules Picard said to her when he seized her for a second dance.

"I like my ladies to have a good time. *Laissez le bon temps rouler*, as we like to say. Let the good times roll!" Her trustee gave her a small squeeze and appeared a little annoyed when a masculine hand tapped on his shoulder.

"Now look here, we just started this dance! Oh, it's you, Bob. I guess you got prior claim. I been keeping her warm for you. Well, *laissez le bon temps rouler*, Laura." Jules danced himself off the floor and went to get a fresh bottle of champagne for the table.

Dizzy with drink and dancing, Laura's impulses returned. When Robert held her close, she pulled him even closer and whispered, "Why did you give me this necklace?"

"I wanted to give you the ring that matched it."

"But you took the ring back."

"No, you dropped it."

"I came to you in the barn."

"And I ruined the moment. But not tonight, Laura. Tonight, I will give you romance. Tonight, I shall whisper amorous French phrases in your ear."

He did. His French even worse than Laura's, he began with "*La plume de ma tante*"—the pen of my aunt—murmured passionately into the hollow of her neck. She laughed, and her laughter took her back to the first day in Chapelle: ogling his ass in Domengeaux's café, calling him Little Bob and treating him like a hired hand in his own barn, going on his irreverent tour of the Chateau. For a while, all that kept them apart vanished.

No one interrupted them as they danced all the remaining dances together, sometimes with champagne flutes in their hands, sometimes sipping wine from each other's glasses. A fairy tale night, Laura reflected. Not a Barbie doll night, she thought, as Denise whirled by propelled by a pimply youth. She and Robert were like Cinderella and her prince on the old music box she'd had as a child. When wound, it played *Someday my Prince Will Come* as the couple twirled under a glass globe nothing could penetrate.

They took a bottle of champagne outside and danced beneath the stars. The night remained strangely balmy for February, and other couples stood here and there in the dark until people began to leave the hall.

"You going to midnight Mass?" Robert called to an acquaintance who passed waving a wine bottle.

"Hell, no, we're going to Broussard's Barn! Come along!"

Chapter Twenty-Four

Robert took control of Laura's car. They bucketed along the back roads, part of an entourage of well-dressed and drunken revelers. "I sent Tante Lil and Angelle home in the Lincoln. I thought tonight you might just give me a lift," he said.

Laura didn't answer. Perhaps, the time had come to put a new man in the driver's seat, but she wasn't about to say so. Excessive indulgence in champagne had a way of making decisions much too easy.

They came to a crossroad where an old country store stood, its flaking metal sign reading "Broussard Grocery." Enough vehicles crammed the field next to the store it might have been mistaken for a used car lot. The sports cars and sedans of the Mardi Gras set joined the pickup trucks and motorcycles. Robert carried Laura across the muddy lot and up the creaking cypress steps, stumbling a little, and not nearly as agile as he had been during the pageant. Setting her down on the porch, he said, "Just practicing for later when I carry you off to have my way with you."

"Do it," Laura challenged.

"Not now! Later. I promise. Come on."

They entered through the store, a real country store with a grated window that served as a post office and had a small sign reading "Justice of the Peace" to the left of that, plus a jumbled array of canned goods, some with labels faded with age, to the right. The only sales taking place seemed to be for cold drinks and occasional jars of white liquid served from under the counter by a fat man in a soiled T-shirt with stained yellow armpits.

Robert led her straight ahead down an aisle and into a huge metal building attached to the store. Here a mass of people danced spasmodically to the beat of an all black band playing an exotic blend of rock, Cajun, and country music. The crowd was mostly white, except for a few colored women in very short crocheted dresses with little on beneath, who passed in and out of two large open doors in the rear of the place. Laura could see the dim form of an old motel behind the building.

Before she could take it all in, Robert's friend with the wine bottle beckoned them to a table. He generously shared his bottle with the group. Laura took a big swallow. Not wine. The fire spread from her throat to her toes. She coughed and the friend snickered. "I had Broussard fill it with some of his white lightning."

A tall, brown-skinned woman, large in the breasts and barely covered by orange crochet that matched her hair, leaned over Robert. "How's it hanging, Bob? You alone on Mardi Gras Eve? Need a date?"

"Not tonight, Sugar. Miss Sugar LeDoux, I'd like you to meet our parish librarian, Laura Dickinson. I guess you don't get to the library too often."

"No, sir. I use the one at the university." The hooker winked. "Anything I can do for the rest of you gentlemen?"

"How about me, Sugar? I'm lonely." The wine bottle wielder ran his hand under her short dress and snapped the elastic on her bikini pants. His petite blonde date, his wife actually, glared.

"Well, maybe on my poker night."

Working the room, Sugar passed along to another table.

"Hey, you know her real name is Beulah. I'd change that one, too. She took the LeDoux from the sheriff's name. They're not really related like everyone says. Good joke, huh, Sugar LeDoux, Sugar the Sweet." The drunk laughed, and his wife speared him with another look he was too numb to feel.

"That's Pearl's..." Laura said slowly because her lips felt clumsy and her mind slow. In a moment of insanity, she'd taken another sip from the bottle.

"Just an old friend of mine," Robert interrupted. "Let's dance."

They danced now to a primitive rhythm as unlike the sedate music of the ball as possible. The band made the most out of a strange assortment of instruments: fiddles, two electric guitars, drums, a triangle and an accordion. One musician became an instrument himself, strumming a corrugated metal sheet worn over his shirt.

"They call this music Zydeco, meaning string beans. I can't even guess why," Robert shouted over the beat.

"The Broussards used to have a real barn out back, used as a speakeasy in the Twenties, but the place burned down in the in the Fifties when the family ran a little short on money. They got enough from the insurance company to pay off some debts to a group of pretty shady characters. Later, they put up this metal building. Everyone still calls it Broussard's Barn."

Making it easier for Laura to dance in her long

gown the band swung into an electrified two-step. Sweat trickled between her breasts and her skirts stuck to the back of her legs. Robert caught a trickle of perspiration on her neck with his tongue. She said, "I wish I could take off this dress."

"Oh, you can. But not until after the wedding. Didn't your mama ever tell you that?"

"I want to do it right now!" Laura insisted, reeling with white lightning.

"I accept your proposal." Robert held up his arm signaling the band. "A wedding march, please!"

The band, also available for receptions as their advertising said, actually did know the wedding march. Robert led Laura grandly into the store to the electronically distorted chords of Handel. The word passed from table to table, "A wedding, a wedding." It reached the front counter where Broussard put on a black coat hanging on a nail behind him and shoved an already knotted tie over his head and around the fat creases of his neck. Ceremoniously, he moved from behind the bar to behind the bars of the post office window. "Will the happy couple please step forward?" he intoned. The crowd gathering behind them pushed Laura and Robert to stand before the justice of the peace.

"Just fill in your name when I get to the blanks," Broussard instructed and began reading. When he got to the part about anybody knowing why these two should not be wed, he paused and scanned the mob for sober friends, but found none. Broussard shrugged. It made no never mind to him.

The small blonde woman, whose very intoxicated husband seemed to be acting as best man, took Laura's left hand and said, "If you are sure you want to go through with this, I'll witness for you, honey."

Laura nodded. "I do, I do."

"No, no! You say that at the end," Robert joked.

When the moment came for a ring, she presented her left hand unsteadily to her groom. Surprisingly, he had a ring—even if the box did catch in his jacket lining twice before appearing. Broussard put back the box of cheap bands he kept under the counter next to the stamps for such occasions. The ring in the box matched the necklace the bride wore. Taking note of the expensive jewelry, Broussard grew uneasy. Few came so prepared to marry at the barn. His eyes shifted around the crowd, always wild on Mardi Gras night, as if he searched for plain clothes cops who might be lurking, trying to catch him with stolen goods or ready to shut off sales for his home brew.

"Okay, you married. Sign here. One hundred dollars." He charged twice his usual fee, and the guy in the tux paid willingly, drawing out an accordion folded hundred dollar bill and declaring blearily, "My lucky hundred, never go anywhere without it."

Old Broussard blessed them with a wave of his fat hands toward the door. "Now go on home. Happy honeymoon!" Father Ardoin would not like to hear it, but Broussard's makeshift marriages lasted almost as long these days as the ones performed in the church.

The best man tucked the shakily signed marriage certificate and a pre-dated license to marry into Robert's pocket. Two of Broussard's bouncers helped the happy couple to their car. They returned to Chateau Camille by the shortest route the groom could remember. Laura dozed. Robert rolled down the windows and let in the breeze, then drove on speedily until the shell drive of Chateau Camille crunched beneath their wheels. The wedding party entourage streamed by as the couple's car turned in the driveway, sounding their horns in celebration.

The bride said not a word. Robert had the insane idea she'd overdosed on alcohol, and he had lost her again. He shook his new wife, asking if she was all right, and when Laura laughed, teasing him by pretending to be asleep, he put his cold hands on her warm breasts. She fought him off, still laughing, while he carried her across the threshold.

"See, I did need the practice," he said as he headed toward her room. Laura's wide skirt caught on every outcropping in the hall and draped inconveniently over his hand when he reached for the doorknob of the bedroom. He cursed.

"Quiet, quiet, shhhh," cautioned Laura, still giggling.

Robert bumped the door to the bedroom closed with his hip. Putting her down, he took the marriage certificate and license, propping them on the dresser where Angelle had burned her candles hoping for what had now come to pass. He turned to Laura, the laughter gone, that serious dark look in his eyes she always shied away from, avoiding the passion and the longing of his gaze. He did not appear drunk anymore or joking.

As for herself, she still felt giddy and lightheaded. When she did not drop her eyes from that black stare, he came to her, put his arms around her and slowly slid the zipper on the back of her dress down until the bodice could be pushed aside. He gathered her breasts in both hands, licking her nipples, massaging their mass until she felt the tingle under her skirts overcome the numbness caused by the alcohol consumed.

He ran his tongue down to her waist, levered the zipper again and knelt in the pool of her silver skirts as the dress slid from her body. He clasped her buttocks and buried his face in the scrap of black lace panties he had bought for her at Miss Helen's boutique. His hands slid the lace downward. His lips kissed the spot where she throbbed. His tongue laved her until her legs grew weak from the heat spreading through her body. He caught her and carried her, wearing only the garnet necklace and her wedding ring, to the big four-poster bed where his LeBlanc ancestors conceived their children.

Laura cried out for Robert to fill the void of nine long months of widowhood. Her nails pressed into his back, and her legs wrapped around his waist. She drew him closer, guiding him inside a body starved for his presence with hands that found the zipper in the tuxedo pants and all the good things ready and waiting inside. When he stopped for a moment to rid himself of the impediments of formal wear, she continued to move beneath him, urging him on. On he went and on, until she cried out so loudly he had to cover her mouth with his and let her absorb his own shout of completion. They did not separate that evening, but slept still twined together until sometime in the night when Laura turned and fit herself into the curve of his body.

Chapter Twenty-Five

Dawn came with the incredibly raucous babble of a mockingbird staking out his territory as he perched on Laura's windowsill. Slowly, the bride raised her eyelids. The early light pierced directly to the back of her skull rebounding inside her brain causing incredible pain. Laura shut her eyes and attempted to reclaim sleep, but now something else prodded her awake.

Men, she thought hazily. Why do they always have the urge at six a.m.? Just like David to want it now.

The prod moved down her buttocks and slipped between her legs where reluctantly she'd come wide awake. A hand slid beneath the barrier of her arm, captured a breast and fondled until it, too, grew alert.

Laura opened one eye. Something was wrong—the hand tanned even in February, wrong—the scattering of black hair on the back of that hand, wrong—the calloused, blunt fingers—wrong! David had the fair hands of an artist. David, her husband! Laura rolled away from the man trying to enter her, away from the rough, dark hands. She slipped from the bed and stood dizzy and naked among the crumpled clothes and stray studs discarded the previous night. Robert LeBlanc, staring at her from the bed, willed her back under the covers with his bittersweet brown eyes, his bedroom eyes. She gathered up a swath of silvery cloth from the floor and held it in front of her. "We can't do this."

"Even Tante Lil wouldn't expect us to be doing anything else the morning after our wedding." Robert grinned and ran his hands over the still warm spot next to him in Caroline Montleon's big, canopied bed.

"Wedding?" Laura's head throbbed, blocking out all recent memories.

"There's the certificate." Robert waved toward the dresser. He seemed very amused.

"But there have to be licenses and a ceremony and a ring," Laura babbled like the mockingbird who would not shut up.

"Old Broussard kindly pre-dated one just for us and one lucky hundred dollar bill. Truly quite a bargain. We've had the ceremony and got the ring. Sorry you don't remember it." He glanced significantly at her left hand where the antique garnet ring gleamed. "I hope you haven't forgotten all of last night though."

He rose, still erect, from the bed and rubbed against the thin sheet of material separating them. Laura backed away. She suddenly felt sticky and unclean between her legs. "Let me alone. We aren't legally married."

"Then half of Chapelle isn't legally married. Everyone the church won't recognize goes to Old Broussard. Everyone in Chapelle accepts these marriages." Robert no longer smiled.

"Goddammit, Laura, I waited. You took one step forward and two steps back so many times I didn't know which way you were going, so I had to make up your mind for you before you could do something stupid like marry that guy back home. Last night, you said you were willing."

"I was drunk out of my mind. And Benny Schweitzer is a jerk! I wouldn't marry him in a million

239

years! We never did—this." She gestured feebly toward the bed.

Laura started laughing, even though it made her head ache, at the thought of Benny Schweitzer with his beach ball belly and toupee as an object of jealousy. When she couldn't stop laughing, she realized she rode the fine edge of hysteria. Tears rolled down her cheeks, and she blotted them with a handful of silver silk. Robert didn't get the joke. How could he? He snatched the marriage certificate from the dresser and left the bedroom, naked as he was, to retreat to his own room before her laughter woke the household.

Laura fell back across the bed and muffled her laughter until the tears took over completely. After they dried, only the throbbing in her skull remained along with the knowledge that something that should have been right had gone all wrong again. Exhausted, she slept.

****

Securely wrapped in her flannel nightgown and robe, Laura crept into the kitchen. Nearly noon according to a clock that ticked too loudly. No quiet digital timepieces for Chateau Camille, no sirree. She felt shaky and weak from a night of excess. Pearl, wearing her pink chenille bathrobe, sat at the breakfast table. Her hair lay in a grizzled, frizzy mess around her shoulders. She leaned over a glass full of tomato juice caged between her hands like the elixir of life. She toasted Laura.

"Hair of the dog. Can I get you a Bloody Mary?"

"Just coffee, very black."

"That's the only kind I make." Pearl poured a cup from an insulated carafe and shoved it across to Laura.

Some sloshed on the tablecloth, but Pearl only eyed the stain wearily.

"Miss Lilliane will be in bed all day. I took her a tray, but she only pecked at it."

"Where's—Angelle?" Laura covered her hesitation with a sip of coffee.

"At school. I swear I had to dress that child asleep and spoon feed her to get her on the bus at eight. Can't figure out why anyone would put that holiday on a Tuesday. They must have lived different lives back then."

"Yeah, why not Friday Gras or Saturday Gras? I'll have to look that up at the library. The library. It's Wednesday!"

"Just sit down, honey. I already phoned you in sick. 'Course, half your staff is sick this morning, but a few good Baptists showed up for work. Don't matter. Won't nobody be coming to the library today." Pearl chuckled slowly as if it hurt her head to laugh.

"I picked up your room while you slept. Looked in to see if you wanted a tray, too, you know. That tux has to go back to the rental place today, and they sure ain't gonna be happy about the tears where he couldn't get the studs out fast enough." Pearl waited with her usual patience for a comment and got no answer as Laura tried to drown her face in the coffee mug.

"Ain't nothing wrong with what goes on between a man and a woman, especially when they been working up to it for over six months. You white folks sure are slow. So, when's the wedding?"

"It's over."

"I'd say it just started." Pearl chuckled again.

"No, I mean the wedding. I think we were married

241

last night at Broussard's Barn." Laura peered shyly over the rim of her cup to assess Pearl's reaction.

"Why some of the best marriages in Ste. Jeanne Parish had their start at Broussard's Barn. My own sister, for one. Ruby coming from strict Catholics, and George Senegal from dyed in the wool Baptists, and him a shade too dark to suit our folks, they ran off to Broussard's when old Tubbs Broussard had the place. Burned down under his care, but the family rebuilt. His son runs the Barn now. Don't matter. All of them Broussards is interchangeable. Bands, booze and whores has always been their business. Anyhow, my sister has the best marriage I know of. I always did envy Ruby for knowing what she wanted."

"Most of us don't."

"No, honey, most of us don't," Pearl agreed. "But I can tell you one man who does. He ate a mighty big breakfast today and went out to the barns. He seemed kind of cranky for a man who finally got what he itched for. He'll be back in for lunch any time now."

"I think he's really, really mad at me, Pearl. I got a little confused this morning and sort of laughed him out of my bedroom."

"Oh, Mr. Bob has a quick temper, but it flares up and then it's gone. He ain't one to rake over old coals to stir up the fire again. Give him half a chance. Give yourself one."

"I think I'll go get dressed." Laura retreated to her room and hid out there for the rest of the day.

By dinnertime, she had sorted her thoughts and conceived a tentative plan. She would act casually as if nothing significant had happened. After all, Miss Lilliane and Angelle did not know about the pseudo-marriage for the moment. Acting calmly, she'd announce the time had come for her to stop intruding on the LeBlanc hospitality and find a place of her own. Then, she'd move out as soon as possible, away from the influence of Chateau Camille and the yearning eyes of Robert LeBlanc. A quiet annulment based on her inebriated state or the fake pre-dated license—that was her ticket out.

Of course, she would have to endure some embarrassment. In a town the size of Chapelle, the marriage at Broussard's Barn had likely been discussed breakfast, lunch, and dinner at most of the tables in the parish. She could brush the event off as Mardi Gras madness and go about her duties quietly and efficiently until the gossip faded away. Perhaps, she would look for another job, far, far away. As soon as she entered the dining room, the bride knew her plan would fail.

Miss Lilliane occupied Laura's place across from Angelle. The child beamed. Her first words were, "May I call you Mama now?"

Unable to answer, Laura smiled painfully at the girl who took that grimace as a yes and rushed to hug her new stepmother around the waist. Robert looked at his wife as if he expected more from her. When she appeared to be frozen in a tableau with Angelle clasped against her, he stood and held the chair at the head of the table for her. That gesture released Laura's power of speech.

"Oh, no! That's Miss Lilliane's place."

The old woman, who wore her dressing gown and slippers like a royal robe, declined grudgingly with a shake of her head, "You're married to the head of the family now. The place opposite him is yours."

Laura could guess the aged librarian's true thoughts. "First you take my job; now you take my place at the table."

Her own thoughts weren't any kinder. She stared at Robert, who had taken his accustomed place, and willed him to understand—How could he? How could he tell the child! How could he use his precious daughter as a weapon against her?

He avoided her eyes and pretended to have a great appetite for a chicken leg resting on his plate in a nest of rice and gravy. Laura had no intention of pretending. After a few bites, she pushed her chair back and announced that last night's festivities had been too much for her while looking pointedly at the other end of the table where Robert hid in the act of eating. She was going back to bed.

Angelle pleaded, "But Pearl and I have a surprise for you!"

"It will keep!" snapped Tante Lil, the only other person in the room besides Laura willing to admit anything was wrong.

Laura made her escape to remain sleepless in the night, her head filled with fruitless plans to retreat from Chateau Camille. Early in the evening, Angelle tapped on their adjoining door and asked "mama" to kiss her goodnight. Laura went to the child and tucked her in, though she'd heard Robert's low voice a moment before as he carried out the same nighttime ritual. In the late hours, he tried her locked hall door very quietly and whispered "Laura" in that deep, strong voice of his. He left her undisturbed when she didn't answer. All in all, she passed a torturous evening as unlike her wedding night as she could imagine.

Chapter Twenty-Six

What a hideous Thursday! While stopping for gas at Thibodeaux's station, the old man looked at Laura slyly, winked and said, "Can I look under your hood, Mrs. LeBlanc, or is T-Bob taking care of all dat now?"

At the library, coffee break turned out to be a surprise bridal shower complete with a white frosted coconut cake, tiny net sacks filled with pastel candied almonds and numerous small gifts ranging from handmade potholders to a set of peach-colored towels monogrammed with the letter "L" presented by Ruby.

Of course, Pearl could have told Ruby and alerted the staff, but when questioned, her clerk replied coyly, "Oh, the whole town knows. We could all see it coming—Mrs. LeBlanc."

Laura gladly left the festivities to take the phone call from Lola Domengeaux, though she suspected the reason for the summons wasn't a happy one.

"Oh, *cher*, my husband passed dis morning. It's been coming on a long time, so I was ready, holding his hand at da end. Can't ask for more den dat. No more suffering for my Louie. Now, da wake is tomorrow night at Duchamp's starting at six, wit' a rosary at seven and funeral, Saturday, at ten in da church. I don't mean to spoil your happiness. One marriage ends and another begins as *le Bon Dieu* wills it. I'm selling my house, I t'ink, and going to live wit' my daughter up by

245

Baton Rouge. But we see each other before I go, heh? I got lots of calls to make. You tell da library people. God bless you and Bob and T-Angelle and all dose little LeBlancs you gonna to have. Bye-bye, *cher*."

Laura returned to the uncomfortable party with a piece of news guaranteed to deflect the attention from her marriage. It did. Her staff lingered over their cake and retraced the course of Louie Domengeaux's health over the past ten years, reminisced about Miss Lola's miracle baby and praised her pralines before returning to work. By the end of the day, a car pool had been arranged to the wake and a collection taken up for flowers and Masses. On her way out the door, Ruby hugged her boss and assured her that sometimes good news came with bad as she placed the neatly packed cartons of shower gifts in Laura's arms.

****

Delighted by the small boxes of wedding gifts as if they proved Laura was really her mother now, Angelle dragged the cartons into the kitchen to show Pearl. The housekeeper soon evicted her, however. Though the entire mansion smelled of baking and roasting, Pearl served an unexpectedly light dinner. Only the atmosphere at the table remained heavy. Laura mistook it for Robert's guilt over forcing their marriage and Tante Lil's ambient anger.

Unable to capture Pearl's attention again after dinner, Angelle settled for poring over the gifts in Laura's room. Who gave this, and who gave that? Angelle admired the potholders and shook out and refolded the towels until Laura began to lose patience with the child.

Laura found herself experimenting unwillingly

with parental powers. "It's nearly eight. You should have your bath and get ready for bed, Angelle."

"Oh, I can stay up late tonight," remarked Angelle casually. Then, she clapped a hand over her mouth.

"Who said so?" Laura interrogated.

"Tante Lil and Pearl," confessed the child.

"Angelle!" Tante Lil's cracked voice outside the door summoned the girl. "Come help me in my room. At once!"

Reluctantly, the child went.

Laura, alone at last, took a hot bath, slipped into her comfortable flannel nightgown and sought escape in a murder mystery, no romances tonight. Fortunately, the plot was absorbing and frightening as a serial killer stalked a young woman, peering into her windows while the heroine slept in her bed. Something blundering in the shrubbery near the house unnerved her enough to make her take her book out to the parlor. Strangely, at eleven p.m., Tante Lil still sat reading in front of the closed pocket doors shutting off the other side of the room.

Beyond the divider, someone moved furniture, and Pearl chided Angelle for "getting into the food." Before Laura could ask for an explanation, noise enveloped the Chateau. The air rattled with a little French ditty about a bullfrog who puffed up when he saw his lady love sung as loudly, raucously and salaciously as possible by a chorus of men accompanying it with a banging of spoons on pots and pans. The irreverent choir circled the house once and began a second chorus even louder than the first.

Laura turned to Miss Lilliane for an explanation. The old woman, very pleased with herself, replied, "It's a local custom, my dear, a *cherivari.* When two people, widowed or divorced, marry again, the old men like to make it official this way. It says your marriage is accepted and celebrated by them—though how you are going to explain why the bride is dressed so drably and sleeps apart from the groom, I don't know. We'll have to let them in soon."

At that moment, Pearl drew back the partition to expose a table cluttered with trays of tiny meat pies, plates of cold sliced boudin sausage and mounds of crustless chicken salad sandwiches. Bottles of wine and beer poked out of a tin tub filled with ice sitting at one end of the dining room on an old, brown cotton rug. A small wedding cake with attendant of plates of cookies—sugar, chocolate chip, and Mexican wedding dredged in powdered sugar—sat in the center of the array of foods.

Angelle jumped up and down in time to the song now completing its third round and pointed at the cake. "Our surprise! We saved it for tonight."

The groom appeared almost overdressed for his role as a new husband in pale blue pajamas, deep burgundy robe and leather slippers. Laura ran to her room. Robert pursued her. Standing by the locked door, he pleaded, "Please Laura. It's an old custom. They wouldn't do this if they didn't like the both of us. Come and greet them if only for a moment."

Laura rooted furiously in the bottom of the armoire, too hurried to answer. There it was, still in the box. She shook out the outrageously frilly peignoir and its matching gown. Discarding her flannels, she slipped on the shower gift intended for another wedding night and another groom and shoved her feet into the matching satin slippers. Passing through Angelle's and Tante Lil's vacant rooms, she paused in the bathroom, applied a touch of lipstick, blusher and eye makeup, combed her hair, and then, as an afterthought, mussed it again. Bedroom hair, that's what she wanted.

As Robert opened the doors of the Chateau to the *cherivari* prepared to face the crowd of well-wishers alone and bear their jokes, Laura slipped into his bedroom, rumpling the bedding as she went. As the first tin pan bangers surged into the hallway, Laura stood dressed as a newlywed should be, in the doorway of the master's bedroom. Showing neither lust nor longing, but gratitude, Robert's eyes met hers over the throng.

"Sorry to interrupt anyt'ing," quipped old Thibodeaux, eyeing the bed rumpled behind Laura, "But you gonna be married one long time, yeah. Let's have us a little party to get t'ings started right."

Jules Picard led the chorus in another round of the bullfrog song and told ribald stories in French that made the men guffaw and Laura blush, even though she had little idea what they said but could judge by the tone of his voice. Even old DeVille, the snoozer from the library, attended. He soon settled on the floor by Miss Lilliane's wheelchair and dozed off with his head in her lap. She stroked his white hair tenderly as if DeVille were a favorite pet.

An elderly man so fat he used a pair of red suspenders to pull his pants almost to his armpits clasped Laura to his huge belly and hugged. "Tubbs Broussard, pleased to meet you. Don't get by da library much, but always glad to celebrate a union made at my Barn. Best wishes to you and T-Bob."

He took a swig from a dripping beer bottle after his

toast and finally released Laura from his bear-like grip. He'd copped a feel in the process. A wizened geezer took Tubbs' place, but offered a politically proficient handshake instead of a hug. She recognized this one.

"Leroy Mouton, your police jury representative. Seen you at the council meetings. Good work with the library. Not that Miss Lilliane wasn't great at her job, too. Anything you want, you call me, you hear?" He attached a "Vote For Leroy 'Lamb' Mouton" button to her peignoir. "I hope I can count on your vote."

Robert came to her rescue with an offering of red wine. She accepted the glass as he snugged her against his hip with one strong arm. He stayed by her side for the remainder of the party.

At one a.m., Robert and Pearl put the guests, full of beer, boudin and cake, outside. The groom felt obligated to drive the drunkest home. By the time he returned, Laura slept in her unlocked room. He noticed she'd been too exhausted to discard the provocative gown. Vulnerable in sleep and thin white nylon, she tempted him to get in beside her. But, she'd been generous to him this evening, hanging on his arm, laughing and blushing at the jokes, as if this were the most wonderful night of her life, saving him from embarrassment before the community. Vivien would never have done the same. Laura deserved to be left in peace. He kissed his bride lightly, whispered, "I love you," and locked himself out of her room.

Chapter Twenty-Seven

Friday evening brought the wake of Louie Domengeaux. Indicating this sort of affair was best left to women, Robert refused to go. Laura volunteered to drive for her own subversive reasons. Her new husband thanked her for looking out for Tante Lil. His aunt was getting too elderly to drive at night, he said. The old woman glared at her nephew as he packed her, the wheelchair and Pearl into Laura's small vehicle and waved them down the drive. His outraged aunt provided the only conversation on the way into town.

"He thinks I can't drive after dark anymore, but did he concern himself about that at the Mardi Gras Ball? No! I'm good enough to get Angelle home while he had his little fling. I sat out there in the drive honking the horn until Tony came from heaven knows where to help me inside and find Pearl to get me undressed. I suppose T-Bob knew I wouldn't get drunk and do something stupid on Mardi Gras eve like some people I could mention."

Miss Lilliane muttered and coughed along the same lines up to the door of Duchamp's Funeral Home. Somewhat mollified by the personal attention of Armand Duchamp who erected her wheelchair, she rolled up the ramp where the caskets usually rolled down to the waiting hearse.

Laura followed them through the door of the

251

converted Victorian mansion, down its thickly carpeted, sound-muffling hallway and into the viewing room. She shivered a little at the sight of Louie Domengeaux in his coffin. Not knowing what else to do, she stepped up to the open coffin and gazed on the corpse, such a spare little man in death, hardly making up half of his widow's bulk. He slept eternally now with his spectacles still set on his nose as if he might wake up at any second and need them handy for reading the sports page. Laura bowed her head for a moment, and then moved to the back of the room to make way for other mourners.

She turned to see Miss Lilliane tap a woman who had been praying intensely by the side of the coffin and take her place, pulling a rope of rosary beads from a pocket and beginning to say them fervently. Even Pearl went to her knees on the padded kneeler placed in front of the coffin and swayed slightly as she prayed. The mourner who had been relieved and whom Laura assumed was close kin to the dead man turned out to be the telephone operator, Myrtle Hill. The operator moved away from the candlelit coffin toward the discreetly dim area of electrical lighting where Laura stood searching for Lola Domengeaux. She noticed the town gossip too late for retreat. Miss Myrtle seized her arm and started right in with the chatter.

"Can you believe I been here for two hours? My knees are just killing me, and I could use some food, couldn't you? Mama is taking care of the exchange. I should take her a plate."

"I'm looking for Mrs. Domengeaux." Laura's escape plan failed.

"Well, she's right back here with the

refreshments." Myrtle dragged her along to another room where Lola Domengeaux, entirely clad in black except for a white apron, supervised trays of fried chicken drumettes and poured small cups of black coffee or sweet punch depending on the preference of the mourner. Such a normal scene, so routine, so like the old days at Domengeaux's store—Laura's eyes filled with the first real tears of the night. She hugged the large woman and blinked her eyes to control her emotions. As usual, Miss Lola was the one who consoled.

"Don't cry for Louie, *cher*. He suffered, now it's over. My daughter, our Suzette, stayed right by me to da end, and I know my Louie was a good man who had his las' rites said by Father Ardoin. A few more prayers and he'll pop straight t'rew to heaven and be waiting for me dere. Now, tell me how you doing, little bride. I knew you and T-Bob was meant to be from dat first day you come in my shop. I seen you checking him out. If you had fed him my gumbo las' fall, it would have happened sooner, I tell you me."

"I'd like to speak to you—alone." Laura rolled her eyes toward Myrtle Hill piling a plate with drumettes and pastel mints.

"Troubles already? Let me give you my gumbo recipe. Dat'll fix things up. He got to expect you can't cook Cajun yet."

"No. It's about your house. I'd like to buy it."

"T-Bob wants some rental property? He don't have enough responsibility with da cattle and dat big house? What he want wit' my little place?"

"No. It's me. I need a place to live."

"No, no, no, *cher*. Dat's da worse t'ing you can do

if you fightin' is to move out. You stay put and make him see how wrong he is, den when he good and sorry, you take him back in your bed. My Louie could tell you how good dat does. I already heard you not sleepin' wit' him, but dat's none of Miss Lilliane's business. I tell her to let you two alone. It will come right, heh?"

Filled with rancor for Miss Lilliane and embarrassment for herself, Laura nodded and pulled away from Lola Domengeaux. She had some coffee but refrained from eating because she persisted in imagining she could smell formaldehyde scenting the room. The others chowing down didn't appear to notice any unusual odors.

Feeling calmer after listening to Myrtle Hill's mind numbing chatter for an hour, Laura returned to the wake and expressed her condolences to Suzette Domengeaux Prioux, a stout woman like her mother. Abruptly, she jerked Miss Lilliane's chair away from the casket. None too gently, she shoved the old woman into the car with Pearl's startled aid. Before starting the engine, she made an announcement to all passengers. "What goes on between Robert and me is a private family matter, and as long as I am living at Chateau Camille, it will stay that way."

She raced the engine and swerved onto the road, leaving a spray of gravel in her wake. No mutters came from the backseat on the drive home. In the chill and silent atmosphere, Miss Lilliane went to sleep, only to be jerked awake when Laura braked forcefully in front of the Chateau. Without a glance into the backseat, Laura announced, "I'll send Robert out to get you."

"I can handle it," Pearl intervened.

"Fine!" Laura marched into the mansion and

feeling perverse, entered her husband's room without knocking and slammed his door intentionally so that Miss Lilliane would be able to hear it in the drive. She would give the old hag another kind of rumor to spread. How about bondage for a start? She could leave silk scarves tied to the bedposts as evidence for the old lady to find. Let her tell her friends about that!

Robert was packing. An open suitcase lay on his bed.

"You shouldn't be the one leaving. This is your house. I'll go." Laura made the offer automatically, not sure why she'd come to his room now. The heat of her anger drained into a small, chilly puddle in the pit her stomach.

"It's funny," Robert said without a smile. "I've been waiting for you to come here, and now you come when I decide to go. Don't worry about making other arrangements. I won't be back for two weeks. I'm going to do a little fishing and some thinking out at Ed Montleon's camp. When I get back, we'll either start all over again fresh, or we'll call the whole thing off and get an annulment. I'd give you longer Laura, but calving is starting soon. I breed my cows a little later than some because blue ribbons for size at the fall shows don't mean as much to me as healthy calves born after the last chance for a cold spell passes. Calving is a wonderful time, Laura. I hope you will be here to see it."

Without looking at her, he continued to shove balls of heavy socks into the pockets of the suitcase. "Besides, if I stay here another night, I might just knock down that locked door. As it was, I nearly molested a sleeping woman last night. You'd better get to bed. I'll be gone by five a.m."

Laura turned to go, then hearing Miss Lilliane's chair in the hall, she stayed and faced Robert. "It's just that I don't want to be pushed by loneliness or drunkenness or convenience. I want to know this marriage is right by my own conscious decision. Do you understand?"

"Yes, I do. But let me tell you, Laura, we are all pushed by something—revenge, lust, loneliness—and we must hope we are being pushed in the right direction. Now go to your own room before I close this suitcase and leave space on this bed for other activities."

As he snapped the case, she ran away.

Chapter Twenty-Eight

Laura heard Robert leave before dawn. Sleeping brokenly, troubled by dreams of open coffins and the flaring flames of hellfire, she'd tossed all night. After his truck rattled down the drive, she slept more soundly, one source of turmoil removed from her mind.

She took breakfast with only Angelle. Miss Lilliane did not feel up to dining at the table, Pearl said. That did not stop the old woman from waylaying Laura as she passed her door on her way to work. Beckoning from her room, she called out, "Come in here. Please."

Laura sighed and went to stand by Tante Lil's bed.

"You were right, you know. You are family now, no matter how it came about, and by talking behind your back I betrayed the LeBlancs." The old woman groped in her night table drawer and handed Laura a small key. "Here, read all the diaries. The Leblancs weren't saints. Most of the skeletons in our closets are real. Caroline LeBlanc saved this house with her mind and her body and maybe lost her soul in the process. When I sit by a casket at a wake, it's mostly her I pray for. A lot of the men weren't worth a damn. That's not to include T-Bob. Don't listen when they say he slept with Sugar LeDoux. But plenty of the others took after black women, even the high and mighty Charles. Our blood is tainted, but never, never admit that to anyone else. You're family now. Read the diaries."

Her shriveled hand remained on Laura's long after the key was passed. Now she took it away. "Get to work. You'll be late. I was never late." The old woman settled down into her pillows, dismissing Laura with a frail wave.

Speechless, Laura drove to work, did her job as thoroughly as Miss Lilliane could have wished and returned that evening to take down a diary, openly for the first time, from the library shelf. She read it while Tante Lilliane and Angelle watched television, careful only that the old woman did not note the dates on the pages. After all, the books were in the same type of binding except for the copy Laura had made, shelved now, probably by Pearl, with the others. The year was 1876.

"I greet this year of our nation's centennial with joy. We are healing into one nation again. My general does well in his law practice, some thinking that having a Yankee lawyer will prove to be an advantage in the courts, and others who do not know us well, assuming that Alexander fought with the Confederacy and will defend their southern rights more vehemently. We raise a few fine horses and enough food and livestock for our needs. I fear I am growing a trifle stout for food and the pleasures of the bed taste so much better to one who has done without.

"Alas, we do not raise children for ours are grown, and no more come. I know that dear Alex would like a son of his own. He can do nothing with mine, but Tante Inez says I am beyond the years of childbearing. When I argue, saying everyone knows Camille LeBlanc gave birth at my age, she looks at me slyly and says Madame Camille did not have my sinful nature, so God blessed her with a son. I understand and become silent.

"Indeed, I have enough children to cause me problems. Felice is sweet and unscarred by the war, but ripe for a man at the age of seventeen. I fear she will marry the first to offer, and many are beginning to show interest. Charles shows no interest at all in marriage though he is twenty-four. I know he keeps a Negress in town and flaunts his virility with other dark women, so my worst fear about him is unfounded. Why, if he loves the company of the opposite sex, does he not then marry?

"As for Lucinda Bell Moore, my stepdaughter, she is a hopeless spinster at twenty-one. When she came to me in her seventeenth year, I arranged her hair and dress more becomingly, though she would not allow false curls and or extra lace to increase the size of her bosom. But, how can one teach the art of flirtation or the mastery over men with feminine wiles? Poor Lucy would rather argue law with her father, and she does make herself useful at his office. Now and again, she convinces my husband to defend a Nigra in her mother's memory. How ironic the servants insist on calling her 'Miss Lucy Bell.' 'Belle' she is not. They have no way of knowing Bell was her mother's maiden name, and staunch New England abolitionist stock it was, bred to a more easy-natured Pennsylvanian. What a pity Lucy refuses to embrace the Catholic Church and allow herself the choice of the convent as Catherine did.

"At least, Catherine is settled. She has confessed to me that for the good of her own soul she no longer prays I will burn in Hell as she once did, but pleads with God to spare the souls of her misguided parents. I believe she realizes Alex and I pay only lip service to the Church for social reasons. Enough! These diaries contain too many secrets. I must see they are burned before I die despite the relief they have given me in times of confusion. Where else can the mistress of a plantation bare her soul and not do penance?

"January 7, 1876. A solution at last! We have been invited for the Mardi Gras season to New Orleans by my brother Armand. The wounds heal at last. Perhaps, Armand has finally acknowledged he survived that bitter war only because he was fortunate enough to be captured by the Yankees. Heaven knows, the war took its toll on the Montleons, two brothers dead, one sister widowed, the rest pinched old maids or aging nuns. My way of surviving might have been the best of all.

"February 5, 1876. The gowns are ready! We prepare to leave for the city. I have exhorted the young people to search seriously for appropriate matches. It is their duty, I tell them, to rebuild the South. Charles shrugs sullenly, as is his way. Lucy Bell merely stares at the floor. Only Felice, blushing, is likely to take my orders to heart. Dear Alex has declined to go, giving his practice as a reason, though I believe he sees himself as an impediment to reconciliation and the future of the children. I bless the day my lands were conquered by him.

"March 15, 1876. We return to our beloved Chateau, having neither failed nor succeeded. Armand and I have reconciled with tears and embraces as it should be, but our truce might be strained by the devotion of his eldest son, Jean, to my Felice. The lad eagerly accepted an invitation to return with us for a visit issued by Charles who wishes to explore the return of the land to cane planting by a method called sharecropping. Jean has been schooled in this method by his father. I oppose both this idea and the marriage of cousins. It reeks of a return to the old days of inbred aristocratic families ruling the land. Look at what those times brought upon us!

"April 30, 1876. There is no help for it. Young Jean refuses to return to his home until he has spoken to us.

"May 1, 1876. Jean Montleon has asked for his cousin's hand in marriage from both his adored aunt and the esteemed general. He claims to have his father's full agreement. How can we refuse? Charles stood at the young man's elbow adding his voice to the plea and then, asked to speak for himself for the hand of Lucy Bell Moore. We were stunned indeed, but promised to deliver an answer after we had spoken with the young women. What to do? What to do?

"May 5, 1876. It is clear Felice is deeply enamored of her cousin. Theirs may be a happy union as the boy seems equally infatuated. We have sent her suitor home bearing the good news. The wedding date has been set for early October before the harvest when the weather has cooled, and travel is more tolerable. I have quizzed Lucy Bell and am convinced there is no mutual attraction between her and Charles.

"Quite coldly, she told me that she and Charles had hit upon a solution to both their problems. He would no longer be hounded to marry, and she would receive the status of a wife. In other words, they created a legal contract between themselves. I argued that marriage is far more than a legal contract. Once I married for status and wealth, overlooking the weaknesses of an attractive man, and came to regret my impulsiveness. Lucy pointed out that while I may have had other opportunities to wed, she has none. Then she drew out an actual contract written by herself in which she granted Charles all marital rights. The paper included a clause saying she would embrace the Catholic faith and raise her offspring, should there be any, therein. In return, he is not to hinder her participation in her father's legal practice and is to settle all of his belongings on herself and her offspring, should there be any. I was appalled.

"Having seen the lengths to which Lucy and Charles are willing to go and considering both are of age and could not really be stopped Alex and I could do nothing but consent. Lucy, herself, set the date of the marriage to be the last Sunday in June, saying she was no young girl to be months preparing and would wed as soon as the banns had been said a sufficient number of times and herself confirmed into the Holy Catholic Church. I have bad feelings about all this.

"June 19, 1876. The wedding of Charles and Lucy Bell has been accomplished. The girl looked as good as possible in gray silk. I gave her the silver and garnet necklace her father presented to me upon our marriage and, though it looked overlarge on her spare frame, I could see my gesture touched her. For a bouquet, the bride carried blood red roses from our gardens. She and Charles rode from the church to the Chateau in a buggy draped with the same. The young men dashed ahead on horseback creating the required havoc, and Felice and her friends crowded into another carriage and admired their antics.

"With dining and dancing on the lawn, a stranger would have assumed this to be a joyous occasion—had not the groom drunk overmuch and the bride not at all, not even the toasts to the happy couple. Even my dear Alex imbibed too much and for the first night since our own marriage, had to be carried to our bed. How glad I was for his stupor. The room we decorated for the newlyweds sits directly above our chambers in the house and throughout the night, I head small cries and furious poundings.

"In the morning, I berated Charles for his poor treatment of an innocent, and he greeted my comment with laughter, saying Lucy Bell is as narrow and uncomfortable as a church pew. As for Lucy, when I tried to console her, assuring her future times would be better, she looked away and replied, 'What is done is done.'

"September 20, 1876. I have long been concerned about Lucy Bell's health. The poundings from above continue. Some nights they are so intense Alex cries in my arms. Lucy has asked him not to interfere—even when she comes pale and bruised to the breakfast table. She applies rice powder and goes off straight and spare as ever in the buggy to practice law vicariously with her father. I have told her there is such a thing as too much pride. I would send Charles, my own son, away for the things he does to her, but she says she is fulfilling her part of the contract. During the day, she is free, I must understand. I do not!

"Now the vomiting has started, so intense the girl keeps nothing down but broth. I have called in Tante Inez, who in her old age rarely leaves her cottage, for I am sure that this is a female complaint and nothing a doctor could treat.

"September 21, 1876. Lucy Bell is with child.

Never have I seen such symptoms, though Tante Inez tells me it can be so, especially if a child is unwanted or the act of making a child feared. I did not confirm this to her, but Tante Inez knows—as she has always known the secrets of this family. Her dotage has been made quite comfortable because of it. The midwife says Lucy will feel less ill as the child settles in her womb and to expect the little one by early April.

"September 22, 1876. Charles has removed himself from Lucy Bell's chambers and taken up his old quarters next to the library. We are all greatly relieved, so relieved I have tried to overlook my son's announcement that he has now fulfilled his obligation to rebuild the South, and he will leave Lucy Bell alone to swell to the size that her name implies. I am afraid I lost my temper and accused him of being an unnatural son. He replied sharply that it was to be expected when one had unnatural parents, a father who abandoned his son and a mother who whored through the war. I struck him, I did, and I do not regret it.

"October 15, 1876. The days are better now. Lucy seems less ill and will be able to participate in Felice's wedding in a few days. Charles is preoccupied with planting his inherited arpents in cane, supervising and driving the darkies who are 'sharing' their labor with him. I have heard him discussing the purchase of Felice's holdings with Jean after the crop comes in, and he has approached Catherine, here in her black robes, about paying the convent for her portion of the land. My arpents will come to him eventually through Lucy Bell because of my marriage to her father. I begin to see it all now and understand far too well.

"October 20, 1876. We have seen the young couple

aboard the steamer for New Orleans. The wedding was perfection, though I have been too busy to write of it. Felice looked as happy as her name implies in her white lace and pink fall roses. There was joy in the dancing, and the bride and groom were drunk on each other's smiles. This is as it should be. I wish them well.

"December 20, 1876. We have curtailed our holiday activities and visits for the sake of Lucy Bell who has swollen to great size. I do not recall ever having been so large or awkward in my sixth month. Her limbs and face have an unhealthy puffiness about them, but despite all this, she persists in accompanying her father to the office where her obvious condition embarrasses the clients. Still, Alex will not deny her. He says it is Lucy's only joy. That I believe since she will not knit or sew for the infant or talk about the child except to say that if it is a male, it must be called Alexander, Alexandra if a girl. Charles who will accept only the idea of a son has settled on a second Aurelien LeBlanc, and so they are at odds as usual.

"I have allowed myself two thoughts concerning Lucy Bell. One that she may bear twins; the other that Charles had his way with her before the wedding. I doubt the last, though many in town, seeing her difficulty in kneeling at Mass, believe it is so. I will call in Tante Inez and hope she confirms the former.

"December 31, 1876. The year that began so well ends in misgivings. Tante Inez says Lucy Bell will not bear twins or possibly any child at all for the girl is very ill. I was forced to call in Dr. Arceneaux when Lucy suffered an attack of vertigo on the stairs and had a slight fall. The fall did no damage, but the doctor saw what Tante Inez has seen. Lucy Bell suffers from a poisoning of the system and has been confined to bed where she suffers nobly, patterning herself on her deceased mother's last months without doubt. Does she fear death or welcome it? Such morbid thoughts for the year's end!"

Laura bent over the closing entry, trapped in the past until Tante Lilliane, wheeling close, coughed in her ear and read over her shoulder.

"Lucy Bell. Well, you certainly picked a strange place to start, though I've always felt a close kinship toward that woman. Given another hundred years, she would have been a lawyer, a career woman, not a spinster, not dead at twenty-two from complications of childbirth. She wasn't a breeder the doctor said later, all wrong for it, suffered a torturous two day labor, gave birth to a slightly premature but healthy boy, and lay in her grave three days later. She got her way on the name though, Alexander Aurelien LeBlanc, A. A. LeBlanc, my father.

"He married so late in life I remember him only with gray hair. It's no wonder, caught as he was between two strong characters like Caroline and Charles. He was quiet and scholarly, lean and stooped over, nearsighted, too, a real disappointment to his father who never bothered to remarry. Charles had that 'servant's staircase' built to the housekeeper's room when he added the new kitchen to the house and installed his current colored mistress there. Charles raised cane, outside and in." Tante Lilliane snorted at her own wit.

"I'll give this much to him. He put the plantation back on a paying basis and had a fortune to leave my daddy, though I know that's not why he did it.

Somewhere, we have a snapshot of Charles taken shortly before he died, holding a riding crop and astride a white horse, overseeing the cane cutters. Some say he rode with the Klan, and I believe it. The old days, that's what Charles wanted."

"How did they die, Charles and Caroline?" Laura wondered out loud.

"As they lived—Charles dramatically in the old manner and Caroline in bed," Tante Lilliane replied with a nasty chuckle. "Charles went before his mother, sent to hell by a black man with a knife after raping the man's fourteen-year-old daughter. Of course, the black man hung. Charles would have been so pleased. By then, Caroline was bedridden. A stroke took her suddenly and left her mostly paralyzed for nearly two years before the end. The servants spoon-fed her and changed her diapers like a baby. When they told her about her son's death, she didn't even bat an eyelid to show she understood. My father said he'd read to her in the evenings, bringing books from the old library in the house. He tried to pick things he thought she'd read in her youth. He said she'd become excited, blinking her eyes and making noises whenever he said he had a new book from the library. He considered it her only pleasure in her last days." Tante Lil laughed and coughed at the same time at the joke fate had played on her great-grandmother.

"I see. She was afraid he'd read the diaries," Laura inserted.

"So true! A.A. never did read them, though. He would not have pried into a lady's personal affairs. Really, the old general raised him, saw he got to the right schools, taught him law, and left him his practice

267

when he passed on. A.A. was raised as a Moore, not a LeBlanc, not a Montleon either. Daddy used to say when Aunt Felice visited with her eleven children, he felt like it was him against the world. After a while, there were so many Montleons, we couldn't keep track of them and sort of lost touch with the New Orleans branch of the family. You can imagine how it was when T-Bob brought Vivien, already pregnant, fact accomplished, home to marry with her airs about being descended from one of Caroline's sisters who had married a cousin. Brother and I almost swallowed our tongues. You see, we knew it all."

Tante Lil dabbed at her eyes where tears had gathered in the corners. "Can you believe, my gentle daddy, knowing how proud I was of being a LeBlanc, gave me the diaries all wrapped up in a big box for my seventeenth birthday. Caroline, Charles, Aurelien and Camille had passed into legend before I drew my first breath. They were in the local history books, all of them: Aurelien LeBlanc, builder of Chateau Camille; Caroline Montleon LeBlanc who saved the old plantation; Charles LeBlanc who rebuilt the family fortune. Opening that box ruined my life."

"Why did you let it?" Laura found herself taking the old woman's age-spotted hand. With the television turned low, contemporary news created background music for the tragedies of the past. The child, Angelle, unconcerned about her ancestry, slept curled on the rug in front of the screen.

"I was too young. Dear impractical Daddy might as well have given me a bomb. Within days, I knew why the DeVilles didn't want me seeing their son. If all this was true about my monumental ancestors, then the whispers I had heard all my life about there being black blood in the family was also true. Before the diaries, Lionel and I defied his family. Afterwards, I understood their reasons. I thought all the coloreds knew, too, and some did. She's no better than us I thought they said just out of my hearing."

Tante Lil leaned her head back in her chair and closed her eyes with lids as thin as parchment paper. She continued to talk. "My mother, God bless her, was a French woman. Gave birth to me upstairs in this house after she'd taken a fall. Miss Roz, the white midwife, delivered me. I was so tiny I could have fit in a shoebox, but of course, I had a lacy bassinet. I was Mama's treasure. She told to me, 'It does not matter, *cherie*, you are you, and in France, a little black blood, some scandals, makes one more *exotique*, more sought after by men.' If she had lived, I might have come to believe it, but Mama died of pneumonia back before penicillin came into regular use, you know. She was in her forties, and I only eighteen. Daddy packed me off to Normal School to become a librarian, something to make up for losing Lionel and Mama, because up 'til then he always opposed my going away.

"Poor Daddy, he never got over Mama's death. He was twenty years her senior and should have died first. He called her his war prize, his *'prix de guerre'*. Can you imagine a staid, established lawyer of nearly forty dropping everything and running off to fight the Kaiser? Of course the army gave him a desk job. He spent more time in France after the fighting then during, helping to settle affairs because he spoke the language. He told me once he fancied himself another General Moore going off to win a trunk full of medals and the heart of a beautiful woman, but he only accomplished the second, which was enough for him. Oh, he held on during the Second World War while my brother, Robert, went off to fight. He said he had to make sure Robert had sugar for his coffee over there in Europe, and something to come home to besides. But after the war, he passed on as gently as he'd lived."

"He must have been a good man." Laura averted her eyes from the old woman's face because tears washed down its wrinkled grooves now, but she continued to hold the fragile hand. She kept expecting her own Robert to come from his desk and break the moment as he bundled Angelle off to bed. Laura remembered, then, that tonight it would be her duty alone. She loosened her grip on Tante Lilliane, but the old woman wasn't finished with what she had to say.

"I wanted you to know about one truly good LeBlanc man. There's a lot of my father in T-Bob, though he never knew him. But make no mistake there is some of Adrien and Charles in him, too. He won't be shut out much longer."

Laura stooped to lift Angelle, but now she turned to resume her old battle with Miss Lilliane. Before the acid could flow, the old woman held up the hand that Laura had been clutching. "I can say that because you're family now. You've read all the diaries. I know it because I had Pearl bring me the locked one. I was going to give it to you with the key, but I saw the scratches on the brass. It doesn't matter. You're a LeBlanc, too, and won't betray us." Tante Lilliane wheeled toward her room, and then paused.

"Maybe it would have been better to burn the diaries. They blighted my life, and I know their secrets hurt T-Bob and caused Angelle, innocent that she is, real harm. Maybe they should still burn." The old woman glanced at Laura's shoulder where Angelle rested her head, more than half asleep. "Good night, *cher* heart."

Chapter Twenty-Nine

The two weeks of Robert's absence should have passed quickly enough. The calves began to come, and he phoned daily to check with Tony or later in the afternoon to say "hello" to Angelle, but he never called in the evenings when Laura was home. With all the pressure removed, she began to resent her husband's neglect. Laura laughed at herself. Now that she had the time to think about what she wanted, she no longer wanted the time and space he had given her. Laura waited with toe-tapping impatience for the day of Robert's return to tell him yes to the marriage, yes to staying at Chateau Camille.

She smiled on the last evening of their separation when the telephone rang at eight p.m. She allowed Angelle to scoot ahead and grasp the receiver. He was surely as eager to have her answer as she was to give it. Pressing her lips together to suppress a smile, Laura calmly followed Angelle into the hall. The child's look of disappointment caused an identical emotion to well up in her stepmother.

"It's a strange man asking for Mrs. LeBlanc." The little girl handed over the receiver abruptly and giving Laura a pouty look, returned to her television program.

"Mrs. LeBlanc?"

"Yes," replied Laura, thinking the name sounded strange and he must mean Miss Lilliane.

"This is Dr. Alvarez calling from Ochsner Hospital in New Orleans. Your husband was brought in a little while ago, a hunting accident. He'll be fine." The doctor spoke smoothly but in haste to quell the fears of the next-of-kin. Obviously, he had done this often.

"What happened? May I speak to Robert?" Laura's mouth had gone dry and her pulse pounded. The call was too similar to the one she'd received telling her David's helicopter had crashed.

"He's sedated right now, but he was conscious when they brought him in. He had all his papers, driver's license, insurance card, wallet, so it wasn't necessary to call before we made him comfortable. He was fishing near some heavy brush by the edge of the lake, and some kid hunting out of season mistook him for a deer.

"It would have been a minor accident if the boy had called an ambulance, but he ran off and left your husband to walk back to his car alone. Seems Mr. LeBlanc thought he could drive himself to the hospital. He might have gotten killed when he blacked out and hit that embankment. Fortunately, he was driving very slowly. The police called for medical assistance and wrote up a report.

"What we have here is mostly blood loss. A shoulder wound, no major organs were pierced. We'd like to keep him under observation for a while, at least until his blood pressure stabilizes, and we're sure we've headed off any infection."

"Certainly." Laura gave the consent automatically, all the while wanting to jump into her own car and go screeching off into the night toward New Orleans.

"As I said, your husband will be fine. There's no

use your making the trip to New Orleans tonight. Mr. LeBlanc gave us the name of some relatives in the city. Their doctor is going to examine him in the morning. Why don't you call around noon and check his condition? I understand you have a young daughter to take care of. The Montleons said they would keep a good eye on your husband if you can't get away."

Laura obediently wrote down the telephone number given by the doctor.

"Any questions I can answer for you, Mrs. LeBlanc?"

"No. Yes. When will he be home?"

"That's hard to say. A week or so depending on how well he responds."

"Of course. Thank you, doctor," Laura said without thinking. She stood listening to the dial tone for a moment before she realized the conversation had ended. She went for a glass of water in the bathroom before facing Angelle and Tante Lilliane.

The child, too young to fathom the meaning of medical complications and secondary infections, accepted Laura's assurance that her Daddy would be "fine soon" and "home again in no time at all." Angelle did sulk when told that seven-year-olds, even on their best behavior, were not encouraged to visit hospital rooms.

"It's not fair!"

"I know, but that's the way it is," Laura told her.

So far she had focused all of her attention on her stepdaughter, reading a message from Robert into the doctor's words that the child was to be her special concern. Turning to Tante Lil for reinforcement about hospital visiting rules, Laura was shaken to see the elderly woman trembling and on the verge of a coughing fit.

Miss Lilliane, oblivious of the child, wondered aloud, "What if he dies? If T-Bob dies, what will happen to us? Cane, I know about cane. I grew up with cane. Oh, Daddy wasn't much of a manager. He had too many Yankee scruples about exploiting the blacks, but he hired an overseer to do for him. We could handle cane. But cows. Cows don't make enough money. We'll lose it all, the house, the gardens, the damn cows!"

Seeing Angelle's eyes grow wide with alarm, Laura rushed the child to bed. The inevitable question came as she snugged the blanket around her stepdaughter.

"Is my daddy going to die?"

"No way, honey. And until he gets better, I'll be here. I guess I can take care of a few cows."

"Do they teach you that in library school?"

"Well, no, but I can always look it up in a book."

A small smile and a relaxing of the little body rewarded Laura's feeble joke. She sat for a few minutes with the child until Angelle curled into her favorite sleeping position. Then dutifully, Laura returned to care for her elderly in-law.

Miss Lilliane had gotten herself more or less in control. She poured sherry from the decanter that usually gathered dust on the sideboard. Her shaking hand kept missing the lip of the petite glass making up part of the set. Droplets of wine spattered on her robe like blood from a nosebleed. Laura took the glass, poured and handed it to the woman.

"I'm sorry, truly." Tante Lilliane gulped her sherry

and asked for more. "If anything happens to T-Bob, you and Angelle will inherit his share of the house. Like as not, you'll pack up and leave, and the Montleons will come for Angelle. I can't buy you out. I can't do for myself. It scares the hell out of me."

The old woman stared at her glass of deep amber sherry, not at Laura. "I wish my brother were alive. He was the best of my daddy and old Charles LeBlanc put together, a good lawyer, a fair judge, even the blacks trusted him. He mechanized those cane fields, and the hands he kept on got a decent wage during cutting season, but T-Bob couldn't see it. Those family stories turned him from cane the way they turned me from marriage."

"Robert will be fine and until he is, I'll be here." Laura echoed the words just said to a small child.

"Still undecided? Make up your mind girl! You get on my nerves!" Miss Lilliane slammed the fragile sherry glass back on to the sideboard, hard enough to make her point, but not hard enough to damage the crystal.

"I want to tell Robert face to face before I speak to anyone else."

"Ah. So for tonight you're still family and will be for a few more weeks at least. Pour me one more sherry, please. Want to hear another family story, one not in the diaries?"

Thinking the wine had addled the old lady's brain but willing to go along with any distraction, Laura nodded.

"My daddy, old A.A., had this craving in his youth to go to Paris, but every time he tried to get away, his grandmother Caroline would think of a reason he had to stay on the plantation. 'You can go after this year's planting,' she would say. Then, it was after this year's cutting, then after graduation from law school. She was feeling poorly and just might die with him so far away. Of course, he knew Adrien LeBlanc had died over there, so finally he said he would put a wreath on Adrien's grave for her if she'd let him go. How Caroline laughed, he told me. 'It's not likely you'll find a marker on a pauper's grave,' she said. 'But you might find a few cousins. Look up Martine LeBeau and her family when you arrive.' With that comment, she gave her consent at last.

"Daddy's bags were packed when the general took ill, and Daddy lacked the heart to leave the old man who lingered on for several months. After General Moore's death, A.A. inherited the law practice and never did get to Paris until the war. He looked for the family of Martine LeBeau without any luck in those unsettled times. He had never read the diaries, and really had no clues to go on. Still, Caroline's laughter and words stuck in his head. When Brother went off to war, he told him the same thing, 'If you get to Paris, look up the family of Martine LeBeau—you may have some cousins over there.'"

Tante Lil helped herself to more sherry after a dry cough or two.

"Well, Brother got to Paris after D-Day. He had a college degree and spoke the standard French they teach at the university, so he ended up as an aide to a general, but he never tracked down the LeBeaus. He came home, married a sweet girl from Lafayette and had a son to follow in his footsteps. Just about the time Robert, Jr. graduated from college, the Viet Nam war really heated up, and T-Bob's future daddy got called up for service. Brother used all his influence to get his son sent to a European embassy rather than a battlefield. He knew refusing to serve would mean no political career for Junior, but he wasn't about to let his only child be killed in a war everyone hated. Junior found the LeBeaus while he served as an aide at the Paris embassy.

"Evenings, he'd go to these little cafes looking for companionship. One night he came across a bistro featuring a real chanteuse, Aurelie LeBeau. The bar was tacky and had bad wine, but a better than average singer. She liked those American blues and sang in English, which attracted a lot of students and servicemen, but she lured Junior with her name. This is the only family I know of where Aurelien has achieved any sort of popularity as a given name and linked with a LeBeau in Paris naturally it drew Junior's attention. The chanteuse declined to drink with him or any other serviceman, but when he asked if she knew the family of Martine LeBeau, she greeted him like a long lost cousin—which he was."

Tante Lilliane took a gulp of sherry, hiccupped and pressed her fingers over her lips for a second. "Pardon. Turned out Martine LeBeau used Caroline LeBlanc's money prudently, setting herself up as a high-priced courtesan and eventually becoming the mistress of one wealthy man. Adrien LeBlanc had acknowledged his daughters, and they bore his name. Beautiful women and well-educated in convent schools, they reigned as the toast of the demimode in turn-of-the-century Paris. On the advice of the wise Martine, each bore a son to their wealthy lovers, thereby insuring life-long income.

The French woman, Caroline's namesake, in fact gave birth to two sons. Old Martine cautioned her that while one child insured security, too many children would drive a man away. As an old woman, Caroline's counterpart in Paris greatly regretted taking her mother's advice because she lost both sons in the Great War and had to live off her sister Aurelie's generosity. She served as nursemaid to the new Aurelie when her nephew's wife gave birth. Nevertheless, she cherished the child as she had no grandchildren of her own."

Slopping some wine over the rim, Miss Lilliane refilled her glass. "By then, the family had achieved respectability, and their name was neither LeBeau nor LeBlanc. Her great-aunt saw that little Aurelie studied voice and the arts, but when the girl decided to sing in the cafes instead of going into opera, her grandmother accused her sister of bringing out the wild LeBeau streak in young Aurelie and threw the woman out of her house. Her devoted grandniece went with her and literally sang for their supper during the war in Nazi occupied France. The girl used Aurelie LeBeau as her stage name, partly to spare her family and partly to shame them. Singing wasn't all she did. She slept with men for stockings and chocolate and just for the pure pleasure of it. She had a girl child, father unknown and raised her in the cafes and clubs, took over her mother's act and adopted her mother's name when the older woman's voice began to fail.

"Jesus, this is dry work. Pour me another." Tante Lil held out her glass with a trembling hand toward Laura who hesitated to refill it. "Pour! Okay then, where were we? Well, Junior and Aurelie spent nights trying to untangle the family tree and mostly likely doing other things as well. By the time they finished, Junior fell in love. He brought home his long lost, many times removed, cousin as a wife. When I met her, she said, 'Aurelie, it is a dreadful name, no? Please call me Auree.' That's how the whole town knew her and little else about T-Bob's mother.

"At first, they all suspected she'd married to get out of France and perhaps, pursue a singing career here in America. Oh, but the woman possessed charm and good sense, inherited or learned from the LeBeau women. She valued the security Junior gave her and the home. She soon made herself adored by giving her husband one son, but not another to ruin her figure. Cigarette smoking eventually destroyed her voice and took her life, but she reigned as Chapelle's one claim to sophistication during her life. She had style and wit, and I miss her to this day."

A coughing fit shook Miss Lilliane. This time Laura brought her water. The hour grew late, and she presumed the story to be over, its moral being that if Auree LeBlanc had lived, her son would not have tangled his life so badly. If Miss Lilliane intended the tale to raise sympathy for Robert, it did succeed. Mostly, Laura wished she could talk to someone as worldly wise as her long dead mother-in-law. But, Tante Lil had not run out of air yet.

"Only Junior and I knew Auree's background. There was talk enough in Chapelle about the LeBlanc ancestry, so we kept Adrien LeBlanc's little Parisian adventure to ourselves. Then along came Vivien, flaunting her lily whiteness, neglecting her child because of rumors heard. She knew nothing! One day when Angelle kept crying and crying in her room,

Vivien forbid me to pick up that 'little black bastard'. I told her it was true. Angelle had three streaks of blackness, one from Robert, one from Auree, and one from her, too, because she'd descended from Adrien exactly like them. I could prove it using the church records. What I said caused her to hurt Angelle, and I think Vivien tried to kill me in my bed. No cigarette fire flares up like that in a wall of flame. No cigarette fire leaves the smell of lighter fluid in a room. There, you know it all now, except maybe the part about Sugar LeDoux."

"I know all about her."

"Just make sure you know it right. T-Bob slept with her to get rid of Vivien. I'd have slept with the Devil myself to get that woman out of Chateau Camille. But you, I want you to stay and take care of the place after I'm gone…if the stories don't scare you away. I'm going to bed now."

Tante Lilliane wheeled crookedly toward her room, hit the doorframe, then the wall and cursed. She raised an imperious finger at Laura. "You may push my chair this evening and help me into bed. That's what family is all about. Hurry up, girl. I have to pee!"

Laura took her place behind the wheelchair. "You and all your stories don't scare me one bit."

Chapter Thirty

Laura called the hospital early and was told her husband's condition remained satisfactory. She tried later, and they put her off with "resting comfortably." At last in the afternoon, she reached Robert directly only to be shocked by the dullness of his voice like a knife that had lost its edge. Yes, he felt better. No, don't make the drive to New Orleans. Yes, he would be home soon. Good-bye.

Taking painkillers would account for the change, Laura assured herself while she told Angelle, Tante Lilliane and Pearl how well Robert sounded. He was not up to talking to them all yet.

When Tony came in the night to report one of the heifers having trouble with her first calf, Laura called the veterinarian, pulled on jeans and trod the gravel paths of the garden to the cattle barns. The vet provided the skill to turn the calf, and Tony the muscle to pull it from the exhausted animal. Laura stood nearby providing permission, support, and buckets of warm soapy water while she learned a few things about livestock that might be of value if Robert did not recover. After all, she'd promised Angelle she could handle a few cows. She could not bear thinking about the rest.

She overslept the next morning and berated Pearl for creeping into her room and turning off the alarm clock set for six a.m. Breakfasting on a biscuit, refusing grits and eggs in spite of Pearl and gulping strong black coffee to fuel her day, Laura raced to work. The coffee gave her heartburn all morning. She brewed tea for break, and after delaying as long as possible, called the hospital well into the afternoon. She dreaded hearing that lifeless voice again and prayed Robert would be better, more himself, knowing prayers are rarely answered, especially selfish ones.

"Laura," he said before she had spoken a word—as if he had waited all day for the call. The conversation ran on for such a length of time the librarian knew she would owe the parish a wad of money for making the call from her office. She told about having to phone the veterinarian, asking really for his assurance that she had done the right thing. She had.

"So now you know more about cows than just a roll in the hay with a cattleman," he teased, his voice deep and rich with laughter.

Laura laughed, too. The ladies of the staff turned to stare at her through the glass-walled office and smiled knowingly among themselves. Laura swiveled her chair around so only the back of her head showed to the audience.

"Seeing new life come into the world is a wonderful experience. You sound more like yourself today."

"I told them to shove the painkillers. A little pain is good for a person. Lets you know you're alive. Speaking of pains, Vivien came to see me. She brought me a bunch of flowers arranged in one of those baskets they use for funerals. I tell you that woman still loves me."

"What did she want?"

"Mostly gossip. She said she was disappointed I hadn't sent her a wedding invitation until she heard the sordid details from an old friend in Chapelle. Since Vivien has no friends, old or new, in Chapelle, I suspect she called the exchange and pumped Myrtle Hill. She said getting married at Broussard's Barn was exactly my style, and how many months pregnant are you? Charming woman, Vivien. But she did bring me a present, some of her special medication from her spa. She wanted me to take a capsule right away to help me feel better."

"You didn't!"

"Hell, no. I flushed them as soon as she left. It's not like Vivien to be concerned about others, especially if the other is me. She might have sent me on a one-way trip."

"You're smarter than I thought."

"I got you to marry me, didn't I?"

"All right, if you're so smart, you can wait to get home and see if I'm still there." Laura hung up, laughing to herself. Robert LeBlanc was getting well. He knew she'd be waiting.

****

Greatly relieved after the long conversation, Laura wondered when Pearl's strong coffee caused heartburn again the next morning. When Thursday's breakfast of eggs fried in bacon grease rolled over in her stomach and returned to the outer world, she made an appointment with a gynecologist in the city. She selected a doctor from the phone book in the library because his office lay near the university.

Laura had the perfect excuse for going to

Lafayette—hauling the last of the Ste. Jeanne Parish records for microfilming. Once they concluded filming this batch, both the university and Chapelle's small library would have the complete records saved for posterity. The archives librarian mentioned the possibility of a joint venture into selling the records with their rich resources on early Louisiana settlers statewide. Those first Catholic settlers traveled for days to be married by a priest on the only piece of holy ground in a hundred miles. Laura suspected the brides insisted and wondered how many honeymoons had been celebrated on the road to Chapelle and how many babies conceived during the journey.

As for herself, she'd never missed a period since adolescence and only one had been delayed—the month David died. A little late, a trifle nauseous, she hadn't taken birth control pills since last June. This time, she wanted to be completely sure and doctor-certified she carried a child before saying anything to Robert. She'd fooled herself before and wasn't about to trust any home pregnancy test.

The thought of a baby lifted her spirits though she dreaded admitting to everyone she had conceived during the orgy of her wedding night. Of course, people like Vivien would discredit even that, watching her belly grow each month and nodding knowingly if the infant made an appearance even two weeks early.

In making the appointment with Dr. Gray, she outright lied about her condition to thwart the ever-vigilant ears of Myrtle Hill who put the call through to Lafayette. Laura announced loudly to a startled nurse-receptionist that Dr. Bourgeois in Chapelle had referred her to a specialist for undiagnosed female complaints.

When the nurse inquired about her symptoms, Laura lowered her voice and whispered she felt she could confide only in the doctor.

"Oh," said the nurse, "we aren't accepting any more OB cases right now. Are you sure you aren't simply pregnant, Mrs. LeBlanc? It is Mrs.?"

"Yes, I'm sure!" Laura snapped using the same sharp tone she'd developed to fend off pushy book salesmen. The nurse made the appointment for Tuesday.

The remainder of the day provided enough material to amuse Robert in his sick bed for a week, but Laura decided to wait until the next Wednesday to tell him anything. Restless all morning and unable to wait for her appointment, she drove to the next town to buy a pregnancy kit, peed on the stick in the restroom of the gas station out on the highway, read the positive indicator, then took the whole kit wrapped in an old lunch bag and buried it deep in the oil drum holding used paper towels and the remains of the fried chicken box lunches sold by the diner down the road. Back at the library, she laid her head on her desk for a short nap and barely noticed when Ruby closed the blinds in her office and tiptoed off to lunch with the rest of the staff.

Most of the library's women drove home at noon and spent their hour watching a soap opera or checking up on elderly mothers, children, or daughters-in-law by phone. When Laura awoke in a puddle of her own drool and opened the blinds, she watched the current of gossip flowing from Bobbie to Berta to Ruby and on to the janitor—who told the bookmobile driver and clerk. Something was wrong with Miss Laura, sure enough.

The late afternoon coffee break started off quiet

and gloomy until Bobbie Meaux told a story about this woman she knew, a cousin twice-removed, but she forgot her name now, who had this awful problem with her female parts. Her condition ruined her marriage because she couldn't have normal relations, you know. But after she got fixed up, why she gave birth to twins.

That anecdote stirred the conversation from ashes to embers to flames as each woman tried to give Laura hope and comfort without admitting each and every one knew she had a special, possibly fatal, female problem—as Myrtle Hill informed them.

Berta Migues said she'd once heard of a woman who married a man with such a big organ she couldn't accommodate him down there. This woman went to a specialist and had herself stretched and all went well, except the woman couldn't cheat on her husband because after that no other man could satisfy her. Ruby rolled her eyes at Laura after that tall tale, but on her way back to the circulation desk, she patted the younger woman on the hand and assured her everything would be fine.

The humor of the situation, along with hot tea and dry biscuits got Laura through the weekend. She almost confessed when Pearl sent Angelle along to the cattle barns, counseling the child to "keep your new mother out of the pastures where all those jealous cows have their calves, and don't let her lift nothing heavy, you hear?"

Even if she hadn't heard the rumor, Pearl probably suspected the real truth as she watched one good spicy meal after another go uneaten. She served a positively bland Sunday dinner: roast chicken without rice dressing, creamed potatoes without garlic, green beans without bacon and onions, and custard for dessert. Laura ate heartily, choking once on a piece of white meat when Tante Lilliane shushed Angelle for complaining about the tasteless food.

****

Tuesday came, and Laura had to confess her lie to the nurse with the coal black hair who guarded Dr. Gray's office. Totally disgusted, Nurse Marks grudgingly filled in the preliminary paperwork, name, age, height, weight, blood pressure, no previous pregnancies, miscarriages, diseases, or allergies. None. Good.

"When was your last period?" Nurse Marks queried, the deep lines around her eyes and mouth belying her black hair.

"First week in February." Laura kept her answers humbly minimal.

"Are you usually irregular?"

"No, only once after my husband died." Laura flinched in her chair.

"Look, honey." Nurse Marks' hard lines softened. "We're near the campus. We get unwed mothers all the time. You don't have to lie. Take the test. The results will be back by four. If it's positive, you can discuss your options with the doctor. We can recommend an abortion clinic, but a lot of nice couples want babies. We can refer you to a lawyer who arranges private adoptions."

"I am married. I've been remarried for a month. More than a month." Laura babbled in self-defense.

Nurse Marks' features stiffened. Her facial lines seemed deeper and more forbidding than ten minutes ago. "After you have the baby, the doctor will discuss proper birth control measures. You Cajuns are always in such a hurry to get started."

"My husband's family isn't really Cajun, more French, really—with some other interesting bloodlines thrown in."

Looking as if she could care less now that the opportunity to place a baby in a proper home had vanished, Nurse Marks thrust a laboratory slip with the appropriate boxes checked at Laura. "Down the hall to the left. Call back at four."

Leaving both blood and pee behind, Laura emerged furtively from Dr. Gray's office. The early spring sun shone down on the small circular dot of the bandage stuck to the inside of her elbow. Besides the urine specimen, the technician took what seemed like an excessive amount of blood, three full ampules, so one ordeal out of the way. Daffodils and early tulips set out by the agriculture students brightened her way. In a week or two, the mountainous azaleas clumped around the neoclassical red brick buildings would burst into bloom. Fat, deep pink buds weighted the branches of the dark green bushes. If the test came back positive, she would be heavy with bud herself during the worst heat of summer.

With such whimsical thoughts occupying her mind, she nearly missed the greeting thrown at her from the library steps. Looking up, she saw Denise DeVille, her majesty, Queen Marie Antoinette, gracefully descending the stairs. Laura switched the sweater she'd been carrying to cover the patch inside her left elbow.

"Well, congratulations! I heard you and Bobby made your arrangement official on Mardi Gras eve. That certainly will be a night to remember for all of us.

My mama said it was about time with you living out at the Chateau and all, but I said, 'Mama, don't be so old-fashioned'. An experienced woman that age knows exactly what she's doing. I do hope y'all are very happy," the co-ed gushed, shaking her blonde curls in the light breeze.

Laura concentrated on the black roots showing ever so slightly in her rival's scalp and replied, "I *am* very happy, thank you."

"That's not what I heard, but then you didn't have much of a chance. Imagine Bob going on a fishing trip right after the wedding and getting shot to boot. I just poo-pooed Mama when she said maybe Bobby couldn't face two bad marriages and tried to do away with himself out in the woods. I mean, he seemed fine when we were dancing at the ball—though I did have to tell him that night he and I could never be together. He said he understood completely. You don't think Bobby tried to kill himself over little ole me, now do you?"

"No, I don't, especially since some kid shot him with a deer rifle." Laura deliberately removed the sweater covering her bandage. "I've just come from the gynecologist's office. Can you believe I'm pregnant already? While you were soaking your feet after the ball, we made our first child, truly a night to remember."

Denise turned red all the way to her dark roots. Suddenly, she spied a beefy young man in a letter jacket climbing the steps. "Oh, I have to run. Cliff and I have a study date. Congratulations again!" She waved one royal hand and grabbed the passing athlete with the other. The boy appeared a little startled but pleased at his unexpected luck.

Laura watched the couple pass into the halls of learning with Denise firmly attached to Cliff's bulging biceps. She felt queasy again, and the sun burned hotter on her face. Two big "what ifs" filled her mind. What if she was not pregnant and had to admit it to damned Denise one of these days, and what if Robert had tried to kill himself? The first, she decided she could endure, but the second was unthinkable. How Robert would react to this baby, she wasn't sure, but she did know how well he took care of Angelle. Robert LeBlanc knew how to nurture cattle or children or women who couldn't make up their minds and would never take the easy way out.

Laura took refuge in the cool of the library, taking the elevator to the Archives where certainly Denise and her beau for the day would never penetrate. Having a Pepsi in the staff lounge settled her stomach and passed the time, but at last, she had to find a book in the Louisiana Room to occupy the hours until four.

One scholar hidden behind a stack of volumes with cracked leather bindings served as her only companion. From a closed room nearby, she could hear the click and whir of the microfilming equipment as Dr. Andrus transposed the Ste. Jeanne Parish records from paper to film, leaving the desk unstaffed. Relying on the same professional privilege that allowed her a parking space and use of the staff lounge, Laura helped herself to an early history of Louisiana from the closed stacks and sat at the librarian's desk. Familiar enough with the procedures after months of hauling and photographing records, she could help any patrons while Dr. Andrus stayed closeted in the microfilm room.

Only one person claimed her attention during the

next three hours. A tall black woman approached the desk. At nearly three-thirty p.m., Laura hoped her sole customer would not need a lengthy search for material. Still, the only other work she'd done was to reshelf the leather bound volumes when the scholar left at two. She could delay her personal business until she'd helped this patron. Putting on her best smile, Laura greeted the woman who returned the grin with a set of strong white teeth.

With her hair shaved close to her scalp and large gold hoop earrings piercing her ears, the woman obviously favored an African look. A tawny sheath printed with black designs swathed her body from neck to ankle where two sandaled feet with long brown toes emerged.

Laura, playing a game she had contrived while working in another university library, guessed that this one wanted either early slavery accounts or black genealogy material. The woman stood waiting, and then held out a hand. Her grin tightened the lustrous brown skin over her high cheekbones, making her very attractive indeed.

"You don't recognize me, Mrs. LeBlanc. I attended your wedding. I'm Beulah Segura, also known as Sugar LeDoux."

To Laura's credit, she shook the hooker's hand without hesitation. She offered Pearl's daughter the chair next to the desk as if this were simply another reference interview. "May I help you with something?" she asked, falling back on professionalism to keep her mouth from hanging open wide enough to let in flies.

"Not really. I saw you sitting in here alone when I came out of the law library across the way. I'm doing a paper on the insanity plea from the psychological aspect."

"You're a student here?"

"Yes, student by day, ho by night. She worked her way through college. Sounds like a porno flick, doesn't it? I'm a psychology major. After I straighten out myself, I'm going to straighten out other people, maybe some of my old customers."

Laura liked the dark woman immediately and completely, much preferring her to darling Denise DeVille.

"Look, I've wanted to talk to you, but Mama hates having me come to the Chateau, and you don't exactly frequent Broussard's Barn. I know you and Robert have gotten off to a rough start."

"Doesn't everyone?"

"Chapelle is a terrible town for gossip—not much else to do. There's a story you should know that might make things easier for you."

"It's a great town for stories, too. I'm not sure I can handle any more of them," Laura replied. The room was as quiet as a chapel on Monday.

"I wanted to put in a word for Robert LeBlanc."

"Doesn't everyone want to do that?"

"I guess you know how he got his divorce so quickly. We had it all set up, the judge, Robert, and I, and a photographer who had his own darkroom. Robert came to my room around six. We undressed, got into the sack and waited to be caught. We waited stark naked for two hours, just talking and passing the time. The photographer caught a flat tire, and then took a wrong turn on the back roads. Finally, the man walked in on us. We struck a few poses, and that was it, except

Robert stayed awhile afterwards."

"He's an attractive man, Robert, bedroom eyes and all that. I guess I can't be surprised he stayed with you afterwards," Laura said neutrally. Inside, she felt the sinking sensation of disappointment. Years ago, this happened years ago, she rationalized.

"Oh, he is all that and he paid in advance, but what we did was talk some more. He told me I was pretty and smart and quite possibly a distant cousin of his, and he hated to see me wasting myself. He had to pay old Broussard three hundred dollars in cash for our little performance since we ran over into prime hours, but he gave me a bankbook with a twenty-thousand dollar deposit in it. My mother was a co-signer, so I couldn't spend the cash myself. The money belonged to his father, he said, but the idea was his own. That nest egg paid my tuition the first few years."

"Now, I work for Broussard weekends and holidays and I stay with old Tante Lu the rest of the time. My uncle, who knows how to handle trash, makes sure I get my cut. He'd give me my living expenses, but I've got to make my own way, you know. I screwed up my life early on, and it's not like I haven't been doing it for money all along. One of these days, I'll leave Chapelle and Broussard's Barn. Sugar LeDoux will vanish—or become one of those born again virgins. Before I go though, I'm going to stop by Chateau Camille and give your man one big kiss. I don't want you to misunderstand when I do."

"I won't." Laura stood when Pearl's daughter did. "Good luck, Beulah."

"And that's another thing I'm leaving behind in Chapelle. Beulah! I think I'll get me a new name—

something classy like Laura." As Dr. Andrus emerged, blinking like an owl in sunlight, from the microfilm room, Sugar left.

"Here are your originals, Mrs. Dickinson. The project is complete."

"LeBlanc. Mrs. LeBlanc. I've remarried."

"Well, congratulations. You're one of us now." He handed over the last of the bound volumes. "Do consider the publishing venture." He raked his hands through his thinning gray hair, adjusted his glasses and red bow tie as he fished for further conversation.

"May I use the phone for a moment, Dr. Andrus?"

"Certainly. No long distance now! I'll go clean up the stacks. We close promptly at five, you know." He tapped his watch with a neatly trimmed fingernail.

Taking the hint, Laura called Dr. Gray's office immediately. An anonymous young voice answered the phone, gave her the news that Mrs. Robert LeBlanc was most definitely pregnant and scheduled her first pre-natal examination.

The full service Shell station where Laura stopped for gas on the way back to Chapelle was definitely not the best place to make a romantic or important call. A slack-jawed attendant in greasy overalls peered intently into Laura's radiator while wiping off the dip-stick as the telephone rang in Robert's hospital room.

"You sure know how to ruin a person's dinner!" her loving man said when he answered the ring.

"I'm sorry about that! Mine hasn't been going down so well either," Laura snapped, her eagerness to tell about the baby sapped by his bad mood and the suffocating heat radiating off the concrete.

"Oh, it's you, Laura. You can't ruin anything that's

already ruined. They don't seem to know about pepper sauce in this place. I'll be glad to get back to some of Pearl's deep fat fried chicken with a little cayenne in the batter. I intended my opening remark for the staff dietician. Obviously, she isn't going to return my call."

Just thinking about the fried chicken and the deep fat made Laura's stomach roil. "If you are that irritable, must be time for you to come home. You might be disappointed in the Chateau Camille cuisine though. According to Pearl, we are having a nice chicken gumbo without sausage or too much onion and pepper and all the grease skimmed off tonight."

"What the hell is wrong with Pearl!"

"It's what's wrong with me, Robert. I'm pregnant, and I expect to be pampered all through the summer heat until October when our child is due."

She hoped she had put it well, lightly but positively. He did not answer. He'd accused her once before of being with another man and maybe he still believed that, certainly more plausible than her getting pregnant on their wedding night. Laura's knees went weak, and she gulped in the fume-filled air of the gas station. The sound of a truck passing obscured Robert's voice when finally he spoke.

"What! What did you say?" Laura shouted frantically.

"Calm down. It's not good for expectant women to get excited. I said I hope this doesn't interfere with our sex life."

"Oh, Robert! Is that all men ever thing about?"

"It is since I met you. If you still blame me for the way we married, you don't have to have this child or me or Angelle, but I want it all—all or nothing. This decision is yours, and you never gave me an answer."

Laura shouted over the noise of the traffic as the rest of the world raced by.

"All. I want it all. I'm staying. We're staying. And don't worry about your sex life. It will be more than you can handle in your weakened condition. When will you be home and well enough to resume where we left off?"

"Yes, to the marriage, to the baby, to unlimited sex! Cha-ching, call me a winner! With that incentive, I plan to get out of here tomorrow. I've been badgering the doctor. I believe he'll release me into the custody of the Montleons if I promise to stay in the area for a checkup. For some reason, they feel responsible for me. I wonder if Thurston can be bribed to chauffeur me directly back to Chapelle. The doc thinks I'm still too weak from blood loss to drive all that way, but what does he know?"

"Come home no sooner than the doctor allows. I want you well."

"You sound like a wife already." A big rig pulled into the station venting its air brakes. "But where on earth are you?"

"At a truck stop/casino/gas station between Lafayette and Chapelle. I didn't want to call from home because of Myrtle Hill. This time, I wanted only you to know."

"What about Pearl and the tasteless meals?"

"She's only guessing."

The attendant waved at her, signaling that two cars driven by elderly ladies raring to get into the casino waited in line behind hers for full service treatment.

"Laura, I love you."

"And I love you, Robert."

Laura gently placed the phone into its cradle. She had no desire to say good-bye.

Chapter Thirty-One

Laura discovered the joy of hugging Angelle without reservation and the wonder of being fussed over by Pearl who had greeted the news of Laura's pregnancy with, "Don't I already know." Even listening to Tante Lil's warnings that Robert had been a colicky baby and Angelle a fretful infant brought out a special kind of happiness. The greatest joy of all came in having made the decision to stay. No more retreating, running or hesitating for Laura LeBlanc from the moment she acknowledged those two names belonged together.

Casually, very casually, she mentioned at the morning coffee break that she had been worried about her health and as it turned out, she was only pregnant, the most natural thing in the world. That remark turned the afternoon break into a party with a pink and blue iced cake special ordered by Ruby during the lunch hour from Pommier's Bakery down the street.

The conversation ran toward questions. Yes, she would continue working, at least until the baby came. No, they had not picked any names yet. Yes, she had called her mother who was surprised—especially since Laura announced her marriage at the same time, a fact she neglected to tell her audience. Yes, Mother, I'm married and pregnant in that order, honestly! Boy or girl, it did not matter. Angelle seemed thrilled, not jealous. On and on the chatter went until Robert called to announce his release from the Medical Center, and the group decided they had to return to work.

Staying at the Montleon's home in the Garden District, he felt certain he could manage to return to Chapelle by the weekend, perhaps sooner. Vivien helped things along with her hostile reaction to his announcement of impending fatherhood and her making the members of the household miserable.

"I thought they'd ship me home immediately when Vivien started raving about my black blood being passed on because of my unbridled lust for white women. Instead they gave her a sedative and reservations for a nice, restful vacation in Hot Springs. I wish they felt less responsible for my welfare. It's not their fault some tall, skinny kid in a camouflage jacket went hunting out of season on their property."

"Tell them I'll take good care of you."

"I have, I did, and I will again. I'll escape by Saturday, maybe sooner. I love you."

"And I, you." Laura ended the conversation shyly aware of the office listeners. A less pleasant call came at quarter to five.

"Hello, Laura. This is Vivien. I wanted to congratulate the new Mrs. LeBlanc on her marriage and on her condition. How happy you must be. I know I was—at first."

"I thought you were on your way to Hot Springs, Vivien."

"Did Robert tell you that? As a matter of fact, I am. I've finally persuaded Daddy I can drive myself. My health has been poor, you know, and he worried, but I absolutely refused to leave home unless he allowed me to go alone. I am regretting that now. I'm so fatigued I decided to stay the night at the Hilton near the university. I really do want to know you better, Laura. I feel you must know certain things about Robert for the sake of your marriage. Could we get together tomorrow? I know. Meet me in the church about three. It's so close to your work you could simply slip away for a while without anyone noticing. We could have a nice quiet chat, just the two of us before I go to Hot Springs."

Laura had no desire to meet, speak or have anything to do with the ex-Mrs. LeBlanc. Honestly, that woman was worse than the racist David Duke and all his clones. She started to give an excuse to get out of the meeting, but then recalled how good it felt not to run, retreat, or hesitate.

"I'll meet you, Vivien. I'm sure we will come to an understanding."

Better to settle with Vivien now than endure her accusations year after year. Though more cordial than Denise DeVille over the phone, Vivien certainly would be more acid in person. Her imaginary grievances had fermented like damp hay in a silo, liable to burst into flame at any moment.

"No more loose ends after this, I promise you, Laura. At three, then. Good-bye."

****

The hands of the clock crept slowly toward three and the confrontation with Vivien LeBlanc. Laura's tension made her irritable. She snipped at Bobbie and Berta for their incessant chatter as they entered new titles into the computer and was short with Ruby over a simple shelving error.

"Hormones," she heard Bobbie whisper to Bertha. They repaid her with a hot cup of tea, a box of saltines to settle her stomach and a number of tales about how nervous they'd been with their first pregnancy. Heaven knows, their husbands were not in the hospital at the time. What a relief to escape all that sympathy by announcing she wanted to go over to the church to return the last of the records she had borrowed.

"Now don't strain yourself with those heavy books," Ruby called after her.

The warmth of the afternoon at the end of March amazed Laura, accustomed to wading through slush this time of the year. The air had a spring-like balminess, and the live oaks on the green sprouted pale green leaves and dainty tassels along their branches. Laura found herself delaying the confrontation by taking the long way around the church instead of entering at the side altar where the image of Robert's supposed ancestress impersonated the Virgin Mary and received the homage of votive candles glowing at her feet.

She passed St. Francis soliciting a little rain water for the birds from the blue-black patch of clouds on the horizon. A clump of burgeoning ferns covered the hole where a black kitten named Snake greeted her on her first visit to Chapelle. Snake grew fat and happy mousing the cattle barns at Chateau Camille. Fat and happy, words she could soon use to describe herself. Already her breasts felt heavy, and if she pressed both hands against her abdomen, she could feet the small hard ball where her baby grew.

Across from the church lay the empty lot where Domengeaux's store and briefly, Laura's home once stood. Miss Lola, gone to her daughter's in Baton

Rouge, had donated the space to the church for a parking lot. She must write Miss Lola, or better, call her with the news. Laura wanted to hear her former landlady's voice say, "Me, I told you, *cher*, it would all come right."

At the church doors, Laura lingered again, feeling very much like Saint Joan on the edge of martyrdom. She stiffened her shoulders like the statue on the edge of the green and entered.

Vivien waited halfway down the aisle by the marble slab marking Pere Blaise's former resting place. A beige snake skin handbag sat next to her in the pew. Always fully accessorized, Vivien looked calm and prepared for the coming encounter. She welcomed Laura by taking one of the two heavy volumes from her.

"Ah, the church records. You have an interest in them, too. I once spent hours poring over them. They're incorrect, you know. Caroline LeBlanc never had a daughter named Felice. Felice was her sister. But today, we set all the records straight, Laura. There will be no more misunderstandings. Why don't you put that heavy book down over there?"

Laura turned toward the small marble-topped table in the center of the aisle where the wine and the hosts rested before being offered at the altar. She laid down her burden and took a small breath before turning to face Vivien, but the woman had followed her. The former Mrs. LeBlanc seized the heavy volume and bashed it against Laura's temple sending her rival to her knees before Father Blaise's grave. Laura clutched at the marble table for support while her head spun with vivid images of the blue and gold ceiling of the church.

When her eyes focused again, she stared at Vivien's khaki skirt and olive drab knit top fashionably covered by an army camouflage jacket and accented for the full military look with a small chrome pistol.

"You shot Robert."

"Yes, Daddy would be so ashamed if he knew I only wounded my prey. We used to hunt swamp deer together out at the camp. Guns and ammunition are stored there. Robert never cared for blood sports. Another thing we didn't have in common like our ancestry, but today all errors will be corrected. I could have let you go, dear. After all, Robert deceived you just as he did me, but now we have another little error to correct."

The pistol pointed directly at the spot in Laura's belly that her hands sheltered minutes ago. "I could shoot you in the gut and correct that error now. But bullets are so unclean, and this building, too, is full of flaws bullets can't remedy—these records, that statue. Fire cleanses all with white hot flames."

Laura estimated her chances of grabbing Vivien by the ankles without being killed. When she saw no chance at all, Laura prayed silently from her place on the floor, the cold edge of Fr. Blaise's tomb digging into her knees.

"Now Laura, dear, I've done half the work prying up this stone. It was so loose, such sloppy maintenance on Father Ardoin's part. You move it aside. See where I've placed the wedges. Good girl! Now simply slide down there and join Pere Blaise. He can keep you company until you are freed of your impurity."

Thinking she might catch Vivien off guard with a thrust of her elbow, Laura balked on the edge of the grave, but Vivien moved swiftly and shoved hard. Laura fell three feet beneath the floor of the church of Ste. Jeanne de Arc and caught herself on her hands and knees. She was not entombed with the dust and bones of the old missionary, but Vivien, preoccupied with covering the dark hole, did not appear to notice or care.

The ground beneath Laura felt cool and damp. A slight breeze passed beneath the church ventilating the old building with the original form of air conditioning. The remains of Father Blaise and his stone coffin had been removed to the cemetery during the renovations, a fact Vivien did not know, but one that gave Laura hope of survival.

As the marble slab grated into place blocking off the final view of Vivien's pale, crazed face and the blue vault of the chapel, Laura's heart slowed from a panic to a steady beat. She tried to empty her mind of the claustrophobia of being in total darkness, pressed beneath the bulk of the church, and of sharing the space with things that slither and creep in cool damp places. She would lie still, and when the stiletto sound of Vivien's spiked heels left the church, she would push away the stone, or failing that, wait. At six o'clock, the worshippers would come and hear her screams.

Laura heard Vivien moving the heavy marble table, scraping it along the floor until it weighted the lid of the tomb above her. Wondering why Laura did not scream or perhaps wanting to enjoy the moment more, Vivien tapped the stone with her heel. "Laura? How does it feel to be buried alive? Tell me."

"Please, please, let me out," Laura begged, catering to the woman's ego and hoping to hurry her exit. She would not be able to lift the slab now and must wait three long hours to be discovered, but she felt safer beneath the stone than under Vivien's gun. Absolutely. Laura told herself that several times. She lay on her back and let her eyes adjust to the darkness.

"Sorry, Laura. I have work to do and can't talk now, mistakes to correct here and at the Chateau. A number of things need cleansing out there."

Above her, Laura followed the click of Vivien's heels as the ex-wife moved toward the Mary altar and its rack of prayer candles. Through the small cracks in the old flooring, she heard the tearing of paper—so many hymnals and prayer books to provide fuel for an arsonist, not to mention the brittle and ancient church records. The odor of a bonfire burning drifted down to Laura. Vivien's footsteps retreated from the building.

Laura stayed quiet, praying silently. "St. Joan, St. Francis, anybody up there? Hear my prayer. Save my life and the life of my unborn child. Help me to find the way."

Suddenly remembering Vivien's mention of mistakes to be corrected at Chateau Camille, she added, "And please save my daughter, Angelle."

Then, Laura screamed in earnest.

Chapter Thirty-Two

Freshly home from school and playing with Snake on the gallery, Angelle saw her mother's car turn into the drive. Her daddy said she should never see or go anywhere with her mother unless Thurston or another adult came with her. She ran to tell her great-aunt, but Tante Lilliane napped in her bed before dinner, and she knew better than to wake the old woman because it made her grumpy. The child dashed to Pearl fixing a potato salad in the kitchen.

"Mother is coming up the drive, Pearl. Please, please, please hide me."

"Calm down, child. Look, we'll both go to my room and shut the door. She'll think no one is home and go on her way. Quiet now." Pearl hugged Angelle close to her side as they listened to the front door slam and measured Vivien's progress by the sharp tap of her heels on the wooden floor, down the hall and into the kitchen.

"Anybody home?" the mad woman called pleasantly. "I know there must be since the door is unlocked. My, my, potato salad in the making. Such a pity I never touch carbs. It is one of your better dishes, Pearl. Come out, come out wherever you are and bring the child with you. I saw her scoot into the house. What a way to greet her loving mother. But then she was always a mistake, a terrible mistake since birth."

The kitchen door opened and closed. Pearl and Angelle breathed easier.

"Do you think she's gone, Pearl?"

"You stay here. Let me just take a peek." The maid opened her bedroom door a crack only to have it kicked back into her face. She stumbled against Angelle but regained her footing and her senses in time to shove the child behind her.

Miss Vivien waved a small pistol at them. "Naughty, naughty child to hide from your mother again. I almost got rid of you when I burned down Domengeaux's store. You have as many lives as that black cat you adore. A bullet will be less painful, but not as cleansing as fire. Fortunately, I still have a full clip since I didn't have to waste even one shot on that passive wimp, Laura. Step aside, Pearl. This doesn't concern you."

Pearl stayed put before the child and talked soothingly to her former mistress, telling the demented woman what she wanted to hear. Maybe she did have Tante Lu's talent for telling tales after all.

"Miss Vivien, you sure are right about those errors. Why, I found a whole new batch of diaries in a secret compartment when I cleaned out that old closet upstairs. They say Caroline LeBlanc was a crazy person who made up all those stories. I know you want to see them. They in my closet right here."

Watching Vivien and blocking her view of Angelle, Pearl moved toward the hidden stairway and shoved her small sewing machine out of the way. When the door stood half way open, Pearl pushed Angelle before her and jumped in after, slamming the closet door shut. They made the fourth step before Vivien fired into the wood.

"I know where it leads, Pearl. I'm blocking this door, you hear? You won't get out."

From their place on the tenth step, they heard the sewing machine being shoved back into place and jammed against the wall. A vacuum cleaner stood in the way in the upstairs closet. The housekeeper and child on the thirteenth step shoved it aside. Shielding the girl, Pearl moved into the empty bedroom first, but Vivien did not wait for them. In the kitchen below, the maniac broke glass, bottles of cooking oil, liquor, anything flammable, Pearl guessed. Miss Lilliane called from her room for Pearl to stop that racket.

Footsteps sounded in the hall and up to the first landing. Leaving Angelle hidden in the closet, Pearl risked taking a glimpse from the Judge's room. Miss Vivien gleefully sprayed a can of peanut oil on the frayed runners of the stairs. She lit a wooden kitchen match and touched it to the soaked fabric. Even before that, Pearl smelled something burning in the kitchen— grease, alcohol and paper toweling maybe. Vivid orange and blue flames shot up from the pool of oil on the stairs. That crazy woman meant to burn them alive.

On the other side of the veil of flames, Vivien shouted, "I do see you, Pearl. Much as I'd love to watch you and the child fry, I must go pay my last respects to Miss Lilliane. She won't need her wheelchair after today. It is cruel to leave your prey half alive, but LeBlancs are tough to kill. Must be your primitive black blood. Who knew she would jump out a window rather than burn. After today, only Robert will be left to spread the lies, and I am sure I can find him easily at my father's house and finish the kill I started at the camp."

Pearl half shielded by the door watched Vivien retreat down the stairs. "*Bon jour*, old woman. May you dance in hell," Angelle's mother called out merrily to Tante Lil. The mad woman returned quickly with the wheelchair, went outside and threw it down the verandah stairs. She did not return to the burning house.

Chapter Thirty-Three

Father Ardoin saw the smoke upon his return from the other side of town after attempting to administer last rites to a person in very good health. He considered the false phone call a very cruel joke at best and sacrilege at worst. He contemplated preaching on the matter this Sunday, but the smoke escaping in small wisps around the stained glass borders of the windows drove his sermon from his mind.

The priest woke Chief Fontenot, chair cocked back against the fire station wall, from his doze in the spring sunshine. Once the Chief cranked the siren, a host of volunteer firemen gathered rapidly like a heavenly army, their slickers flapping like golden wings as they ran. Even Robert LeBlanc, who was supposed to be half dead down in a New Orleans' hospital, came running from the library. He didn't look too bad for a sick man, but frantic, very frantic. Father Ardoin had no more time to worry about T-Bob who could surely take care of himself. The sacred treasures of the church must be saved without delay.

****

Beneath the flaming chapel, Laura lay on her back duplicating the cruciform shape of the church with her body and trying to be sensible. The short bout of screaming had done no good. She had to think this through. If she crawled to her right among the brick

311

supports that raised the building off the damp Louisiana earth, she would reach the side of the church where St. Francis had provided one small hole in the siding for the shelter of a kitten and the possible salvation of Laura LeBlanc.

She rolled over and crawled, smashed her hands painfully into one of the brick supports in the darkness, altered her direction slightly, prayed she would not move in a circle. A papery shed snakeskin disintegrated beneath her hands. She hoped its owner had moved to other quarters. Thankful the smoke rose upward, Laura saw small chinks of light ahead. She reached a barrier of boards, boards too thick to break with the frenzied blows of her fists. Moving along those boards on raw hands and knees, she sought to find that small weak spot in the wall obscured by ferns and ivy. She came to a corner.

Oh Lord! The wrong direction! She'd arrived near the arm of the church holding the Mary altar. She raised her hand. The floor felt warm and the smell of ashes seeped between the cracks in the thick old cypress boards. Laura retreated, one hand on the wall, the other feeling for the brick supports mushrooming up at regular intervals in the darkness. Having to pass them by removing her hand from the guiding boards was like being forsaken by God each and every time. Then she found salvation—the hole just big enough for her left hand to grope through into the patch of tall wood ferns. Her right hand beat on the siding, her mouth screamed until it became dry and cracked, but neither could be heard above the sirens wailing on the green.

****

Robert LeBlanc stood on the green arguing with

Chief Fontenot. Pretty much like trying to make a point with a tub of lard, he knew.

"Now Bob, your wife's not in there. Any minute now, she'll come along here from the bakery or La Boutique and be on me for letting a sick man get in the line of danger. That church has four wide doors, and I'm sure she went through one of them a long time ago. If she were in there when the fire started, why, she'd have come to get me, right?"

"Then let me work the hose line."

"No way, boy. You are sidelined until further notice. Crack open that wound working for the city, and you could sue me. Yes, you could."

"What's that?" Robert directed the chief's attention to something flailing in the ferns by the feet of St. Francis.

"Must be an animal trapped under there. We find 'em all the time roasted to a crisp under these old places. Now get back. Shit! Someone hold on to Father Ardoin. He's going into the church."

By the time the chief turned back to the argument, Robert had seized an axe from the fire truck and raced to the siding determined to make some effort to fight the fire. The chief was probably right about Laura being safe somewhere. Certainly, he had enough strength in his arms to free some poor entrapped cat or dog.

"Thibodeaux!" bellowed the chief. "You go tell LeBlanc I'm chief here. He's outta this fire."

Old Thibodeaux tapped Robert LeBlanc on the shoulder, "Chief says..." Both saw it at the same time, a woman's left hand beating at the wood ferns, a hand with a ring finger bearing an antique silver and garnet wedding band. Thibodeaux ran for another ax, but

Robert keep hacking at the boards until his wound broke open and bled through his shirt.

He didn't notice the pain. What he did feel was the warmth and softness of Laura's body as he pulled her free of the church. She coughed and touched the side of his face, unable to do more until her lungs cleared. He carried her and his child-to-be away from the flames. She'd lost her shoes and bled from scrapes on her knees, elbows, hands and chin. Her dress was covered with dirt and green stains from her crawl under the church, and her snarled brown hair smelled of smoke as he buried his face in it. He put his mouth over hers, wanting to give her his breath, but she pushed him away and struggled to her feet. Laura saw the hurt in his bittersweet brown eyes but had no time to waste apologizing. She tried to talk over the commotion of high-pressure hoses and collapsing timbers, but could not make herself understood with a voice raspy from smoke and screaming. She took his hand and drew him from the fire toward the library.

"That's what I told you to do, T-Bob. Go on home and rest. See a doctor, whatever, and let me run the show," Chief Fontenot shouted as he orchestrated the fight to save the church of Ste. Jeanne d'Arc. "Just 'cause you right this time, don't mean you always right."

At least, the library staff gathered outside to watch the fire applauded his heroics and called for a kiss. Robert tried to embrace her again, but Laura batted him away. "Vivien has gone after Angelle. I do love you, but later! Ruby, send the police and another fire truck to Chateau Camille just in case she set another one there."

He needed no more explanation. They took the

Mercedes the old black chauffeur, Thurston, had driven from New Orleans with Robert as his passenger. With the keys left in the lock, they snatched it right out from under him as the driver, shaking his head and muttering about "crazy Miss Vivien" who ought to be put away, watched the fire.

****

Pearl retreated to the closet and filled her arms with the old sheets stacked on the shelves. Taking Angelle's hand, she led the child to the library. Too scared to do anything but cling and hinder the housekeeper, the girl stuck to her like ivy to an oak tree as Pearl knotted the sheets into a rope.

Oh yes, she could see the mad woman waiting in her car down below. Oh yes, she knew Vivien had the gun, but what other choice was there? Keeping low, hoping the slats of the upper gallery would provide protection Pearl moved to tie the sheets to the banister nearest the corner column. The child hung on her, weighing her down like a baby nine months in the womb. They would have to go down together or not at all. And now, Miss Lilliane's voice cried out, not from her room but closer, near the stairs. Pearl noticed the cries captured Vivien's attention and made the arsonist smile. Small child up here, old woman down there. Good Lord, what to do!

"Look here, Angelle. I got to get Miss Lilliane. You be safe here for a few minutes. Just squat down real quiet, and don't move till I get back." The girl hung on her and had to be pried off and tied by the sheeting to the rail while Miss Lilliane called louder and louder from the stairs.

There she was, that tough old woman, pulling

herself hand over hand up the stairs toward the smoke and flame. Two more sheets from the closet went into the tub of the modern bath by Charles LeBlanc's old room. Pearl, draped like a Klan member, wore one wet sheet and carried the other. Thanking the Lord for long legs, she jumped the flaming runners and swathed Miss Lilliane in the sopping sheet.

Up was harder, made harder still when Vivien opened the front door. The flames soared higher relishing the fresh air. As best she could, Pearl drew the old woman through the fiery barrier, thanking Jesus for the smoke that obstructed Vivien's aim as the bullets shattered the finely milled newel posts of the staircase.

A powerful car, crushing the shells as it sped up the driveway, created enough diversion for Pearl to drag Miss Lilliane into the library, slam the door and hoist the woman into the judge's ancient caster-wheeled desk chair. Far way, a siren howled on the trail of the smoke.

"Help's coming, Pearl. You take Angelle down. I'll wait here," rasped Miss Lilliane.

"No, ma'am. Smoke's getting worse." Wisps of it slithered under the library door.

"Get her, get her!" Miss Lilliane pointed to where the slim child, free of the bulky knots, stood ready to jump from the outer edge of the balcony, a perfect target for her insane mother.

Pearl got out there in time to save the child. She made a grab. They lost their balance, but the housekeeper grappled at the knotted sheets one-handed and swung the child down with her. Their good luck ended. Vivien was waiting. Behind the demented woman, T-Bob and Miss Laura ran to help, but not fast enough, Pearl knew, to save them. She twisted the sheet and offered her back to the former mistress of Chateau Camille. Vivien fired her last shot and watched Pearl fall the final few feet with Angelle clutched in her arms. Without enough bullets left for the child, Vivien went and stood over her daughter clicking the trigger of her pistol in frustration, unable to stop trying to correct the errors.

Robert seized his ex-wife's arms, but she kicked him with those sharp high-heeled shoes of hers, and when he lost his grip, she smacked him with the pistol in the center of the bloody spot staining the front of his shirt. Robert crumpled over his wound. Vivien ran free through the gardens laughing gaily as if she played hide and seek among the blooming camellias

Pearl lay dying. She knew it. She had saved one child; the one clinging to Miss Laura, now came the time to save another.

"Laura, Miss Laura."

"I'm here, Pearl. The police are coming. They can radio for an ambulance."

"No need—'cept for him and the old lady. Miss Lilliane still up there."

She nodded toward Robert. He'd taken Angelle into his arms, but leaned heavily on the child, his strength giving out as his blood flowed.

"You tell my daughter I got money saved up in the bank. Her inheritance, all I got to give. She's to make herself a new life. You tell her I love her no matter what name she goes by."

That said, Pearl rested in Laura's arms and let her soul slip away.

Chapter Thirty-Four

Only the all black Nebo Volunteers came to turn their hoses on Chateau Camille. The Chapelle firefighters had their hands full trying to save their two-hundred-year-old church. Only the charred timbers of both landmarks remained by the time help arrived from neighboring communities, but the Nebo men had a tale to tell that rivaled the one about Father Ardoin going into the church to save the cypress carving of the Virgin. They swapped the stories in some of the neutral meeting places around Chapelle, the post office and the bank.

"There she was on the balcony, this old, old white lady in a fancy nightgown, sitting in a desk chair, her lap full of little brown books. She threw them books out in the bushes away from the fire. 'Why, that's the old librarian, Miss Lilliane, I sez.' Before we could get a ladder up there, she uses that chair to push herself along the walls and back inside.

"She wouldn't come out wit' us 'til we took the rest of them books, too, so we did. The whole time she was gasping and choking and between coughs, telling us not to get water on the ones she threw in the bushes. Well, we got her down the ladder and slapped a oxygen mask on her. Did the best we could. I was real sorry to hear she didn't make it, a tough old lady like that, willing to die for her books. Lungs jus' gave out, I guess.

"Had to take Mr. Bob to the hospital in Lafayette, he bled so much. I'd a thought we were gonna lose him, too. Sent him off with Miss Laura and T-Angelle, 'cause he wanted them by his side just in case. But he made it, yes, he did.

"The police caught that crazy bitch, Vivien, out in the cattle barns trying to set fire wit' no matches. They took her off to the nut house, and she won't never get out this time. Yessir, this is a story to remember."

****

The entire community remembered Miss Lilliane and Pearl Segura on Sunday at a special Mass. Baptists and Methodists also attended, black and white, small children ordinarily sent to the nursery during services and old people taken from the rest homes for the day. The Baptists provided the folding chairs set up on the green beneath the sheltering oaks. All the chairs were taken and some small children perched on the low-slung branches while their parents leaned against the broad trunks.

Three people in the front row gave up their seats next to Ruby Senegal and her husband when the LeBlancs arrived from Lola Domengeaux's old house where they stayed until they could rebuild. The three of them wore clothes so new none had been washed yet because, of course, they'd lost everything but a box of little brown books in the fire.

On the edge of the crowd stood a tall black woman in a yellow and brown patterned sheath. With her hair wrapped in a turban made of the same material and large hoop earrings hanging to her shoulders, she appeared to be one of those African-American types, a big city reporter maybe, definitely not a local.

Father Ardoin stood before the crowd between two statues. On his right sat the cypress Virgin, her tawny skin blackened by smoke, on his left, the effigy of St. Francis pried from its spot near the ruins of the church. Potted Easter lilies, already being sold at the K-Mart, surrounded the Virgin, and St. Francis' bowl held coins, dollar bills and checks. Father Ardoin had a new majesty about him. He wore the cassock singed by the fire.

"Dear people of Chapelle, we come together this day to remember two women, one white, one black, who directly or indirectly, fell victim to the flames which have ravaged our heritage. They were human and had their flaws, but in the end, they were strong. So we must be strong. Our church will be rebuilt on this site, and our own unique Virgin of the Flames, symbol of our past, will be housed again within it. St. Francis shall have a special shrine in our new building, because at his feet a living woman bearing within herself a child that is a symbol of our future was pulled from the fire. The sacrifice of Pearl Segura spared yet another child." Father Ardoin rolled on, loving the moment in the present as colorful as anything in Chapelle's past. Laura smiled very slightly remembering her first meeting with the verbose priest.

Robert sat with one arm around his daughter and his other hand clasping hers. Absently, he rubbed her silver and garnet wedding band. She worried about him. He still looked gray beneath his usual tan and heavy close-shaven beard. She fretted about Angelle who gave them no rest at night with the violence of her dreams. Yet, Laura felt strong as if the toughness of Miss

Lilliane and the vitality of Pearl Segura had been seared into her. She would be able to care for the ones the flames had damaged. She leaned toward Robert, and he leaned against her.

Chapter Thirty-Five

Angelle pulled her parents up the cracked walk to a little white frame house with a screen porch and a plaster Virgin Mary residing in the half shell of a buried porcelain bathtub painted blue on the inside decorating the yard. A cluster of bells chimed as the child pushed open the screen door to the porch and towed Laura behind her. Laura stumbled over the doorstep and her husband caught her.

"I'm getting so clumsy," she said.

Robert ran his hands over her firm, bulging belly and kissed her cheek. "You don't have to do this if you don't want to, Laura," he whispered.

"No, no. It will be good for Angelle. She wants to know," Laura replied.

Angelle stood at the front door, calling inside, "Madame Leleux, Madame Leleux, we've come to have our fortunes told."

A small, aged woman looking like every Cajun granny Laura had ever met came from her kitchen wiping soapsuds from her hands. "Well, well, T-Angelle, a former client of mine. I heard you got good results with the powder I give you."

"Yes, ma'am. And now I want to know what kind of baby we're having and lots of other things."

"T-Angelle, the doctor can tell you that."

"They want to be surprised," the child replied in

disgust. "I want a baby sister."

"Well, come into my special room, and we see."

Madame Leleux led the way to what might have been a sewing room in another house. The space was small, cluttered with tiny bottles and virtually papered with holy pictures and cards. It had the scent of home-baked cookies rather than incense. Madame seated herself on one side of a square table with most of its varnish worn off where people had placed their hands over the years.

"You first, Mama." She took Laura's hand.

Laura felt a warm surge as the old woman searched her palm. "You know, telling the future is against my religion. Been Cat'lic all my life, and the priest says only God can know what's to come, and it's bad to take God's place. But if God, he tells me the future, it's not so wrong to pass it on, I think. I got the gift, the gift from *le Bon Dieu*, praise the Lord."

"Amen," Laura felt compelled to say.

"Well, T-Angelle, I got some news for you, and don't you give me no *bouderie* lip. You have a baby brother on the way and more to come, all boys." Angelle's pouty lip came out for all to see. "But you will remain the only daughter, the favorite, best-loved only daughter."

She took the little girl's hand. "After the bad times, come the good. It's all good ahead. I see you traveling and coming home. I see another man in your life, and he ain't a brother."

"But I don't like boys!" Angelle whined.

"You'll like this boy and your little brothers, yeah. Now go out in the kitchen and get a cold drink from the icebox."

Madame Leleux took Robert's hand. "You want to know if all is well. It is. The ones you miss are in a fine place where black and white don't matter."

The *traiteur* frowned. "One exists in the flames she started. I didn't want the little one to hear that part. There is nothing you can do for the damned one. It is God's will."

Laura shivered. Robert placed both his hands over hers.

"And God's will for you is to love what you have been given and not to regret what has been taken away," concluded Madame Leleux. "Now, I never charge for my services, but you may leave whatever you see fit at the feet of the Virgin in the yard. There's a rock off to one side you can use so it won't blow away."

The little wren of a woman went spryly back to her kitchen. As Laura and Robert passed out of the house, they heard Madame urging a freshly baked chocolate chip cookie on Angelle. "Take two, take three."

The couple paused at the statue of the Virgin. "What do you think, twenty?" asked Robert.

"Let's see, she has a fifty-fifty chance of getting the sex of the baby right. The odds are greater on the theoretical brothers. Chances are Angelle will go away to college and marry. Madame probably heard the gossip about Vivien setting her mattress at the asylum on fire after they caught her and locked her away and knows she died in the flames. We were given some traditional comfort and good advice. Make it forty."

At that moment, Angelle joined them, clutching a paper napkin stuffed with warm chocolate chip cookies. "For the new family, Madame said."

Epilogue

"I tell dem folks what come to see da church dat ain't da real one, no. It's just a copy for da tourists. I tell dem, me, Old Thibodeaux, da old one, she burn down. Dey called me Old Thibodeaux even den, but I'm even older now. And I can tell you a good story, me. Not so good as Tante Lu who passed on at one-hundred-two, but she gone now, and dey got only me, heh."

"I tell dem 'bout Miss Laura who is our librarian lotsa years now, how I saw her pulled from under da church. I tell 'bout old Miss Lilliane who usta be librarian, and how she t'rew dem books off da balcony of Chateau Camille."

"'Course, dere ain't no more Chateau Camille. Da gardens is dere, and dey can go see dem if dey want to. I tell how da police cotched crazy Miss Vivien trying to set fire to da straw in da cattle barns, but she ain't got no matches to burn 'cept inside her head, so dey took her to a place for da criminal insane where even her rich folks from New Orleans couldn't get her out again. Why, she hated being in dere with colored folks and such so much one day she fired her own mattress and put a end to herself. No one here cried, not wit' what she done."

"I felt sorry for dat little girl, T-Angelle. Turned out to be an artist, she did. First she painted only flames, Sainte Jeanne burning up and such t'ings like dat. But da doctor says it's okay. She workin' t'ings out, and so she did. Went away up nort' to study art. But she come back to see her people. Does real good, fixes up old paintings and such. Did all dose copies of da old LeBlancs dey got out in da Visitor's Center at da gardens. Once she even done one of Pearl Segura who saved her life and won a prize wit' it. Miss Angelle, she gave dat one away to dis black lady from New York City, a Dr. Roberta Segura, who maybe was Pearl's cousin or somet'ing, up dere working wit' runaway girls like."

"*Mais*, we still got LeBlancs in Chapelle. You can read about dat family in Miss Laura's book. Tells about dem all da way back wit' no fixin' dem up. I tell you, me, it's as good as one of dem paperback books, only wit'out da half-naked ladies on da cover. I got my own autograph copy. Dey sell dem out at da gardens, too."

"Sure, we still got LeBlancs. Dere's T-Bob's t'ree boys by Miss Laura. Dey named Robert Francis, Alexander and David, but dat first one called 'Smokey' mos' of da time on account of his eyes. Dey gray like Miss Laura's but got dis dark ring around da outside. Madame Leleux say it is da mark of smoke from da church burning. Dos las' two boys, dey twins, but not alike. Dat little one, David, he calls himself a horticulturist and fools wit' da plants. Alex, he's a cattlemen like his daddy, but Smokey, he played pro baseball, yeah. Come home rich. Dat Smokey, he might jus' marry old DeVille's great-granddaughter. Times sure is changin'. I tell you, me, you got to read Miss Laura's book."

A word about the author...

Once a librarian, now a writer of romance, Lynn Shurr grew up in Pennsylvania Dutch country. She attended a state college and earned a very impractical B.A. in English Literature. Her first job out of school really was working as a cashier in a burger joint.

Moving from one humble job to another, she traveled to North Carolina, then Germany, then California, where she buckled down and studied for an M.A. in Librarianship. New degree in hand, she found her first reference job in the Heart of Cajun Country, Lafayette, Louisiana. For her, the old saying, "Once you've tasted bayou water, you will always stay here" came true. She raised three children not far from the Bayou Teche and lives there still with her astronomer husband.

When not writing, Lynn likes to paint, cheer for the New Orleans Saints and LSU Tigers, and take long road trips nearly anywhere. Her love of the bayou country, its history and customs, often shows in the background for her books. She is the author of the Sinners sports romance series: *Goals for a Sinner, Wish for a Sinner, and Kicks for a Sinner;* the Roses Series; and the single title, *A Trashy Affair*.

You may contact Lynn at www.lynnshurr.com or visit her blog—lynnshurr.blogspot.com.

www.ingramcontent.com/pod-product-compliance
Lightning Source LLC
Chambersburg PA
CBHW071526260626

47170CB00002B/522